Clubbing Together

Clubbing Together

Helena Pielichaty

Illustrated by Melanie Williamson

OXFORD
UNIVERSITY PRESS

OXFORD
UNIVERSITY PRESS

Great Clarendon Street, Oxford OX2 6DP

Oxford University Press is a department of the University of Oxford.
It furthers the University's objective of excellence in research, scholarship,
and education by publishing worldwide in

Oxford New York

Auckland Cape Town Dar es Salaam Hong Kong Karachi
Kuala Lumpur Madrid Melbourne Mexico City Nairobi
New Delhi Shanghai Taipei Toronto

With offices in

Argentina Austria Brazil Chile Czech Republic France Greece
Guatemala Hungary Italy Japan Poland Portugal Singapore
South Korea Switzerland Thailand Turkey Ukraine Vietnam

Oxford is a registered trade mark of Oxford University Press
in the UK and in certain other countries

'Starring Sammie' first published 2003
'Starring Brody' first published 2003
'Starring Alex' first published 2003
'Starring Jolene' first published 2003

First published in this edition 2005

British Library Cataloguing in Publication Data

Data available

ISBN 978-0-19-275430-1

5   7   9   10   8   6

Typeset by Palimpsest Book Production Limited, Polmont, Stirlingshire

Printed in Great Britain by Cox & Wyman Ltd, Reading, Berkshire

to Connor, Michael, Louisa,
Claudia, and Mathilda
with lots of love

Contents

Starring Sammie...

... as the girl who becomes a big fat liar (but whose pants don't catch fire!)

Chapter One

There are two parts of my day I don't like very much. The first part is before school; the second part is after school. They're so bouncy since Dad left. I don't mean bouncy like when you're on a bouncy castle and everyone's jumping up and down and bumping into each other and it's a good laugh. I mean bouncy like when you're on a bouncy castle and everyone's jumping up and down and bumping into each other but nobody's in control so you're scared in case you fall off and get hurt. That kind of bouncy.

When Dad lived with us, which was until five months ago, I didn't bounce much because I knew where I was. We all did. Ever since I can remember, he would come in from working nights at the furniture warehouse just before Mum started out for work at the knitting factory. He would make us our breakfast, have a chat, take us to school, then go to bed. After school, Dad would collect us, make our dinner, have a chat, wait until Mum got home, have a row with her, then go to work again. So we were never alone. We didn't need childminders or babysitters or nothing.

Now it's all changed and I don't like it one bit. I've told Dad a million times I don't like it and he says all Mum has to do is ask and he'll be back in a blink but she hasn't asked yet and says she never will. I keep hoping she will change her mind because everything's a mess. Take this morning, right? Our kitchen at quarter to eight. It was already feeling bouncy. One reason was Mum wasn't even up yet.

She should have been—she's supposed to set off for work at eight but she'd just kept snoring when I called her earlier. I suppose she's very tired—she was at 'Mingles' with her friend Bridget until one o'clock this morning. Mum and Bridget go to Mingles for Singles three times a week to find Mr Right because neither of them found him first time round.

This time round Mum says her first choice is the actor Ross Clooney because you might as well aim high. She has not had much luck so far, which is good news as far as I'm concerned. The sooner Dad comes back the better, and he doesn't need competition from American film stars.

Another reason I'm feeling bouncy is I'd just asked my two sisters, Gemma and Sasha, to sponsor me for *Children in Need* but they're being really mean about it. 'But it's for little children who haven't got nothing, no clothes or food or nothing,' I said, showing them the cute picture of Pudsey Bear with his little eye bandage on in the corner of my sponsor sheet.

'Little children who haven't got *nothing*?' Sasha tutted. 'It's *anything*, stupid. Haven't you heard of double negatives?'

That's just typical of Sasha since she started at The Magna with Gemma. She began in September and it's only November now but it's as if she's in a secret society or something and sisters still at primary, like me, aren't allowed to join. Still, I'm not one to give up easy, so I tried again. 'Please sponsor me for the children who haven't not got *anything*,' I repeated.

Gemma scowled. She's in Year Nine and does that

a lot. 'What, like we have?' she snapped, combing her fizz-bomb hair over her Coco Pops.

'Spot on,' agreed Sasha. 'They should be fund-raising for us—look at this crud!' She showed me her knife, which had got the last dregs of orange marmalade clinging to it; except it was more green than orange. 'We have to eat mould. Even South American kids in the rainforest don't have to eat mould.'

Then Gemma goes, 'Anyway, like you'll last twenty-four hours without talking,' and Sasha goes, 'Yeah, talk about mission impossible.'

I'd chosen to do a twenty-four hour silence, if you hadn't already guessed. It was either that or a sponsored spell and I'm no good at spelling so I didn't have much choice. Mr Sharkey, my headmaster, is going to shave his head and Mr Idle, my form teacher, is playing a rugby match dressed as one of the Ugly Sisters from *Cinderella*.

My ugly sister, Gemma, snatched the sheet off me. 'As I'm feeling generous, I'll give you one p,' she said eventually.

'One p? Wow, thanks!'

'One p *an hour*,' she added, as if that made it any better.

Then Sasha went: 'Put me down for that, too.' Copycat.

'You're both mean,' I told them.

Gemma poked me in the back with the end of her comb. 'I'd rather be mean than fat like you. Look, my comb's disappearing in all that flab. Help! Help!'

'Get off!' I yelled, pushing her away. It wasn't like she had room to talk, neither. I hate our Gemma sometimes, I do.

Luckily we heard Mum clattering down the stairs so Gem backed off and returned to slurping her Coco Pops. There was a gap of a few seconds while Mum slipped into her flat working shoes in the hallway. You can hear the 'plat-plat' sound they make on the cushion flooring. At last she came in looking half asleep and struggling to get her arm through her cardigan sleeve. 'Make me a coffee, someone,' she said, her voice as rusty as an old tin of Whiskas.

'You haven't time, you'll be late,' I pointed out. I knew she mustn't be late. At Pitt's where Mum works with Bridget, they give you warnings. Mum had already had a verbal warning and the next stage was a written warning and after that it was a final warning then you were out.

Mum glowered at the wall clock and sighed. She wasn't going to risk being late again. 'Car keys?'

'Treacle tin,' we chanted.

'Ta.'

She grabbed the keys, grabbed a bag of crisps from the cupboard, and grabbed a two-pound coin out of the dinner money jar. Grab. Grab. Grab. Gemma and Sasha looked at each other, knowing one of them would have to do without lunch if she didn't put it back by Friday. I was all right. I took sandwiches.

I saw Gemma mumble something and grew worried in case she started anything nasty. I hated it when that happened so I thought I'd better say something nice quickly. 'Did Ross Clooney turn up?' I asked.

Mum's face softened immediately. 'No,' she said,

smiling, 'he sent his apologies but he had commitments. He said next week.'

'Aw, never mind,' I said sympathetically, but I was glad really.

'Oh, ple-ase,' Gemma sneered.

'Never mind "ple-ase",' Mum said, her eyes alight. 'For your information there's a Lookalike competition Sunday night and there's going to be a Ross Clooney among them. Even if he's only halfway towards the real thing he'll be worth a bit of a smoochy-woochy, won't he?'

'Oh, puke-a-rama,' we all said and she laughed, puckering up her lips and pretending to kiss him. I sighed with relief because she was so happy and I knew she wouldn't bite my head off when I asked her what was happening after school.

I never know, see. Sometimes it's straight to the childminder, Rosie's; sometimes I come home with Nathan's mum next door and wait until Gemma and Sash call for me; and sometimes I'm allowed to walk back on my own. Oh, except Fridays. Dad always picks me up Fridays. I know where I am one day a week.

We've got an after-school thing called ZAPS After School Club but Mum won't let me go to that. She says it's too expensive even though she hasn't even asked. I wish she would let me go because it looks brilliant. It's in this old mobile hut at the back of the school playground. If you stand right up on your tiptoes you can see through the club's windows and there are craft tables and computers and baskets full of dressing-up clothes and a sweet shop and purple sofas and bean bags. It looks really inviting. The supervisor is a lady called Mrs Fryston who comes into assemblies and tells us what's going on that week at the club.

Mrs Fryston has grey hair but a young face so you can't tell if she looks young for her age or old for her age but whatever she is she's always smiling and seems patient and kind, even when Mr Sharkey teases her and calls the club kids 'the mob in the mobile' and her 'the nut in the hut'.

During the last summer holidays, Mrs Fryston did an 'All the Fun of the Circus' theme and arranged for jugglers and clowns to come in and show everyone how to do tricks and fall over properly. I'd have given anything to have been there that week or any week, but first I had to persuade Mum and that's not easy.

'Where am I after school today?' I repeated.

'What day is it?' Mum said, still in her Ross Clooney dream.

'Wednesday.'

'It's Rosie's then, isn't it?' she sighed. 'Pick you up at half-five-ish. Gotta go.'

Blowing air kisses to no one in particular, Mum turned to leave but I stopped her and reminded her Rosie couldn't do Wednesdays no more because she's got the twins and her spaces are used up.

Mum looked puzzled as if it was news to her, which it wasn't, and took a deep breath in as she tried to fasten her coat. The coat stretched and flattened her boobies. She's big, is Mum; we all are, but she's the biggest. Today, she fills the door frame behind her like a soft green leather mattress with buttons. 'Go to Rosie's anyway. What's she going to do, turn a little girl out in the street?' she said.

I know Rosie won't do that but she'll still be annoyed. Mum already owes her three weeks' money. 'Can't I just come home by myself? I promise not to use the deep fat fryer or answer the door to strangers,' I pleaded.

Mum wasn't having it though. 'No, Sam, not with these dark evenings. Just do as you're told or I get confused. I'm off—make sure you lock up properly and someone put the bin out. See you.'

'See you,' we chorused.

'You are the weakest link, goodbye!' Gemma goes under her breath.

Gemma and Sash left ten minutes after Mum. I was last. I like being last. I like it when the house goes quiet and all I can hear is the ticking of the clock and the noise from the boiler when the pilot light whooshes. I like locking the door and checking it is done properly so no burglars can get in. It makes me feel important.

Chapter Two

I can walk it to school easy. All you have to do is go down to the bottom of Birch Rise, where I live, go past Birch Court where the old people live and then cross over at the bottom by the shops and you're on Zetland Avenue and Zetland Avenue Primary School, ZAPS for short, is at the far end opposite the library. Five minutes tops.

I wouldn't say I loved school, exactly, but it's miles better than home at the moment. In class, I sit with Nazeem Khan, Dwight Baxter, and Aimee Anston on the Yellow Table. They wouldn't be my first choice of partners, to be honest, but we're bunched together right next to Mr Idle's desk at the front because we need the most help. We're all a bit rubbish at things like reading and writing. We're also way behind on merit marks. There's a bar chart behind Mr Idle's desk, showing all the different coloured tables' totals, right? You should see the yellow bar. It's only as high as a postage stamp. Everyone else's look like tower blocks. The trouble is, see, as well as earning them, you can have merit marks taken off you for stuff like talking when it is 'inappropriate', being rude, or not doing homework. That's the main problem on our table—Aimee's rude, Dwight never does his homework, I talk all the time, and Naz does all three. We might start off 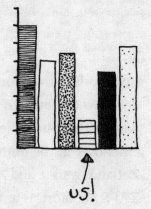 the day with, say, twenty merit marks between us but by home time we can have lost the lot. Mr Idle says we are our own worst enemies.

Anyway, that's the Yellows. When I arrived in class, Aimee was talking about how stupid all this sponsor money thing was. 'I'm not collecting a penny,' Aimee goes, 'it's all a rip-off anyway—the money never gets to the people. The pop stars keep it all.'

Naz pulled a face. 'Yeah, but what about the trip to Radio Fantastico? That's got to be worth two weeks' pocket money, guy.'

Mr Idle knows one of the best presenters at Radio Fantastico—Tara Kitson—and he wangled a slot on her show for us, as part of the radio's Children in Need week. The studios are only small, though, so the whole class can't go, only one tableful. We had a discussion and decided whichever table raised the most money should be the table to go. It was a heated discussion because Sam Riley, who goes to that After School Club I told you about, kept arguing that it wasn't a fair method as the rich kids would win, but not many agreed with him. Sam's usually quiet but he wouldn't back down, even when Aimee said to him, 'So what's your problem? You're a rich kid, aren't you?' His parents own a greetings card shop in the Jubilee Arcade. Sam told her his parents' income was beside the point. Anyway, everyone had a vote and that's the way it went.

Guess what else? Tara Kitson told Mr Idle Radio Fantastico might be linking up live with the *Children in Need* presenters at the BBC but she was not sure when, so there was a chance we might get on telly. Even Aimee couldn't deny she'd like to go on the telly. 'Well, you lot raise the money and I'll come along for the ride,' she sneered. 'Not that we've got a hope, unless Sam takes up stealing again.'

I went bright red. Do you remember Pokemon cards? Well, once, in Year Three, Aimee had dared me to steal some out of the cloakrooms with her or she wouldn't be my friend, so I did. Trouble was, I got caught and she didn't. In fact, she told the teacher she had tried to stop me and they believed her. Aimee is a very good liar. Now she believed it herself and brought it up every so often to make me feel bad. I don't know why she's like that with me. I've never done nothing to hurt her.

Luckily Naz ignored her and said, 'Dwight's got four squids ten and I've got two squids and nought pence and Sam's got—what was it?'

'Thirty pounds,' I said proudly, thinking of all the coins half filling the empty crisp tube on my bedside cabinet. They came from Rosie my childminder and her other mums and going round Birch Court on pension day, which I thought was a stroke of genius. 'Oh, no, wait!' I added, remembering this morning. 'Thirty pounds and forty-eight p.'

Naz nodded wisely. 'Thirty forty-eight. Not bad, guy. But I bet that still means we're well bottom. The Greens have got over fifty and the Reds have got nearly seventy. I don't know about the rest of them but it's gotta be more than us.'

We glanced across the classroom, first to the Red table, then to the Green, then to the rest of them. Everybody beats us Yellows in everything.

'Come on, Anston—you could at least try,' Naz pleaded. 'That Tara is such a babe. She deserves to meet me.'

Aimee finished sharpening a pencil and blew the shavings all over Naz's side. 'Why should I?' she said. 'Nobody makes an effort for me.'

That was such a fib, but never mind—I'm sure

you're getting the picture of what she's like. Then Dwight goes: 'You know Brody Miller in Year Six? She's got over a hundred squid on her own!'

Brody Miller is famous in our school. She's a child model and has been in catalogues and telly adverts and all sorts. If you look in the Argon catalogue on page one hundred and fifteen, she's the one second from the left with the long auburn hair and dazzling smile, sitting on the BMX bike. Not that I'm always looking at her picture, in case you're wondering. She goes to that After School Club as well. It's not fair.

'Well, that's nothing,' I said, glancing at the merit chart, fed up of never getting no recognition for nothing, 'I'll have that easy by Monday.' Don't ask me why I said that because I don't know.

'How?' Aimee goes. 'Your family is always skint. They're not far off being trailer trash, I've heard.'

That really hurt. 'Well,' I said, thinking fast and

fibbing like mad. 'When I got home yesterday, all the residents of Birch Court had done another collection for me—I never asked them or nothing so it was a real surprise—they said they were fond of me and wanted to help. Anyway, that came to—wait for it—fifty pounds.'

'Yes!' Dwight said, punching his fist in the air.

Everyone looked really chuffed, apart from Aimee, who just looked suspicious. I decided to add a bit more. '. . . and then I phoned Dad. I told you he was collecting at the warehouse, right?'

Everyone nodded and I did too because at least that bit was true. 'Well, he told me he's got well over sixty pounds already . . .'

'That's . . .' Naz paused to add up, which he's rubbish at. 'Masses over a hundred. So wicked, Wesley!'

I held my hand up. My mouth hadn't finished yet. I was still stinging from the trailer trash bit. '. . . and he's put a collection box down in The Almighty Cod. You know how busy *that* gets at weekends.' Dad lives above The Almighty Cod now. It's a chip shop on Sandal Road.

Aimee looked at me double-well suspiciously and said: 'You never mentioned that yesterday.'

'I'm not a bragger, Aimee. They don't call me Brody Miller,' I told her, looking her straight in the eye.

'Yellows rock!' Naz grinned, slapping me a high-five.

You won't be surprised to know I was a bit quiet the rest of the morning, wondering what I was going to do. The sponsored silence was on Friday and all the money had to be in by next Wednesday. I'd dropped myself right in it and no messing. I'd just have to come clean at lunchtime, that was all, and put up with all the 'liar, liar, pants on fire' stuff. Aimee would be in her element and get really nasty with me, probably, but I'd just have to take it. I was kind of used to it from her, if you must know.

That was my plan, anyway, until we lined up for assembly and Mr Idle asked us all how we were getting on with our collections. We all muttered, 'Fine', 'OK', 'Not bad'—things like that.

He put out his arm to hold Naz, who was first in line, away from the door frame while the Year Fours trooped past. 'Fine? OK? Not bad?' Mr Idle moaned. 'I want more than that, Year Five! I've got to play rugby dressed in a wig and make-up, not to mention a bikini top stuffed with my wife's old tights. If I'm humiliating myself in front of a crowd of two hundred people, I want "fantastic", "incredible", and "record-breaking", never mind "OK" and "not bad". Understood?'

'Oh, don't get your wife's knickers in a twist, Mr Idle,' Naz goes and everybody laughed.

From further down the line, Sam Riley's voice piped up that he still thought the visit to Radio Fantastico should be made by kids who do something special.

Mr Idle sighed hard. 'We've had this conversation already, Sam, but, for the sake of argument, something special such as?'

'Writing a poem,' Sam said quickly, 'or a catchy verse at least.'

'And I expect you just happen to have one handy?' Mr Idle asked.

'Funny you should mention that,' Sam quipped and everybody laughed. He was quite popular was Sam, though he didn't have one special friend; he just mixed with everybody. I twisted round and could just see the top of his fair head—he's a bit of a titch, height-wise.

'Don't listen to him, Mr Idle,' Aimee called out. 'The table with most money wins it and that's going to be us. Sam Wesley's got way over a hundred pounds all by herself already!' She dug her elbow into my stomach, as if daring me to deny it. Of course, I couldn't then, could I?

Mr Idle beamed at me. Full on, straight in the eyes. 'Is that so, Sam?'

What could I do? Deny it with everybody looking at me? 'Yes,' I said, 'it's true.'

'That's excellent. Well done.'

Aimee winked at me, a massive smirk on her face. She had tricked me into telling another big fat lie and she knew it and she knew I knew it.

Me and my big cake-hole.

Chapter Three

I felt bouncy all afternoon which isn't fair because I don't usually bounce much during school, but I admit it was my own stupid fault this time. Rosie the childminder didn't do much to help the bouncing, neither, when she saw me walking up to her at the gates at half-three. She didn't say nothing to me, exactly, but I could tell by the way she loaded everybody's sandwich boxes into the tray beneath the double-buggy she wasn't happy I was there. I felt treble-bouncy to the point of seasickness all the while I was in her house—as if I didn't have enough to worry about.

When Mum arrived, last as usual, late as usual, Rosie told her straight off she couldn't childmind me no more.

'What's she been up to now?' Mum goes, giving me a deadeye.

'Nothing at all,' Rosie said quickly, 'Sam's a poppet; it's just I want to concentrate on the under-fives.'

'But our Sam's great with little ones. She'd help you, wouldn't you, love?'

I nodded but Rosie had made her mind up. 'Sorry, Eileen, no can do.'

'Fine, fine, I'm not going to beg,' Mum said, clutching my school bag to her chest, and putting on her glum face, 'there's plenty more childminders around.'

'Good luck in finding one that works in arrears,' Rosie said sourly. 'Now, you'll need to pay your fees, please, before you go.'

Mum tried to wriggle out of it. 'I'm short at the moment. Can I post it on?'

'No,' Rosie said firmly, 'you can't.'

She held her hand out and Mum reluctantly pulled out her purse and paid up. It took ages, because she had to scramble about for every last coin she had; then she was forty pence short but Rosie told her to forget about it.

As soon as we got in the car, Mum let rip. 'Oh, that was decent of her, wasn't it? "Forget about the forty p." Stuck up mare . . .'

We set off down the street, Mum ranting on and driving too fast over the speed bumps so I felt my head was going to fall off. 'It's all right for her. She hasn't worked in a factory since she was sixteen, has she, or been married to a loser since she was nineteen? I never had a chance to enjoy myself and let my hair down like I should have done at that age. All I've had is millstones. I'm right, aren't I?'

'Yes, Mum.'

'Millstones' is a Bridget word. She uses it a lot when she telephones. 'Which one of the millstones are you?' she'll say and laugh. I thought it was a compliment at first, like a gemstone, but then Sasha told me what it meant. I don't like Bridget much now. 'That's why I go to Mingles—to catch up on what I've missed out on— it's just for a break and a laugh,' Mum continued.

'I know, Mum. Nobody minds.'

She slowed down behind a queue of traffic at the lights on Batley Road but carried on explaining, even though she didn't really need to. 'I know it's a bit

expensive and I keep telling Bridget I can't keep up with her with clothes and things but, like she says, first appearances count. I'm not going to get Mr Right dressed in seconds from a market stall, am I?'

'No. Why should you? We're not trailer trash, are we?' I agreed quickly, thinking of Aimee's nasty description.

Mum laughed aloud. 'Exactly! We are not trailer trash! Exactly! You're right on my wavelength, Sam. How come you're the youngest but you understand me the most, eh, babe?'

'I don't know,' I said, glowing in her praise. I

paused, then took a chance. 'What's going to happen about me after school now?' I asked.

'Huh . . . I don't know. I'll have to think about it later.'

'I can always go to After School club.'

'What?'

The line of cars moved forward slightly and we nudged nearer the lights. 'After School club—instead of Rosie's. It's really good, Mum. There's themes and a reading corner and a tuck shop . . .' I paused, trying to remember everything I'd heard about it when Mrs Fryston came into assemblies.

'Cut to the bottom line, Sam; how much?'

'I don't know but I don't think it's that much.'

Mum let out a long, deep breath because she knew she had run out of choices. 'What do you do, just turn up?'

'No, you have to fill a form in saying which days you're going to be there and who's picking you up and stuff. Then one of the leaders comes to get you at home time and takes you there.'

'You seem to know a lot about it.'

'I've been observing.'

She sighed hard. 'I suppose you'd better get me one of them form things tomorrow then.'

'OK,' I said, trying not to sound too excited.

At last we got through the lights and headed for home.

The first thing Mum did was go crazy because no one had put the bin out but I didn't mind too much about the shouting because I knew I'd be going to After School club soon and you can stand anything when you've got something good to look forward to, can't you?

Chapter Four

I didn't feel one bit bouncy at school next day. I collected a ZAPS After School Club application form first thing from Mrs Moore, the school secretary, and at break I had a chat to Sam Riley. He looked a bit surprised at first when I walked over to him because we don't mix much. He didn't mind talking about After School club though. He said it was great. He told me he was in charge of the tuck shop and tended to concentrate on that but there were plenty of things to do to suit everyone unless you were a TV freak. 'Mrs Fryston limits that to the last twenty minutes when all the clearing up has been done,' he told me.

'Oh,' I said, 'I'm not bothered. I can watch TV any old time.'

'Exactly,' Sam agreed. He rubbed his chin and stared into the sky. 'Switch the TV off, O Youth of England and Wales . . . It makes your brain go numb and your imagination it jails . . . or fails . . . or—'

'Er . . . very good, Sam,' I interrupted, knowing his poems tended to go into dozens of verses.

'It's a work in progress,' he shrugged, then added, 'You can help me with the tuck shop, if you like. I'm looking for a reliable assistant.'

'Oh, maybe,' I mumbled.

He must have been able to tell I wasn't sure if that's how I wanted to spend my After School club time. I was more into making things. 'You never know, the experience might help you get a job when you're older,' he goes.

'I don't want to work in a shop or a factory!' I told him straight off, thinking of Mum's endless grumbling about Pitt's. 'That would be so boring.'

Sam shook his head at me. 'Oh, you sound just like Luke and Tim—my older brothers—they think that, too. They've told Dad they're not going to work for Riley's when they leave university. Fifty years of tradition gone just like that! I am though. I can't wait until I'm old enough to help out properly and arrange the window displays and serve people and all that. I'm going to design my own range of cards, too. Like Purple Ronnie only different.'

'Oh,' I said, still not convinced.

I guess Sam could tell. He shrugged. 'It has to be in the blood, I suppose.'

I wanted to get back to finding out more about Mrs Fryston but then Naz came up and went, 'Talking to your new boyfriend, Wezz?' and I was forced to chase him across the sandpit to give him a thump and by the time I'd done that the bell had gone and it was mental maths.

Chapter Five

At tea time, Mum agreed to go through my application form with me straight away to get it over and done with before Bridget 'popped in'.

'There,' Mum said, signing her name neatly at the bottom, 'that's you sorted for two hours a day. Now I've just got the other twenty-two to think about!'

'Thanks, Mum, you're the best,' I said happily, leaning across to give her a hug. 'Can I start tomorrow? So I get used to it?'

She shrugged me off. 'If your dad doesn't mind. You know how he is if he misses five minutes with you.'

'I'll phone him now, and ask him, shall I?'

She pulled a packet of cigarettes out of her pocket.

'Ask him if he can pay the first week while you're at it—things are a bit tight for me at the moment.'

'Like that new dress you've got in your wardrobe,' Gemma went.

Dad had just finished having his dinner when I called. Vegetarian goulash. We'd had sausages and oven chips. I told him how Gemma had nearly set the house on fire cooking them. He laughed. 'She'll learn. How was school? Has Aimee been behaving herself?'

He knows sometimes we fall out but I didn't want to discuss Aimee stuff so I began telling him about After School club. He said it sounded 'just the job'. I would have gone into more details but Mum told me to hurry up as money didn't grow on trees. 'Gotta go, Dad. Remember I won't be talking to you tomorrow,' I said.

'OK,' he replied, 'I'll remember. See you at school. Five on the dot. Goodnight, pet.'

'You haven't asked the

question,' I reminded him quickly. He had to ask the question or I wouldn't sleep.

'Oh,' he said, hesitating for some reason, 'erm . . . is she ready to have me back yet? All she has to do is click her fingers . . .' His voice trailed off.

I glanced round, first checking Mum wasn't listening. She didn't know about our little ritual; then I whispered, 'No, but she will, I'm sure. Don't you fret.'

'I won't,' he replied quietly and hung up.

My stomach felt funny straight away. I could have blamed Gemma's sausages but really I knew it was because I always felt funny after I've spoken to Dad. It's because I'm still not really used to him not living with us, if you must know.

Our phone is in the hallway, near the back door. It's where we dump all our stuff as soon as we come in from school. I was just searching in my bag for my maths homework when there was a quick knock on the door and before I had a chance to say, 'Who is it?' Bridget came straight in, bringing the cold with her.

'Hiya, Milly Millstone,' she goes to me, 'is your mum in? I won't be two minutes.'

I scowled at her and followed her through into the

living room. I had wanted to talk to Mum about how I could raise more sponsor money in a hurry but Bridget's arrival had wrecked that. She always said she would only be two minutes but she never was. Two centuries more like. Tonight's two minutes' worth was to ask us what we thought of her new boots.

'Showing off as usual,' Gemma mumbled as we watched her take over.

I don't know what Mum sees in Bridget—she's a bit boring, I think. The only thing that stands out about her is she only takes size three and a half shoes and always wears roll-neck jumpers, even in summer, to hide this birthmark she's got on her neck. It's red and shaped like the Isle of Wight. Other than that she's nothing special.

'What do you reckon?' she goes, moving her tiny feet from one side to the other like a windscreen wiper. The boots were creamy leather knee-highs with a sharp pointy toe and nasty-looking heels.

Gemma and Sasha didn't even glance and just twisted their heads either side of her so they could see the telly but Mum clapped her hands in delight. 'Oh, Bridget, they're gorgeous. How much?'

'I daren't tell you,' Bridget said, then told. It was a lot. A lot a lot.

'Never!' Mum squealed.

'They're Italian—that's what makes them pricey.'

'They are gorgeous,' Mum repeated, her eyes all sparkly. 'What I'd give for a pair of those.'

Bridget smiled tightly and her eyes looked a bit like Aimee Anston's had when she'd told Mr Idle about my imaginary money. A bit shady. 'Well, never mind, Eil, eh?' she smiled. 'Maybe one day when you get rid of the millstones.'

Chapter Six

Next morning was the sponsored silence. I'd started at half-nine when I'd gone to bed so you could say I was already nearly halfway through my twenty-four hours by the time I got to school.

School was easy because I had a perfect excuse not to talk to Aimee. Time dragged a bit, though, I have to admit, until we trooped into the hall to watch Mr Sharkey have his hair shaved off, and then something happened that I had not expected.

A photographer from the *Evening Echo* came and some children had to have a picture taken standing around bald Mr Sharkey. Mr Sharkey asked for teachers to select a pupil from each class and Mr Idle pushed me out before I had chance to mime 'no'.

'Don't forget to say "cheese",' Aimee sniggered.

Guess what? They stood me right next to Brody Miller with her beautiful, long, auburn hair and thick eyelashes and dazzling smile.

I looked straight into the camera, thinking all the time about the crisp tube on my bedside cabinet and how stuffed full of money it was going to be by Wednesday. Somehow, I'd do it. I'd do it for the Yellows and I'd do it for Pudsey. I'd do it, definitely.

Chapter Seven

Before that, though, I had my first experience of After School club. I was really excited when the assistant turned up outside our classroom and felt dead important when she called my name out, then Sam Riley's. She was called Mrs McCormack—I knew that already because her daughter, Alex, is in Year Four and I had seen her loads of times in the playground. I followed quietly behind Sam, first across to Mrs Platini's Year Six class where we picked up Reggie Glazzard but not Brody Miller and then across the playground and over to the mobile on the edge of the playing field.

Sam led the way up the three wooden steps. As we reached the entrance he stood back and said to me:

'*Hope you find that your new home will very quickly bring . . . good luck and happiness to you in simply everything,*'

finally adding, 'New Home cards, price band F next to Good Luck and Congratulations.' I rolled my eyes at him to tell him to shut up but he just grinned and pushed open the outer door.

What got me first was how colourful it was inside the mobile. Staring through the dusty windows didn't show you the floor was such a bright green and the walls so bright orange and yellow. It made me blink a few times, I can tell you. The kids who had already arrived had settled quickly. Some were playing board games, some were setting out paints on the craft table and others were just sitting around, chatting. Everything seemed very relaxed. Reggie headed straight for one of the computers.

I couldn't take much more in then because Mrs Fryston was standing by a desk near the inner doorway and Mrs McCormack said she would want to meet me first.

'I'll come with you,' Sam went, 'and act as interpreter.' I felt really grateful when he said that, because he didn't need to—he could have just gone off to his shop.

'Mrs Fryston,' he said grandly to the supervisor, 'can I introduce you to Sam Wesley, a friend of mine. She's on the sponsored silence, so enjoy the peace while you can because normally she never stops talking!'

What a cheek. It was true, though, so I didn't have no right to punch him or nothing. Not that I would anyway, with him being so helpful.

Mrs Fryston looked even nicer close up than she did in assemblies. She had greeny-blue eyes that crinkled kindly at the edges and pretty silver earrings shaped like snail shells. 'I'll just go over your details,' she said, checking through my registration form with me. I had to nod yes or no to her questions. 'Well, Samantha,' she said when she had finished quizzing me about allergies and stuff, 'would you like me to show you round or would you prefer Sam to do it?'

I shook my head vigorously. 'What, you don't want either of us to?' she asked, puzzled.

I shook my head again. 'I don't think she likes being called Samantha,' Sam said. I gave a thumbs up. Gemma and Sasha always called me Samantha-Panther when they were being sarcastic.

Mrs Fryston paused for a second, looking from me to the other Sam. 'Mm. I've got visions of you both shouting "what?" at me when I call out "Sam" though. How about Sammy?'

I nodded. Sammy would do fine.

'With an ie ending, I think,' Sam added.

I nodded again. This boy knew me well.

'Well, then, welcome to Zaps After School Club, Sammie,' Mrs Fryston grinned, and I felt really warm inside.

'Let me show you the shop first,' Sam said, just about dragging me across the room.  'It's not exactly as I visualize it yet, but I'm getting there.' He guided me towards a wooden market stall with red and white stripy blinds painted down the sides. There was a plastic till and huge tubs full of plastic fruit and vegetables all neatly arranged along the top.

'I'm way behind,' he moaned, scowling at a plastic pineapple which had a caved-in side before he

42

disappeared beneath a curtain at the back of the stall and started getting out more tubs but full of real sweets this time. There were jelly glow-worms and gummi bears and cola bottles and all sorts. My stomach rumbled just looking at them. He added a pile of small white bags, a felt pen, and a margarine tub float to his goods.

Before Sam had a chance to finish his preparations, a little boy with pink yogurt stains on his sweatshirt wandered over and held out a 10p to me. 'Sweets, please,' he said.

I looked at Sam for guidance. He leaned down towards the boy. 'We're not open for business yet, Brandon, but do come back later. You can do me a favour, though. You can tell everyone we've got a new club member. She's called Sammie. Can you remember that, Brandon?'

Brandon stared at me and nodded. The tiny kid shoved out his bottom lip. 'I only want green ones,' he said to me miserably.

'Later,' Sam repeated. 'We have to have a drink and a biscuit first from over there,' he explained to me, pointing to a tray full of brightly coloured plastic beakers near Mrs Fryston's desk, 'and nobody's allowed more than ten pence worth of sweets in one night.'

'My mummy's just had a baby,' Brandon added.

I smiled as if to say 'that's nice' and he walked off.

'He's one of my best customers,' Sam told me. 'He's a full-timer, like me, so I've got to know him really well. I'm a bit worried about him—he's gone very quiet since his new baby brother arrived.' Sam glanced across at Brandon, who had taken a Spot book from a rack and handed it to a boy on a purple sofa. The boy looked about my age but wasn't wearing a ZAPS uniform. 'That's Lloyd Fountain,' Sam said, following my gaze. 'He's another regular, too. He doesn't go to a school—his parents don't believe in it. Has his lessons with them at home then comes here to mix with kids his own age.'

I stared in disbelief at Lloyd Fountain. Fancy not having to go to school. I have never heard of that, have you? I know loads of older kids on the estate who don't go to school because they've been excluded but not any that don't go because their parents actually want them at home. I watched as Lloyd's head of curly hair bent over the book he was sharing with Brandon, and saw how he smiled as he pointed out words to him. At least he can read, I thought. If I had lessons at home I bet I wouldn't even know what a book was until I was fourteen. My mum only ever read the TV guide.

Sam shook a tub of cola bottles. 'They stick,' he explained before continuing. 'The only other full-timers are Brody, who's missing today for some reason, Reggie over there, who always hogs the computer unless it's outdoor activities then he hogs the football, and Alex. Alex's a pain,' Sam hissed, as we stared at her squirting orange paint all over an empty Frosties box. 'She hates coming so she makes as big a nuisance of herself as possible. She gets away with so much stuff

GRRR...EAT!

just because her mum works here. Gets right up my nose.'

I grinned at Sam's serious face.

'What?' he asked.

Glancing round, I took one of the white sweet bags and the felt pen and scribbled, 'And I talk a lot??!!' across the front of the bag.

'Just filling you in on the details,' Sam huffed. 'I haven't even started on the part-timers yet, or the weekly activities. You need to know what's going on, Sammie; you're one of us now, one of the mob in the mobile.'

You probably think I'm being soft, but this glow spread right across my tummy, as if I had just eaten a bowl of creamy porridge. I *was* one of the mob in the mobile, wasn't I? Official.

I scribbled on the bag again. 'YES I AM!! Thanks, Sam.'

That next hour went *so* fast. Sam told me loads more stuff, like how Brody fancied Reggie but Reggie never took his eyes away from the computer long enough to notice and how next time Mr Sharkey 'dropped in' to see Mrs Fryston I had to watch how pink they both went. Sam said he reckoned they were in love which would be cool because Mrs Fryston's first husband had died and she needed a companion. I never knew Mrs Fryston's husband had died. That made me feel really sorry for her, even though it was years ago and she had two teenage daughters and a golden retriever for company.

Do you know what, I think I found out more about people in my school from Sam Riley in an hour than I had in the five years I had been coming here. I couldn't believe it when Dad turned up and it was five o'clock already. He had a bit of a chat to Mrs Fryston and what was nice was everybody waved and said goodbye when I left. After School club was just the best place ever and Sam Riley had a lot to do with that but don't tell him I told you that because I don't fancy him or nothing. I'm not Brody Miller, remember.

Chapter Eight

We caught the bus to Dad's flat and met up with Gemma and Sasha who were already there. They tried teasing words out of me but I still had four hours to go so there was no way I was going to give in to their tricks at this late stage. Not for nothing!

After dinner and an argument about who should get the chair and who should sit squashed up on the bed, because Dad's bed doubled as a sofa, if you know what I mean, we settled down to watch *Children in Need*. At first it was light-hearted and funny but when they showed you short films of where the money was going, we all went a bit quiet. Some of the stories were so sad. One boy called Padraic, who was only my age, had something called arthritis.

Usually it is old people that get it but sometimes you can be born with it, like Padraic. Just walking was agony for him and his finger joints were as big and round as giant marbles.

'That must be horrible to have,' I said. It had gone half-nine so I was allowed to talk again but watching Padraic made me too miserable to celebrate.

'Yeah,' Gemma sniffed gruffly and I looked at her, and she was actually crying, but she gave me a deadeye so I looked away pronto.

'Hey, shall we see how much I collected from work for you?' Dad goes. 'I think we did OK.'

'Yeah,' I said eagerly, 'quick—let's count it now!'

Dad grinned and went to the kitchen unit opposite us to find the collection. My heart leapt as he dropped the box in my lap. For one wild second I thought wouldn't it be great if he had collected so much money he had solved all my problems *and* Padraic's? But I knew as soon as I felt the weight of the box that wouldn't be happening and I was right—it was nowhere near. The warehouse collection came to a crummy eight pounds and seven pence and loads of pesetas. 'Well, I don't know who put those in!' Dad said, holding up the foreign silver coins.

'How much are they worth?' Gemma asked.

'Nothing—Spain has euros now. Never mind, here,' he said, digging into his trouser pocket, 'pocket money time. Don't spend it all at once.'

'Give mine to Pudsey,' Gemma said.

'Mine too,' Sasha added.

'You're not kidding me, are you?' I asked but I knew from their faces I wasn't the only one who felt bad for Padraic.

'Well, if we're being charitable, I'd better add my pocket money, too,' Dad went, and handed me a five-pound note which was the same amount he gave us.

'Can't you do better than that?' Sasha asked.

'No,' Dad smiled, 'I need some for myself. I'm going to the pictures on Sunday.'

'Oooh—hot date, eh, Dad?' Gemma teased.

As if he would. She said such thick things sometimes.

'Er . . . how much will that be you've raised, Sam?' Dad asked quickly.

I mentally added the twenty to the rest in the crisp tube at home. 'Erm . . . about fifty pounds,' I said. There was no point fibbing to him.

'That's fantastic!' Dad said, his eyes all shiny and proud and I thought, any other time, it would have been.

I felt a bit miserable the rest of the night and only got to sleep by imagining I was at After School club chatting to Sam and helping him serve out gummi bears.

Chapter Nine

Mum was already leaving for Mingles when we got home on Sunday, even though it was only seven o'clock. 'I'm going early to get a seat at the front,' she explained, peering into the hallway mirror to check her lipstick. 'There's some sausage rolls and coleslaw in the fridge and I've bought you a big bar of chocolate each, as a treat.' She seemed over-excited and in a bit of a rush. Gemma and Sasha just barged past her without really speaking but I hovered round, wishing she wasn't going out so soon. I hadn't seen her since Friday morning and had stacks to tell her. I knew she'd be fascinated about Mrs Fryston being a widow and Lloyd Fountain having lessons at home, not to mention Padraic's fingers.

I watched as she pressed her lips together over a folded tissue; that's a trick to seal the lipstick, apparently. 'How do I look?' she asked.

She was wearing the new black dress that clung tightly everywhere. It was cut low, so you could see her boobs wobbling out over the top like half-set jellies. On her legs she wore black, shiny tights which looked nice until you got to the battered work shoes on her feet. I thought they didn't really go and I said so, thinking I was being helpful. 'I'll fetch you your black suede ones if you want. They'd be better, I think.'

It also meant a few more seconds with her while I fetched them downstairs, but I got a fierce look and I knew I'd said the wrong thing.

'The heels are too high on those. Men don't like it if you're taller than them,' she snapped.

'Oh, I didn't know that. Sorry. You look really gorgeous anyway,' I told her quickly. 'That Ross Clooney will take one look at you and think "Cor, what a babe!"'

Her eyes sparkled. 'Oh, give up!'

'He will. You're really pretty, Mum. You don't need new boots to get noticed.'

'What's that supposed to mean?' Mum said, flicking her eyes over me for a second before snatching her coat from the hook.

My heart sank as I knew I had said the wrong thing again. 'Nothing. I just meant . . .'

But that was it, she was off, one hand on the door, one fastened round her lilac clutch bag leaving her nothing free to hug me with. 'Don't stay up late, you've got school tomorrow,' she called, banging the door behind her.

'I know—and After School club,' I called after her but she was gone.

In the front room, Gemma was watching telly and Sasha was doing her homework at the table so I went upstairs to get my stuff ready for school and put my sponsor money all together. Guess what? When I got to my bedroom, the empty crisp tube was missing from my bedside cabinet. Ha, ha, Sasha, I thought.

I quickly changed into my pyjamas and went downstairs. 'It's not funny, you know,' I go to Gemma and Sasha, 'in fact it's dead boring.'

'What is, your face?' Gemma mumbled.

'You know what I mean,' I said.

She reluctantly tore herself away from the television screen. 'What do you want, pain-in-the-neck?' she went.

'Hiding my crisp tube. So mature.'

'I haven't seen it!'

'Me neither,' Sasha said, before I'd even asked her. 'Gem, tell me why Galileo was important to science.'

How dense did they think I was? They were always teasing me and I was fed up with it. Especially this time; hiding someone's sponsor money was way over the line. 'Give it back, now, or I'll phone Dad,' I shouted. I meant it, too.

Gemma scowled. 'Dad's going out, remember? And we haven't touched your stupid money! We haven't have we, Sasha?' Sasha shook her head. I waited for the secret look to pass between them but it never happened.

'Where is it then?' I asked. My eyes stung with tears but I didn't care if they saw them or not. It was all right for them. They hadn't told a massive lie about how much they had collected. I knew my collection wasn't much but I had to have something to hand in or I'd look a complete liar. 'I hate you two!'

56

I yelled at them. 'Just because I'm the youngest you think you can do what you want. Well, you can't. Now give me my crisp tube or I'm phoning Dad and if he's not there, I'm calling the police!'

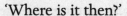

Sasha pushed herself back on her chair and stared at me in amazement. 'Nobody's touched your precious money!'

'Where is it then?'

Tossing down the remote control, Gemma stomped out of the room. 'It'll be exactly where you left it, you big fat cry-baby,' she called, pounding up the stairs. I raced after her, thinking she'd go straight to wherever she had hidden it and pretend she had just happened to find it, but she didn't. Gemma looked in all the same places I had already looked— under the bunk beds, behind the curtains, the back of the wardrobe—everywhere.

Finally, I believed her. She seemed as hot and bothered as I was. I remembered she had given me her pocket money and she had cried at Padraic's fingers, too. I had to think of other solutions. 'Maybe Mum took it into her room for safe-keeping,' I suggested.

Gemma looked at me, then looked across the hallway at Mum's closed bedroom door. 'Yeah,' she agreed, 'maybe she did—it wouldn't surprise me.' For some reason, she sounded angrier than me.

Mum's room was a total mess. There were clothes piled everywhere like in a jumble sale—all over her bed, her chair, her wardrobe door. Gemma ignored all that and dived straight under the bed.

'Aha!' she grunted after a few seconds.

'What is it?' I asked, squatting down to see what she was 'aha-ing' at. Gemma was pulling at a large

white box which had been shoved right back against the wall. Bit by bit, she edged the box out from under the bed, bringing dust and fur balls and screwed-up tissues with her.

'What is it?' I asked again.

'A shoe box, dummy. What do you think it is?' she went, then sneezed.

'So? It's a crisp tube we want.'

'Look at the picture on the side.'

I looked. It was a picture of knee-high boots with pointy toes. 'Why's Bridget left that here?'

'Sam, you're so thick sometimes,' Gemma went but she didn't say it nastily.

'What do you mean?'

'Look at the size of the boots—a seven.'

'So?'

'Do I have to spell it out? Mum's used your money to buy new boots just so she can keep up with Bridget the Widget. It's so obvious.'

'The boots cost way more than I collected,' I went, remembering what Bridget had quoted.

'OK, then put it towards them, then!'

'She wouldn't do that.'

But Gemma wasn't listening. Instead, she flicked up the shoe box lid and let out a long, deep breath. 'Look,' she said, 'now will you believe me?'

I looked. There it was, my crisp tube, surrounded by white tissue paper and totally, totally empty.

Chapter Ten

I didn't sleep much and neither did Mum, judging from the tired way she dragged herself into the kitchen the next morning. She snapped as upright as a newly placed lamp-post in cement, though, when she saw the shoe box in the middle of the table. 'What's that doing here?' she goes, dead angry, looking at each one of us in turn.

I turned to Gemma for help. She had warned me Mum would get all defensive but we had to stand firm. To show me how, she set-to immediately. 'Good question!' Gemma yelled, sticking her chin out defiantly.

'I don't have time for this,' Mum yelled back.

'Make time, Mum. This is important,' Sasha went, dead calm compared to Gemma.

And definitely calm compared to Mum, whose face had gone the colour of cranberry sauce. Even for her, the shouting was way over-the-top. 'Important? I'll tell you what's important—respect! I walk into my own kitchen for a simple cup of coffee and this is what I get—the third degree. Nobody's even asked me how last night went. My big night!'

'How did it go?' I said. Gemma threw me a warning look not to get sucked into distractions but I couldn't help it. It's just the way I am.

'Awful!' Mum wailed. 'Just awful! I bought Ross Clooney drinks all night and then right at the end, when I went to get my coat, he disappeared without a word! The pig!' Mum cried. 'And his real name was Dave Brighouse. Dave Brighouse! That's not very romantic, is it, even for a lookalike?'

Her cheeks wobbled as if preparing for wet conditions but Gemma wasn't having any of that.

 'Who cares? Mum, we know you've been over-spending again—we've found the empty crisp tube,' Gemma said but this time there was no anger in her voice, neither, just hurt and disappointment. 'How could you, Mum? Our Sam's sponsor money? How could you? That is so low.'

Tears sprang into Mum's eyes and she fumbled immediately into her pocket for a hanky. She started crying then and I couldn't stand it. 'Don't, Mum, don't!' I pleaded, dashing round the table and wrapping my arms round her. Her shoulders were juddering but she still managed to hug me back.

'I just borrowed it, Sam, to buy food with . . . you'd have had nothing to eat otherwise . . . those nice chocolate bars . . . I couldn't let you starve, could I?'

'Why didn't you have any money left? You get paid, don't you?' Gemma pressed.

Mum glanced towards the hallway. 'When I bought the boots . . .'

'Aha!' Sasha cried like one of those lady solicitors in court.

Game up, Mum took a deep breath and started to explain. 'When I bought the boots, they maxed out my banker's card so it wouldn't work in the Co-op— you just don't know how embarrassing that was— that snotty Rosie Redfern was stood right behind me

. . . so I came home and remembered the sponsor money and . . . I borrowed it.'

She took my arm. 'I'm sorry, Sam, I wouldn't have done it if it hadn't been an emergency, you know I wouldn't.' Huge tears were rolling uncontrollably down her cheeks and I felt really sorry for her. Sorry and a bit cross, if you must know, but mostly sorry. 'I . . . I just wanted to feel extra special . . . in something new for Ross Clooney. Bridget says you should always buy something new to wear for an important date . . .'

'But it wasn't even a date and the guy dumped you anyway after he'd cadged off you all night,' Gemma said in frustration. 'Mum, you're such a loser. A total and absolute loser.'

'I know,' Mum admitted, 'I know.'

I slipped away then, leaving the house first for once. I didn't want to be there any more.

Chapter Eleven

It was cold outside but I didn't mind. I walked slowly to school, keeping my head down, trying to work things out. But I couldn't. I kept trying but I couldn't. Every time I had one thought about the money it bumped into another one about Mum and got tangled; like those line mazes where you have to trace your pencil along a route to find your way out but all you find is dead ends and in the end you give up and scribble all over the page in frustration. That's how my mind felt as I crossed Zetland Avenue and got nearer to school—like thousands of dead ends with Mum crying at me from some of the ends and Aimee Anston leering at me from the rest.

By the time we were allowed in for registration, I felt really poorly. Being early, I was at the front of the line when I began swaying. 'Are you OK?' Mr Idle asked worriedly. Next thing I knew, I was in Mrs Moore's office with my head between my knees.

'What happened?' I said.

Mrs Moore told me I'd nearly fainted.

'Oh. I've never done that before,' I said. I tried to look up but everything was still fuzzy.

'You look very pale to me,' Mrs Moore goes. 'I've tried calling your mum at work but they say she hasn't turned up yet. Have you any idea where she might be?'

'No. She's always late.'

'You'd be better off at home, pet.'

'I don't want to go home,' I wept.

Mrs Moore passed me a tissue. 'Would you like a friend to come and sit with you then? Aimee or someone?'

The thought of Aimee made me feel even worse. I 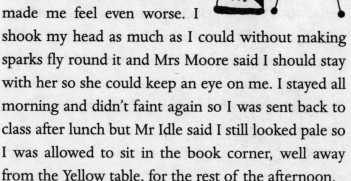 shook my head as much as I could without making sparks fly round it and Mrs Moore said I should stay with her so she could keep an eye on me. I stayed all morning and didn't faint again so I was sent back to class after lunch but Mr Idle said I still looked pale so I was allowed to sit in the book corner, well away from the Yellow table, for the rest of the afternoon.

At half past three, Mrs McCormack came to collect the After School kids and for the first time that day I cheered up. 'You've recovered all of a sudden,' Aimee said as I hurried past her. 'That's good—you'll be able to bring all your money in tomorrow, won't you?'

I pretended I hadn't heard.

As soon as I set foot in the mobile, I felt calm. Don't ask me why. All the fuzz in my head just cleared instantly. Maybe it was because I knew that for two hours I was free. Aimee wasn't here to bug me. Mum wasn't here to confuse me. Gemma wasn't here to stir up trouble. Here I was someone I wanted to be. Here I was Sammie and I didn't bounce.

There were more kids at the club this time, so it was a bit noisier and a bit busier. Brody Miller was there, too. I kept glancing across at her, watching what she did. Sam had asked me to help him in the tuck shop again, so I had a good view of her. Don't ask me why, but I was kind of interested in Brody Miller; she was the nearest I had ever been to a famous person.

'Don't tell me you're another Brody Miller admirer?' Sam said.

'What do you mean?'

'You've done nothing but goggle at her for the past twenty minutes. She's ordinary underneath it all, you know. She slurps her spaghetti and burps like the rest of us—believe me. I've had to sit opposite her in Piccollino's often enough.'

'How come?' I asked. Piccollino's is a posh Italian restaurant in town. Mum and Bridget go there sometimes.

Sam shrugged. 'My parents are friends with hers. Mrs Miller exhibits her ceramics in our gallery—you know, the one above the shop? Mum and Dad have got friendly with her.'

I just said, 'Oh, right, course,' as if exhibiting things in galleries was normal in my family, too.

'And Brody bores for England when she gets talking about Reggie. "Oh, Reggie. Oh, Reggie!" Oh, puke,' Sam grunted.

'She is pretty, though, isn't she?' I went, still staring.

'No prettier than you,' Sam said.

I looked at him to see if he was being funny but he just shrugged. 'Well, she isn't,' he continued, 'it's just that she's got her own personal hair stylist and nail stylist and bogey stylist . . . Besides, her good looks haven't helped her get Reggie to notice her, have they?'

Reggie, as usual, was hammering away on the computer keyboard. 'Shh!' I said, giggling. 'She's coming over.'

'Get your autograph book out.'

'Stop it!'

Brody was first in line with Brandon and Lloyd. 'Hi, Sam, hi, Sam,' she said, ever so friendly.

'It's Sammie,' I said shyly, 'to tell us apart.'

'Oh,' she said and smiled, 'cool.' Her teeth were white and even, I noticed. It didn't stop her having her share of sweets, though. I wouldn't have thought

models were allowed. Brody Miller chose cola bottles and cherry lips. She said 'coh-ler' for cola, like Americans do.

'Ten p, please, Brody,' Sam said in his professional manner.

'And whatever these guys want,' she said, indicating her fans. The two boys said 'Thanks' and smiled at her as if she was a princess.

While they were choosing, Brody took out this purse from a small leather duffel bag. The purse was really pretty—made out of a pink shiny fabric and decorated with sparkly beads and large round mirror-like sequins. I wished I had one like that. She couldn't open the zip at first, though, and she had to tug really hard. 'Oh, my sponsor money keeps getting stuck in the zipper,' she said frowning.

'Haven't you handed it in yet?' Sam asked.

'I kept forgetting. I was late this morning, then Mrs Moore wasn't in the office when I went to put it in the safe at lunchtime . . . you know what it's like.'

Sam tutted. 'You should give it to Mrs Fryston—she'll look after it. You've raised hundreds, I've heard.'

Brody rolled her big blue eyes. 'Oh, the rumour mill's been working overtime again. Not hundreds—hundred—one hundred. Period.'

'It's still a lot. You shouldn't be carrying it around,' Sam told her.

Brody tugged at the purse zip, easing it open bit by bit. 'I will when I get the darned thing open—the plastic bag's caught. Hey, success!'

Finally, she held up a two-pound coin and presented it to Sam.

'I haven't got enough change, yet,' Sam said, shuffling a few 10 p's about in the tub.

'Oh, keep it,' she goes, breezily chewing on a cherry lip.

'Will you play dressing-up with us, Brody?' Brandon asked. I saw he was still wearing the sweatshirt with the yoghurt stains down the front.

'Sure, in a second—you go find something classy,' Brody said, then turned to me. 'Hey, our picture should be in the *Echo* tonight. Fifty p says it will be really gross—that guy didn't have a clue, did he?'

What did she have to bring that up for? I'd been really relaxed until then.

'How did you do it?' she asked.

'What?'

'Raise the cash?'

'Erm . . . I went round . . . collecting.'

A pained look crossed Brody Miller's face and she pressed her hand on my sleeve. I stared down at her nails which were painted dark blue with transfers of white daisies perfectly placed in the centre of each one. 'Oh, I knew it!' she goes. 'You make me feel so bad. I bet you spent hours out in the rain, collecting door to door . . .'

'Well,' I began.

'I feel such a fraud!' she continued quickly. 'India Hevlyn—you know—she's in the Gap Christmas advert—India and me just donated our fees for stomping up and down the catwalk for, like, half an hour at the NEC last week. Is that cheating?'

'Er . . . no . . . you still earned it,' I said.

Her eyes lit up and she smiled widely at me. 'Oh, thanks. People get the wrong idea about me sometimes, you know . . .'

Before she could tell me what sort of wrong ideas, Sam said, 'Does Jake know you've given it all to charity?'

Brody held her daisy nail up to her lip and flung back her hair. 'Really, darling—do you think I'm mad? Kiersten knows though, but shush, OK?'

'Who's Jake, who's Kiersten?' I asked when Brody had gone to the dressing-up area.

As usual Sam was only too glad to fill me in on the details. 'Her parents. Jake Miller, her father, owns Miller's Models and Kiersten Tor's her mother who used to be a top catwalk model but now paints and sculpts. Kiersten's really nice but Jake's a bit tight-fisted. That's why I asked Brody  about the sponsor money—I knew she wouldn't have told him what she'd done—he never gives to charity. I think that's wrong, don't you? If you have wealth you should give some back.'

'Oh, sure,' I sighed, not thinking about that but thinking if I called my mum Eileen or my dad Vaughan I'd get well told off for being cheeky.

'Do you want to join her?'

'Who?' I asked.

'Brody. You don't have to help me every time you come to After School club,' Sam said.

I glanced across at Brody Miller laughing as she fitted a straw hat on to Brandon's small head. He was already wearing a dress fifty sizes too big for him and carrying a pink patent handbag. Lloyd had found a man's oversized tweed jacket and pair of high heels. They reminded me of Bridget's boots. 'No, I'll stay here if that's OK with you.'

Sam looked pleased. 'Good. I like reliability and loyalty in my assistant managers.'

I managed a grin. You can't not with Sam, even if you don't know what he is talking about half the time.

Chapter Twelve

No guesses for who was last to be picked up. Little me, of course. Apart from Alex, that was, who didn't count because she had to be there because her mum worked there. By ten past six, even they had left and I was alone with Mrs Fryston.

I decided to help Mrs Fryston tidy away the dressing-up clothes. 'I bet my mum's forgotten and gone to my old childminder,' I explained. I knew she wouldn't but I felt I had to come up with something.

Mrs Fryston gave me a quick smile as if to say 'it's not your fault'. 'Oh, no worries. I've got to stay late for a meeting with Mr Sharkey anyway.' She smiled again and patted me on the hand. 'Can I leave you to finish this? I need to make a phone call.'

'Sure.'

And that's when I found it. Brody's purse. Lying between a tangerine coloured silk underskirt and the tweed jacket. I could see the edge of the plastic bag containing her one hundred pounds sponsor money caught again in the zip.

Without a second's thought, I slipped it into my pocket and carried on tidying up, intending to give it to Mrs Fryston when she came off the phone. But then Mum arrived, and I knew straight away she was upset, so I just waved goodbye to Mrs Fryston and left. I forgot all about the purse. I really did, especially when I looked at Mum properly under the glare of the cloakroom light.

'Are you all right, Mum?' I asked her as she moved from one foot to the other as if her feet were on fire.

'I'll tell you outside,' she said. 'Wrap up warm, it's windy.'

She didn't speak again until we were reversing out of the car park. 'I've had a nightmare day . . .' she goes. 'First off I get that thing.' I followed her gaze to a brown envelope sticking out of the glove compartment. 'A written warning about bad

76

timekeeping from Pitt's. Bridget got one, too. Can you believe it?'

I could believe it, but didn't say nothing, just listened. 'Sixteen years I've worked there and that's all the thanks I get . . . wouldn't listen when I tried to explain I had to return those boots this morning because the shop closed half day—how was I to know it didn't even open until half nine? On top of that, I couldn't get a refund—scuffed them, they said. Then, to cap it all, I find out your dad's seeing someone,' she goes, 'a woman he met at work. Can you believe it?'

My heart pounded like hail on a glass roof. 'No,' I replied, 'I can't. You must be wrong.'

She scowled and indicated left. 'That's what I said. "How can he find someone before I do, with his lousy dress sense?" I said, but I've heard it from more than one person, so it must be true. Julie, she's called.'

'Well, you'd better tell him to come back quick, then, before it gets serious. All you have to do is click your fingers, remember,' I told her sharply.

She glanced at me and I could tell she changed whatever she was going to say. What she did say was bad enough. 'I don't want him back, babe. Not now, not ever,' she goes, 'so get used to it.'

I remembered Brody's purse again when I was getting into my pyjamas and remembered again when I felt it the next morning as I got ready for school. I know what you are thinking and you're dead wrong. I never planned to keep the money. I had enough to think about with the boots business and this Julie person, didn't I? No, I planned to hand the purse straight in and I would have done, too, if it wasn't for Aimee Anston and her nasty mush.

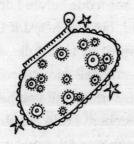

Chapter Thirteen

This is what happened, right? After register Mr Idle reminded everyone about tomorrow being the last day to bring in the sponsor money. He looked at his list and said so far we had a class total of two hundred and sixteen pounds with the Green Table having raised the most with eighty-nine pounds. The Greens cheered their heads off.

'Who's raised the least?' Dwight shouted out. 'Apart from lazy Aimee!'

Mr Idle shot Dwight a dirty look but it wasn't half as withering as the one Aimee fired at him. 'It doesn't matter who's raised the least, Dwight, it's the joint effort that counts,' Mr Idle said.

'Does the top table still go on the radio, though?'

'Yes. It's all arranged for Friday afternoon. Mr Sharkey is going to cover for me while I drive the winners to Radio Fantastico, so the sooner we have all the money in, the sooner I'll know who'll be going.'

Naz sat back and rocked on the back legs of his chair. 'Well, when Sam hands her money in, that's going to be us. Will I be able to tell Tara Kitson my joke about the monkey and the liquidizer?'

'I haven't heard it but I can categorically say definitely not, Nazeem,' Mr Idle goes, then switched his attention to me. 'Nice picture of you in the paper, Sam.'

My stomach plunged a thousand metres. 'I didn't see it,' I said.

Aimee snorted loudly.

'There's no need for that silly noise, Aimee,' Mr Idle said tersely. He hated silly noises.

Aimee scowled at him. She hated being told off. 'She en't got it, so I don't know why you're making such a fuss of her. She wouldn't even have been in the paper if it wasn't for me,' Aimee told him before turning to Naz and Dwight. 'She en't got it, so don't go dreaming of being on radio or telly cos it en't going to happen.'

'What are you talking about?' Mr Idle asked sharply. Between you and me, I don't think he liked Aimee that much either, but being a professional, he wasn't allowed to show it.

Aimee stared coolly at me as if to say 'Your time's up, buddy', then folded her arms and said to Mr Idle: 'The money. She en't got it. She en't collected a penny, just like me, only I en't lied about it.'

Naz leaned across the table and punched Aimee in the arm. 'She has—so shut your cake-hole!'

Aimee thumped him right back, equally as hard. 'No, she hasn't. She's made it up. Ask her before she pretends to faint again!'

There was a pause that felt as heavy as a sack of potatoes pushing into my back. Naz and Dwight looked daggers at her, then me, daring me to tell them Aimee was wrong.

So I did. 'I have got it! I'll get it now!' I burst out. I stood up and walked straight out of the classroom. I know you can guess what I did next but leave me alone. I bet you're not perfect, either.

In the cloakroom, I rummaged deep into my school bag. First I brought out the bit of money I did have—the warehouse collection and the pocket money that were all jumbled together in an old margarine tub—then I rummaged again. From beneath my PE socks, I pulled out Brody's purse, remembering to be careful with the zip as I opened it. I nearly did faint again as I plucked out the neat roll of notes: a fifty, two twenties, and a ten. I had never seen a fifty-pound note before but I knew I didn't have time to gawp, so I crumpled each of the notes up to make them look a bit used and more like Dad's tatty fiver and mixed them in with the coins which still included the pesetas I'd left in for bulk. Finally, I patted down the lid and returned to the classroom.

My heart was hammering away in my chest as I pushed open the door. I felt so angry. Angry with every one of the Yellows for making me do this; angry with Brody Miller for leaving her purse for me to find; angry with Mum for buying those stupid boots; and angry with Dad for going out with someone from work called Julie and not telling me. Most of all, I was angry with me.

I stalked across to Mr Idle's desk and slammed the tub down on top of his pile of marking. 'Here you are, sir. One hundred and thirty pounds, more or less. Watch out for the pesetas!'

'Potatoes? What potatoes?' Naz goes.

'You'd better check it's not come from a Monopoly box!' Aimee fought back but you could tell she was well miffed at the sight of the money.

Mr Idle quickly peered into the tub and smiled. 'No, definitely not Monopoly money. Well done, Sam. And Aimee, I'll see you at break—I don't like your attitude.'

'Who cares? I don't like yours that much, either!' she answered back, going one step too far, as usual.

That meant she was straight to Mr Sharkey's office for the rest of the day and all I had to worry about was facing Brody Miller at After School club.

Chapter Fourteen

The first thing I saw when I walked into the mobile was Brody talking to Mrs Fryston. Brody wasn't crying or nothing, so that was good, but she did look a bit miserable and kept shrugging her shoulders when Mrs Fryston asked her something.

I was prepared for the worst. Any minute now, Mrs Fryston was going to come over to me and question me. As soon as she did, I would tell her everything. It would be a relief, to be honest.

Still, I kept my head down and followed Sam to the cupboard where the sweets were stored, thinking I might as well do something until everything went pear-shaped. 'Is it OK if I help you set up?' I asked.

'Sure,' he said, passing me a tub of flying saucers. 'You put these out and I'll tidy the stock cupboard—it's disgusting. I never get the chance usually but I've got you now.'

He said it in such a taking-for-granted-we'll-always-work-together way. I can't tell you how sad that made me feel.

Mrs Fryston was over at the dressing-up corner now, talking to Brandon and Lloyd. They were both shaking their heads and looking at Brody sorrowfully. Lloyd said something and began taking clothes out of the basket and Brandon joined in, too, thinking it was a game. He began laughing and scattering clothes all over the place until Lloyd put a hand on his arm and calmed him down. At least he's cheerful today, I thought. Finally, it happened. Mrs Fryston and Brody slowly made their way towards the stall.

My heart raced. I felt sick and shaky.

'Sam,' Mrs Fryston goes. We both looked up. 'Sammie,' Mrs Fryston goes, focusing on me, 'do you remember seeing Brody's purse yesterday?'

'Yes,' I mumbled, clinging hard to the plastic container, 'it was pretty—with sequins.'

'I lost it,' Brody said, rolling her eyes. 'Dumb, huh?'

'Can you remember seeing it when you were

tidying the dressing-up clothes last night?' Mrs Fryston asked. 'It's got all Brody's sponsor money inside.'

I opened my mouth to speak, to tell her everything, but nothing came out.

Sam answered instead, 'Oh, Brody, you nit! I told you.'

Brody scowled right back at him. 'Don't bust my chops, Riley. I've already heard it from Mom and Mr Sharkey and Mrs Platini and the world.'

'Well, I did tell you,' Sam repeated.

Mrs Fryston was more patient. 'Where did you last see it, Brody? Can you remember?'

Brody looked fed up, as if she was tired of repeating the same answer. It was a surprising answer though. She sighed heavily and went, 'Well, I'm kind of sure I had it when I left here—I think I remember putting it in my bag as Kiersten collected me. I'm ninety-nine per cent sure I dropped it in the car. I always kind of just dump everything on the back seat when I get in, you know? Kiersten was going to clean it today and phone school if it turned up; she already phoned Piccollino's where we had dinner but nothing was handed in there. Like she said, it could be anywhere. I'm such a Nelly No-brain.'

Anywhere? Nelly No-brain? My heart started thumping against my chest. Brody was blaming herself! She didn't suspect me at all and neither did Mrs Fryston, judging by the look on her face.

'Oh dear,' Mrs Fryston went, giving Brody a quick hug, 'it's such a pity. Well, we'll all have a thorough look in here anyway—you never know.' Without warning, Mrs Fryston clapped her hands together loudly, making me drop the tub of sweets, and asked everyone to listen. As I scrambled after the rolling flying saucers, she explained about the sponsor money and told everyone to have a really good look. While we began the hunt, Brody drew a diagram of her purse on the whiteboard, labelling it with funny captions like: 'Help me, I'm lost' and 'Cranky zipper'

and 'Gunge from squashed jelly belly beans bottom right'.

'See how seriously she's taking it,' Sam muttered. 'Easy come, easy go.'

I didn't say a thing. I held my breath, thinking the longer I kept quiet, the longer I could stay with Sam. I knew I shouldn't. I knew I should have told the truth, but when Brody said, 'I'm sure I had it when I left,' it was like God or someone was saying, 'I'm letting you off this time, Samantha Wesley, seeing as you've got enough to worry about with that mother of yours and that Aimee and that new Julie woman BUT DON'T DO IT AGAIN!!!!' That's what I told myself, anyway. Your mind can tell you anything you want it to when it's desperate enough. Sometimes, you believe it.

Chapter Fifteen

I believed it when I got up the next morning, too. Guess what Mum had done for us all? Only made a cooked breakfast, with waffles and beans. We usually only ever had that on a Sunday. 'Did you hear that?' Mum chirped, turning up the volume on the radio, '*Children in Need* has raised the most it's ever raised. That's good news, isn't it?'

'Yeah,' Gemma goes, 'no thanks to you.'

I shot her a dirty look. Trust her to start spoiling things.

'Don't start,' Mum said, glancing quickly at Gemma then focusing on me, 'I've said I'll pay it back and I will, won't I, babe?'

I was tempted to tell her it didn't matter, that it was

all sorted out, but of course I couldn't, so I just said 'Yep,' and swallowed my last piece of waffle. Mum nodded at me then plodded into the hallway to get ready for work. Coat on, keys in hand, and still only twenty to eight; Mum really was taking her written warning seriously.

Before she left, she stuck her head round the kitchen door, then hesitated. 'Er . . . Bridget's asked if I want to go to the karaoke with her tonight. Would that be all right with you lot?'

Gemma stared at Sasha who stared at me who stared at Mum. This was another turn up. Asking permission to go out. 'OK,' we chorused. Maybe, just maybe, I thought to myself, this whole thing happened to make Mum into a better Mum.

'Thanks, babes. I was going to stay in but like Bridget says, I can't afford to spend time with my millstones when all the good men are being snapped up fast. See you!'

Well, it was a start.

I took my plate over to the sink. Gemma came up and stood next to me. 'So you know about Julie?' she goes.

'Sort of,' I mumbled, scowling at her. From the

way she asked I could tell she had known for ages. Typical. Always the last to know everything, me.

'Dad would have told you but he was worried about how you'd react,' she said as if she could see into my head.

'I don't care,' I shrugged. 'It's his business, not mine.' Angrily I rinsed my plate under the cold tap, shooting water everywhere, thinking maybe she'd get the hint I didn't want to talk about him and stupid Julie. OK, I did really. 'He should have said, that's all. I'm not a baby. It wasn't fair to keep pretending,' I mumbled.

'That's what we told him,' Gemma goes, turning the tap off before I flooded everything.

'She sounds nice,' Sasha added, as if it would help. 'She collects old teddy bears.'

'I'm not ready for details,' I said quickly. 'I have to get used to him not coming back first.'

'Yeah,' Sasha sighed, 'that does take the longest. I still miss not kissing him before I go to school. It was my good luck kiss.' That surprised me, that did.

'I miss the rows,' Gemma added, surprising me even more. 'They did my head in, but at least it meant they were both home!'

I waited, expecting her to follow up with

something sarky but she didn't. 'Maybe we could talk about it tonight, while Mum's out?' I suggested.

I thought they'd say no way, they had better things to do than chat with little brats like me but they agreed straightaway. 'My room, half-seven,' Gemma goes. 'Bring biscuits.'

After they'd left, I made my sandwiches and wiped down the table. I listened to the boiler go whoosh and packed my bag. Everything was quiet and peaceful. As I locked the door behind me, I realized I was looking forward to coming home and being with my sisters.

The bouncing started as I headed for school. It was funny, that, because it was usually the other way round. I told myself it was because Mr Idle was announcing the Radio Fantastico winners today. That meant I wasn't bouncing, really, I was just nervous and sometimes it was hard to tell the difference. It had nothing to do with Brody's purse or anything like that because all that was sorted, right?

Mr Idle made us wait until afternoon to announce who had won the trip to Radio Fantastico. Talk about stretching things out. Don't even try to imagine how I was feeling because you couldn't.

Naz had already worked out the winners. Us. 'I'm going to get Tara Kitson to sign my arm,' he bragged as we waited for registration. Peeling back his sleeve, he showed us a rectangle of dotted lines in felt-tip. 'I've marked the spot for her.'

Dwight goes: 'You should have drawn one on your bum—she'd have had more space!'

Aimee and me laughed at the same time. Do you know, even though she hadn't collected a penny, even though her dad thought it was all a big rip-off, it turned out she was just as excited as Dwight and Naz about the trip to the radio station now that she thought we had genuinely won. 'Dad bought me one of those disposable cameras to take and I've got to ask for a signed photo—one for the whole family,' she said, her eyes shining.

'Do they do those?' I asked. My voice came out low and breathless because I had butterflies in my stomach I was trying to blank out.

Aimee nodded hard. 'Yeah, they do—they're in the foyer as you go in—Dad's seen 'em when he goes to mend the coffee machines.'

'Oh.'

Aimee pushed back my hair and whispered in my ear, 'You can come round to ours for tea tomorrow, if you like. Dad says it's OK, he'll drop you off at your dad's when you're ready.'

'Oh. Thanks,' I said, trying to hide my shock.

She gave me the most enormous smile. 'No worries, Sam. They like me having my best friend round.'

Best friend. That's what she actually called me. You'll hate me for saying it, but that made me really happy. I was in her good books again. Everything was turning out perfect.

Mr Idle walked in then and the whole class stopped talking. Smile, keep calm, I kept saying in my head. Smile, keep calm, no one knows about Brody's money, everything's going perfectly.

'Good afternoon, everyone,' Mr Idle goes, a big smirk on his face. 'In a minute I'm going to announce which table is going to the radio station . . .'

There was a shuffling of bottoms on seats. Naz leaned back on his chair and examined his fingernails, Aimee elbowed me and then linked her arm through mine. It made it hard to concentrate on what Mr Idle was saying when she did that. The butterflies in my stomach had to change direction and crashed into

each other. 'Stop it,' I told them. 'Smile instead. Keep calm, like me.'

Mr Idle carried on explaining. 'I can't give away the total the school has raised because Mr Sharkey is going to announce that in assembly tomorrow. However, I can tell you we have broken last year's total.'

We clapped at that.

'As far as our class goes, I have been staggered by your response. You've been brilliant. Between you, you have raised three hundred and forty-six pounds, on top of which I have added the one hundred and fourteen pounds I made at the rugby club, bringing the Year Five total to . . .'

He put his hand behind his ear and everyone chanted 'Four hundred and sixty pounds,' except Naz, who was still counting.

'That's right! I bet there's not another Year Five in the land that has managed that. Well done. I am so proud of you all. But now for the winning table I'm taking with me to the station on Friday . . . if they can come up at the end so they can take letters of permission home.'

Aimee squeezed my arm really tight.

'In third place,' Mr Idle said, a smile as wide as a banana, 'were the Reds!'

Everyone cheered and I turned round to look at Sam, who put his thumbs up at me.

'What's Riley-Piley looking at us for? Big nerd,' Aimee muttered as she followed my movements.

My smile disappeared in a flash.

'In second place and so close, the Greens . . .'

The butterflies were throwing themselves against the walls of my stomach now. There were hundreds of them—thousands—pushing and pushing and pushing and bouncing and bouncing and bouncing. Aimee squeezed my arm harder. 'Us next,' she whispered, 'we'll bagsie the back seat of the minibus before Naz and Dwight get it, yeah, and I'll tell Tara Kitson all about how I helped you raise the most, right? Oh, and wear your black headband with your name on it and I'll wear mine—we'll look like twins . . .'

A chill ran through me, making the hairs on my arms stand to attention. Pictures of Aimee bossing me about through the years flicked through my mind, like one of those home videos on fast forward. The Pokemon card episode and so, so many others. Then I saw us together at The Magna, her making me smoke behind the sheds or whatever, then dobbing me in when we were caught. I saw her making fun of my clothes and my boyfriends, telling me either they weren't good enough for me or I wasn't good enough for them. I saw her laughing at my kids, telling me they were millstones. The worst thing was, as we got older, I looked more and more like my mum and she looked more and more like Bridget, from a birthmark in the shape of the Isle of Wight to her pointy, Italian boots.

'And, of course, the table going to Radio Fantastico is . . .' Mr Idle grinned and winked at me.

'No!' I screamed. 'No!'

Chapter Sixteen

I am not going to go into tons of detail about what happened after I had confessed about the money not being mine. I don't really want to re-live it, if you must know. Mainly it consisted of Mr Idle going 'Why, Sam?' and me going 'I don't know', and then Mr Idle sending me to see Mr Sharkey in his office and Mr Sharkey going, 'But why, Sam?' and me going, 'I don't know.'

I think Mr Sharkey suspected there was a bit more to the story than I was telling. He kept prodding. 'Has Aimee Anston got anything to do with this? You can be honest with me,' he goes, 'I do know what she can be like.'

I looked at him. I could have said yes. I could have

said she made me do it, with her horrible comments about trailer trash and stuff but I didn't. It was me who had told the first fib and the second one and the third, so it was me who should take the consequences. 'No,' I said to Mr Sharkey, 'it was my own stupid fault.'

'Oh, Sam,' he said, totally disappointed in me. It is not a very nice feeling, knowing your headmaster thinks you have let the whole school down, but to be honest, I couldn't have felt much worse, so I just looked at my shoes and didn't say nothing.

'I've sent for Brody,' Mr Sharkey continued. 'You can explain your actions to her face-to-face. Then Mrs Fryston will need to be informed when she arrives, of course.'

'OK,' I agreed, staring at his carpet, my hands all sticky and sweaty behind me.

After what seemed like a thousand years, Brody walked in, looking surprised and wondering why she had been dragged out of class. Mr Sharkey raised his eyebrows and nodded so I took a deep breath and began.

'Oh, Sammie, I love you!' she goes when I had finished, and gave me a massive hug! I'm not kidding. Talk about strange reactions.

Mr Sharkey seemed as taken aback as I was. 'Brody, this is hardly a matter for celebration!'

'You wouldn't say that if you'd been in my shoes last night when Jake found out I'd lost a hundred pounds. That guy is so going to have a heart attack at fifty!'

'Sam still shouldn't have taken your money in the first place,' Mr Sharkey reminded her.

The Year Six calmed down enough to take things a bit more seriously. 'Well,' she said after a lengthy pause, 'I guess as long as the money went to charity . . .' She gave me a kind of half-sympathetic, half-quizzical smile. 'And I can tell just from looking at her that Sammie's really sorry.'

I decided there and then that if ever Brody Miller needed anyone to die for her, I'd be first in line. Mr Sharkey wouldn't though. 'Well, that's very lenient of you, Brody. I don't think I would be so tolerant if it had been my money!' he goes.

The coolest girl in the world just shrugged. 'Well, the way I look at it is this—Sammie didn't have to own up but she did, so that's a good thing. I got my money and my purse back so that's a good thing,' she said stroking the pink material with her thumb, 'so what's the problem?'

Mr Sharkey rubbed his spiky scalp and sighed hard. 'Right, well, you'd better go back to class. I'll let your parents know what has happened, of course.'

'Sure,' she beamed, then turned to me. 'See you at After School club, Sammie,' she said and left.

Mr Sharkey's eyes followed her out of the room, then he shook his head. 'I need a coffee,' he said, 'the bell's going in a couple of minutes—I'll come back and take you across to Mrs Fryston. I can't promise she'll react in the same way as Miss Miller—After School club is not like here—she can pick and choose her clients,' he said darkly.

Telling Mr Idle and Mr Sharkey what I had done had been hard. Owning up to Brody Miller had been harder, but walking across the playground towards After School club that afternoon was the hardest. The tarmac on the playground seemed to stretch for miles between the main school building and the mobile but it still didn't take nearly long enough to reach it.

Mrs Fryston looked at me with the same expression of surprise and disappointment as Mr Idle and Mr Sharkey had when she found out what I had done. 'Goodness me!' she gasped, as if it was the worst thing she had ever heard of in her life.

I felt a bit choked up then. I hadn't cried so far. I was trying not to because, as I kept saying to myself, I had no right to cry. My eyes began to get blurry though at Mrs Fryston's reaction and I had to look down at the floor dead quick in case she saw. If she told me I could never come along to After School club again, my heart would break, I just knew it would. I loved it here.

That's why I had screamed in the classroom and owned up. I didn't want to spoil it. I bounced everywhere except here and I knew if I had kept quiet about Brody's purse and gone to Radio Fantastico I would have bounced here, too.

Every time I served Brody cola bottles and cherry lips, I would have bounced. Every time Sam talked to me, I would have bounced. Every time Aimee made some snide comment about Sam or the After School club, I would have bounced. And do you know what? I was sick of bouncing. But I had still messed up anyway, hadn't I? Totally messed up, just like my mum.

Not that I knew how to explain any of this to Mrs Fryston.

'I have told Sam that you have every right to withdraw her attendance here,' Mr Sharkey said to her. The three of us were stood in a semicircle near Mrs Fryston's desk, supposedly out of earshot of the others but I could still feel everyone staring at me. Bad news travels fast round our school. I chewed hard on my bottom lip and waited.

'Withdraw her attendance? Well, that's a bit drastic,' Mrs Fryston replied immediately, 'especially in view of Sammie owning up.' She bent down so that we were eye to eye and cupped my chin gently in her hand, making me look directly at her. I could feel a tear roll down my cheek but I daren't brush it away. Luckily, Mrs Fryston had a tissue handy. 'What it does mean is that you'll have to earn your trust back again, Sammie,' she said, dabbing at my face. 'I imagine Sam might not want you helping in the tuck shop for a while, for instance.'

I managed to nod that I understood and she stood up again. I didn't know what to feel. Relieved that I wasn't banned but sad that she didn't trust me to work with Sam. Slowly, I lifted my head to glance over at the sweet stall. If Sam couldn't forgive me, there'd be no point coming to After School club anyway. Sam was the one who had made me feel so welcome right from day one. It wouldn't be the same without him on my side.

Guess what, though? When I looked up, Sam was already at my side, glaring at the supervisor. 'Of course I want her in the tuck shop, Mrs Fryston! Everyone's entitled to one mistake. I told Mr Idle all along making a competition out of who raised the most money was a mistake. I did, didn't I, Sammie?'

I nodded.

Sam began explaining to Mrs Fryston. 'I suggested a poem. Poetry doesn't make people do desperate things . . . unless it's a really bad poem read by a really bad actor, I suppose, or a very sad poem written to a star-crossed lover . . .' He paused and I could tell a million examples of sad poems were now running through his head but Sam pulled himself together long enough to get back to the subject. '. . . but anyway, Sammie's not a proper thief—she gave Brody's money straight to charity and I know she's honest because she hasn't eaten a single thing she hasn't paid for since she's been a helper. Most of them fill their pockets the second they start. Even people who should know better pinch the sweets, don't they, Mr Sharkey?' Sam added, eyebrows raised directly at him. Mr Sharkey was always helping himself to jelly worms, according to Sam.

Mr Sharkey coughed then scratched at a mark on his tie.

'Well, I'm sure that's true but it's not quite the same thing . . .' Mrs Fryston began.

Sam took a tight hold of my hand. I went beetroot straightaway, especially when someone on the craft table giggled, but Sam was too cool to let that distract him. 'Yes, it is; believe me—I am an excellent judge of character. Now, if you'll excuse us, we have a shop to run.' Without waiting for an answer, he dragged me across to the sweet stall and pointed to a box of sweet-and-sour balls. 'Fresh in today,' he told me, '2p each. Watch them—they're exceedingly sticky.'

'I don't like them,' Brandon said, wrinkling his nose. He had been waiting patiently at the stall all the time, ignoring all the fuss. He held out his hand, showing me one of the sweet-and-sour balls almost glued to his palm.

'What's wrong with them, Brandon?' I asked him.

'They're not green enough,' he said instantly, 'and they smash into bits if you drop 'em. I think they should bounce. They're balls, but they're not bouncy.'

I looked at him and grinned. 'Hey, look at me!' I went, patting my sides up and down. 'I'm not bouncy, either! Isn't that great?'

'Is it?' he frowned.

'It is, Brandon, believe me,' I said.

Epilogue

Well, that's my story. I didn't make the best start to After School club, did I? For a few weeks after the purse business I was pretty quiet, for me. I stuck with poor Sam on the sweet stall every night. He must have thought I was a blob of Blu-Tack or something. I wouldn't even go to the toilet in case anything went missing from the cloakrooms and I got blamed. Just before Christmas, though, Sam got that horrible flu that was going round and he was off for two weeks. We sent him cards and everything.

Guess what happened? Mrs Fryston put *me* in charge of the tuck shop. I thought she would have asked Brody or Reggie or even Alex but she didn't—she asked me.

On the first night she gave me the margarine tub float without a word and at the end she just took the margarine tub without a word. 'Aren't you going to check it, Mrs Fryston?' I asked her when everybody had gone and I was last (yeah, I know—it didn't take Mum long to get back to her old habits).

'No,' Mrs Fryston said, shaking her head slightly so her silver earrings jangled, 'I trust you, Sammie.'

That was so nice of her, wasn't it? After that, I really did feel like one of the mob in the mobile and started mixing properly and getting to know the other kids. Sam's still my number one friend at After School club, though, but I don't love him or nothing, so don't start teasing me about it like Gemma and Sasha do. If it's mushy stuff you're after, you need to read about Brody Miller next. Don't get the wrong idea; her story's not all mushy—even child models with dazzling smiles have their problems—but there is a bit of mush, so don't say I didn't warn you.

Luv Sammie

Starring Brody...

*... as the model from the States
(who's in a bit of a state herself)*

Chapter One

Do you have anyone famous in your class? Here's a tip
for you if you do. Treat them like any other regular
person. That's all they want and, believe me, I should
know. Just for the record, my name is Brody Miller and
I'm a child model. You would probably recognize me
if you saw me—I have been appearing in catalogues
and magazines since I was a baby. I am also the
daughter of Kiersten Tor, the ex-supermodel turned
potter and Jake Miller, the fashion photographer. Sure,
we all have a high profile—it comes with the territory,
as does the stalker following me around—but stick me
in a Year Six classroom and you wouldn't be able to tell
me apart from anyone else. Really.

Actually you can cut the 'stalker' thing. It is one

girl at my After School club and 'stalker' is probably not the right word to describe her. I am not sure what *is* the right word to describe Sammie Wesley. All I know is that at three thirty, at the end of school, Sammie would be waiting for me on the top step of ZAPS After School Club. I'm talking every afternoon, rain or shine, hail or sleet, snow or fog, until I got there. No one else; just me. The days I don't come, she doesn't show. I know; I checked with Sam Riley, another club regular she hangs out with. Once we are inside, that is that, she will go off to do her thing, I will go off to do mine. First, though, is always this one-to-one. Tonight was no different.

'I like your boots, Brody,' she began, 'they're well decent.'

'Thank you, Sammie,' I replied, waiting for her to move aside; but I knew she wouldn't. So I waited. Despite the cold February wind blowing round us, she just kept staring at my Doc Martens but not saying anything. I guess they are pretty unusual. They're eighteen-hole DM originals which Mom customized for me—one with a Union Jack design, the other with Stars and Stripes; so my left foot's English like my dad and my right foot's American like my mom. Neat, huh?

Sammie continued to stare at my feet, her hair whipping round her rosy, placid face, still not budging. I figured this greeting ritual with me is something she had to go through, like not treading on cracks in the sidewalk or something. I know from experience she can do odd things sometimes but deep down the girl's harmless so I play along with it. After all, I lived in the States until two years ago. I'm used to weird.

'Do you go modelling in them?' she asked.

I nodded. They had been perfect for the new season's Funky Punk range I had just completed working on. Without giving away too many trade secrets, I told Sammie what clothing style the top guys at Funky Punk would have hitting the high street as soon as Dad finished the shots for them.

'Oh. That sounds dead good!' she enthused. 'I'll tell our Gemma—she loves Funky Punk stuff, though my mum says it's a right rip-off.'

'Yeah, I know what she means—it is way too expensive. Dad hopes his shares will rocket so he can retire and buy a boat.'

My dad's nautical dreams failed to impress Sammie. She seemed miles away, looking at my feet again. 'My mum got some new boots once,' she said.

'Oh?'

'They caused problems.'

'Blisters?'

'No.'

'Oh.'

That seemed to be the end of that but just as I was building up hopes of an early entry into the mobile Sammie looked up and added that my hair looked nice today, too.

'Thanks,' I said patiently, trying not to shiver. Could she not feel this wind at all?

A pained look passed over her face, as if she'd said something wrong and only just realized. 'What I meant was, your hair looks really nice every day but today it looks even nicer than normal,' she explained quickly.

'Thanks,' I said again, 'yours is nice, too. Cool headband.' I like to give a compliment when I receive one. Immediately, Sammie dragged the yellow padded thing off her head and held it out to me.

'It's yours,' she exclaimed.

'No, no, I couldn't, really,' I said in alarm. It was stained and frayed round the edges. A little gross, if I'm being honest.

Sammie gazed at me, her eyes wide and eager. 'Please take it. Please.'

'No, really. I'm fully accessorized. Got slides coming out of my ears at home!' I joked but she looked so disappointed and I didn't want to hurt her feelings. Tentatively I placed the headband on my head and smiled. 'How does it look?'

'Nice,' she said shyly. She smiled at me uncertainly but still didn't move.

I squinted past her and through into After School club. It was already busy. I could see Mrs Fryston, the supervisor, setting up the oven in the corner—it is Wednesday, so it's baking day—and behind her Reggie is standing with his hands in his pockets, looking cool, waiting for the computer to load. I used to have a mighty crush on Reggie but since he told me he didn't plan on dating until Year Seven I backed off and just see him as a friend.

'Anyway, girl in a whirl,' I told Sammie. If I hurried, I could grab the other computer but just as I was about to make a dash for it, I felt something hit me over the head. I twizzled round to see Mr Sharkey, our headteacher, grinning up at me. 'Ah! The famous Miss Miller! Give these to the Nut in the Hut, would you?' he said, holding out a pile of letters still warm from the photocopier. 'And tell her, next time I'm charging!' He strode off back towards the main school building, whistling, and I turned round to face Sammie again but she had disappeared. So snow and ice couldn't budge her but the sight of Mr Sharkey could. Go figure.

By the time I'd dumped my coat in the cloakroom, Lloyd Fountain, the home-schooled kid with the eccentric taste in bright-coloured baggy-jumpers, had taken my place at the remaining computer. I sighed heavily and searched round for Mrs Fryston, the 'Nut in the Hut' as Mr Sharkey had so charmingly called her. She was over at the book corner with little Brandon Petty and is not a nut at all—she is a very nice lady.

Tears the size of pear drops were running down Brandon's pudgy cheeks. 'What's up?' I asked, squatting down so I was eye level with him. He's only five.

'Look who's here, Brandon. It's Brody!' Mrs Fryston said over-

122

cheerfully. 'Brandon can't find his favourite book, Brody. He's looked everywhere.'

'It's been stoled,' Brandon sniffed.

'Oh no! Not *Eat Your Peas*?' I guessed, seeing as I had read it to him about three million times. 'Shall I help you look for it?'

'Would you?' Mrs Fryston said gratefully. 'I need to get the biscuit group going.'

'Sure. Oh, and Mr Sharkey gave me these,' I said holding out the sheets.

She smiled and took them from me, a definite blush appearing on her cheeks at the mention of his name. Let me tell you a secret. Mr Sharkey and Mrs Fryston are dating. I only know because I saw them together at Piccollino's restaurant a few weeks ago. They were so busy playing footsie under the table they didn't notice me over in the corner and Mom said there was no way I was allowed to go up to them and say 'congratulations' in case I was jumping to the wrong conclusion. Since then I have been collecting evidence and I have it in spades. For example, Mr Sharkey just happening to 'pop in' on us in the mobile every two minutes. And when he does, I can tell you for a fact Mrs Fryston automatically does the blushing-thing and this is not a blushing-thing kind of lady. No way was I jumping to any conclusions. Even now Mrs Fryston was stroking the top sheet dreamily with the palm of her hand. It's so sweet! 'Oh, good—the letters home about next week's half-term activities. Will you be coming?' she asked me.

'Yeah—'fraid so,' I sighed, coming back to earth with a bump. Mom was tied up with a new exhibition at The Gallery, a kind of arts studio Sam Riley's mom runs above Riley's card shop, and Jake was in London so I didn't have much choice.

Mrs Fryston glanced at me sympathetically, not offended that I so obviously would rather not spend half-term with her. 'Never mind, Brody, we've got something fun planned. Film-making!'

'Cool,' I said. I felt my spirits rise—film-making sounded better than the usual half-term stuff. 'Brandon and I could give these out for you, if you like, while we're hunting for the book,' I offered to Mrs Fryston as an afterthought.

'Would you, Brody? That would really help. Thank you.'

'Oh, and Mr Sharkey says he'll charge next time,' I told Mrs Fryston as she handed me back the sheets.

Mrs Fryston mouthed a large 'oh!' and faked a scowl. 'The cheek of it. He knows full well I have already paid for his precious photocopying!'

'He's just messing with you, Mrs Fryston. You know what he's like.'

'I do! It's a pity he's nothing better to . . . oh, Tasmim!' she broke off. 'Put the flour down. Not yet!'

I took hold of Brandon's hand. 'OK, buddy, let's go find this book.'

'OK, let's.'

'What's it called again? Eat your knees?'

'No. *Eat Your Peas*!'

'Eat my peas?'

'No, *Eat Your Peas*!'

'That's what I said!'

It took a while to find the thing. Brandon asked everyone about his book and then I followed through with a letter home. Neither Sam nor Sammie at the tuck shop had seen *Eat Your Peas*, nor anyone in the book corner, the dressing-up area, the baking bunch, nor the oddballs with the short attention spans who drifted aimlessly round all afternoon.

We spotted the book by chance in the end, sticking out from under a pile of shiny red paper next to Alex McCormack as we passed the craft table. She must have overheard me asking people for the past half an hour but had let us wander around anyhow.

'I'm using it!' Alex snapped at Brandon as he tried to retrieve the book. She glowered fiercely at the poor kid. Another five seconds and he'd turn into a frog.

I glanced at her work. She was sticking lentils and macaroni to an over-glued piece of cardboard. There was nothing in that activity to do with the book at all. No siree. I bet you she had hidden it on purpose because that's the kind of thing she did. For some reason she got a mighty boost from teasing the little ones, especially the boys, which is weird as I heard she had a brother who had died. You'd think she'd be kinder.

Across the table, her mom was pouring lentils into a jar and she glanced up through her straight peppery-grey fringe, then glanced down again. I knew she wouldn't do anything. That was half the problem—Alex got away with so much because Mrs McCormack allowed her to every time. 'We'll bring it back,' I said firmly to Alex and grabbed the book.

'If he loves it so much why don't you buy him a copy? You're rich enough, aren't you?' she muttered.

'I'm not rich,' I told her calmly.

'But you live up Sandal Road in that massive house with a swimming pool,' she replied. 'You must be rich.'

'As I said, I'm not rich,' I repeated, leaning in real close and keeping a cute smile on my face in case her mommie was watching, 'I'm stinking rich.'

With that, I led Brandon to the book corner, snuggled down with him on the purple couch, and read.

Chapter Two

'Good day, Brode?' Mom asked as I climbed into the passenger seat next to her an hour later.

'Ish,' I said crankily. I was still smarting about what I had said to Alex, plus I had English with my private tutor, Mrs Morgan, next, plus history homework from Mrs Platini once I did get home, plus I was hungry. That's a lot of pluses.

'Buckle up, hon,' Mom instructed.

I sighed hard and did as I was told, thinking about the Alex thing. Why had I said that to her about being stinking rich? I know better than to come out with dumb comments like that. Mom and Dad are always warning me not to sound off about possessions.

The Rich Girl tag gets me every time though.

What was I supposed to do? Sleep in a shed? It's not my fault I live in a big house.

'What's wrong?' Mom asked.

'What? Nothing.'

'You just grunted.'

'Did I?'

'Aha. And I haven't had my kiss.'

'Sorry.' I shrugged all thoughts of McCormack out of my head and leaned across to kiss Mom on the cheek. She smelt shower-fresh and was wearing her black sweater, tan suede jacket, and faded jeans. Just how I liked her. 'Tha looks reet neece, Kiersten,' I said, trying to imitate the Yorkshire accent kids like Reggie had.

'Ta, love,' Mom replied, trying to do one back but sounding really fake. Mom's originally from Kansas and it's not an accent you can easily hide.

'Reet neece,' I repeated for emphasis.

'Ta,' she said again, chuckling.

'Too reet neece to be wasting time sitting outside Mrs Morgan's for a whole hour.'

Mom glanced at me and shook her head. 'Nice try,' she said, handing me my snack of Babybel cheese and a banana before pulling out on to Birch Road and heading downtown to where Mrs Morgan lived.

I tugged at the red wax tab on the cheese and grumbled. 'But why do I have to go, Kiersten? I so do not need extra tuition.'

'Oh, honey, you so *do* need that tuition!'

'I so do not!'

'You "so" do or you "so" wouldn't be saying "so" all the time!' Kiersten laughed. 'Besides, you know you have to keep up, especially now you're going to private school.'

'Stupid Hairy Mary's,' I muttered.

'Queen Mary's,' Mom corrected proudly. 'And there's all the time off you've had recently,' she continued. She means with the Funky Punk thing. Dad did kind of ignore school hours during a job. I hadn't put in a full week for a month now.

'Got me there,' I admitted and chewed my cheese instead. Mom drove on, grumbling about her perspex display units not arriving for the exhibition and how she was sure the whole thing was going to be a disaster, until eventually we pulled up outside Mrs Morgan's large terraced house. To cut a long lesson short, I went in, said, 'Hi', to Mrs Morgan, compiled a list of words ending in -ible and -able and other riveting exercises, said, 'So long', to Mrs Morgan then came out again.

'Right, what next?' I asked Mom, climbing into the car. 'Is there a class in Japanese you'd like me to go to? Or a chimney you'd like me to sweep somewhere?'

Mom switched off her Chili Peppers CD and smiled. 'Next, my poor little munchkin, is the station.'

'Yes!' I laughed. The station meant Dad was coming home. He tried hard to get home one night mid-week but never told us when until the last minute in case he couldn't make it.

'And then Piccollinos?' I asked eagerly. One usually went with the other and the pasta at Piccollinos is just the best in the world.

Mom revved the engine. 'Smell that linguini!' she grinned.

Chapter Three

Dad's train was on time. As soon as I spotted him, I did my usual thing of running down the platform and he did his usual thing of opening his arms real wide and swinging me round until I was dizzy. 'How's my beautiful daughter?' he asked.

'Fine. How's my ugly dad?'

'Still ugly.'

'So I see!'

Dad isn't really ugly, though people round here do frown at his ponytail sometimes, as if it's a crime for a guy of fifty to have one.

'What's that trash on your head?' he asked unexpectedly, lowering me back onto the platform.

'Oh,' I said, reaching up and feeling Sammie's headband. Trust him to notice straight away—he can spot a rogue accessory at two hundred metres.

'Someone gave it to me,' I mumbled.

'It's ghastly—take it off. Or better still, lose it.'

Before I could say a word, he'd tossed it into a garbage can near the sliding doors and without a second thought went straight on to kissing Mom. I peered into the bin after it but Dad scowled so hard I didn't dare retrieve it. I glanced behind me at the garbage can and sighed. Sorry, Sammie.

Piccollino's is just up from the station on Westgate. It's a tall, three-storey, red-brick building brightly painted in green, white, and red. Fredo, the owner, was only just opening when we arrived. He shook hands enthusiastically with Jake, pinched my cheek, and gave Kiersten a long hug before kissing her hard on both cheeks. 'Ah! *bella*, *bella*, Kiersten,' he sighed. 'When you gonna leave this no-good guy and come and live with me, huh?'

Kiersten blushed and laughed him off, as she always did when anyone hit on her.

'You tease!' she told him.

The first thing Dad did when we sat down was to throw a flat brown envelope on the table. I grabbed for it eagerly, knowing it would be the Funky Punk contact prints. 'Are they good?' I asked, remembering the hours of posing I'd had to do. Not just me, either—there had been ten of us altogether, messing about in a freezing cold park in Hertford. Jake shook his head. 'They're not bad,' he mumbled.

'Only not bad?' I said worriedly, glancing from one picture to the other. I hoped I hadn't been the one to mess up.

'What's wrong with them?' I asked, passing the proofs over to Kiersten. They looked fine to me.

'They're all clichéd,' Dad sighed. 'I want something with more edge. Brody, you'll need to skip school tomorrow. I want to take some more one-on-one shots.'

I agreed instantly. 'Sure.'

Mom didn't. 'Couldn't you use one of the agency models? India or Marlonne or someone?' she asked.

'You're kidding me! Pay those pompous wannabes when I've got my little home-grown Jerry Hall right here?' He winked at me and I winked back. I liked being his number one choice.

The waitress, Imogen, arrived to check if we needed drinks. I tried for a Coke but I got nowhere as usual. 'Honey, your teeth,' Kiersten and Jake chorused, shaking their heads in unison.

'Water then,' I mumbled while they ordered a beer each. Modelling

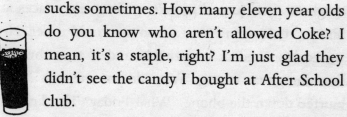

sucks sometimes. How many eleven year olds do you know who aren't allowed Coke? I mean, it's a staple, right? I'm just glad they didn't see the candy I bought at After School club.

Imogen distributed the menus, dutifully recommending the house special.

'Thanks, petal,' Jake said, smiling at her. She smiled back over-brightly before returning to the kitchen area. 'So, how have my two precious girls been coping without the light of their life?' he began. Before either of us could answer, his mobile rang. Dad saw whoever was on the other end off pronto, with a 'Yeah, yeah, action that, fine, fine. Ciao.'

'Oh, Jake, don't you know where the off-switch is

on that thing?' Kiersten complained from behind her menu.

The quick answer to that is no. Within seconds it was ringing again. 'That man's ears will drop off into his soup one day if he doesn't watch it,' Mom muttered to me. 'What are you having?'

I told her I couldn't decide between spaghetti napoli or the calamari. 'Me, too!' she squealed. We had this freaky thing going where we always chose the same things. Finally we both decided on the spaghetti then turned to Jake, pulling crazy faces at him to make him hurry up so we could order. He waved his hand at us irritably and it was obvious something was wrong. 'What do you mean . . . ' he blurted down the phone. 'What Friday? This Friday? I'm not even going to be here. Kiersten? Sure, but she's—' He then stared at the mobile in his hand in disbelief.

'Who was that?' Mom asked.

'She's hung up!' he said, as if he couldn't quite believe it.

'Who was it?' Mom repeated.

'Claire, who else?' he snapped and decided the mobile did have an off-switch after all.

Chapter Four

Just for the record, Claire is Dad's other daughter from his first marriage to a woman called Lynne. He was only young when he got hitched the first time—about nineteen, I think—and he wasn't married to Lynne for long but it was long enough to produce my half-sister Claire who, at thirty, is only five years younger than Mom. Claire lives in a place called Washington, Tyne and Wear, where Dad originally came from and is a real pain. She's always asking for something over the phone—usually money; or moaning about something—usually her kids. She has a daughter called Jolene, who's a bit younger than me, and two stepsons with her new partner Darryl. I'm not sure of their names—isn't that terrible, not knowing? The thing is, I've only met them once, and that was at Grandma Miller's funeral last year, so it wasn't exactly the best time to get acquainted. Whenever I ask why we don't see them, Mom says it keeps things simple and Dad says everyone's too busy. I think there's more to it than that but know better than to 'go roun' diggin' ditches if I can't fill 'em up again' as my grandma Tor used to say.

'What did she want this time?' Mom asked, tucking a strand of hair behind her ear.

'Apparently she's dropping Jolene off on Friday,' Dad growled.

'Where?' Mom asked.

'At the house.'

'Whose house?'

'Our house!'

Mom paled. 'What? Why? For how long?'

'The week!' Dad said, mystified. 'And I can like it or lump it!'

If I'd dared, I'd have laughed, they both looked so totally put-out. You'd have thought Jolene was an escaped convict or something instead of my ten-year-old niece. 'Claire can't just decide that,' Mom frowned.

Dad held his hands up, palms out, which meant, 'It's a done deal—change the subject.'

'But this week of all weeks! Heck, I can't even look after my own child let alone someone else's!' Mom protested.

'I know, I know,' Dad agreed rapidly.

'Why can't Lynne do it?'

'She's in hospital having her varicose veins out, apparently.'

There was a long pause as they both took distracted sips of their drinks. Time for Brody Bright-Ideas to step in. 'Hey,' I said, 'there's not a problem. Jolene can come to After School club with me. It's great—we're doing film-making. She'll have a ball.  Look.' From my pocket, I withdrew the letter home from Mrs Fryston and slid it across the table. Dad took hold of it first, then passed it on to Mom with a shrug. 'Then in the evenings we can chill out and watch videos or swim if the pool's warm enough or . . . ' I reeled off a list of home-based things we could do that wouldn't cause any hassle.

Dad took hold of the letter and read it properly this time. 'It's an option, Kierst,' he said. 'The club's on from nine to six—that's decent enough—and I'll be home all weekend so that frees you up for the exhibition, doesn't it?'

'Does it?' Mom said, staring into her glass.

'Well, the kid's arriving at seven o'clock Friday night. We don't have much choice, do we?'

'No,' Mom snapped, 'we don't, do we, Mister Assertive.'

Chapter Five

Next morning, Dad and me set off to re-take the Funky Punk shots. We drove to a side street off Jacob's Well Road in the city centre and parked outside an abandoned charity shop whose windows had been fly posted to death. Jake thought it was *the* spot for 'edge'. I was already dressed in all the gear. For those who are interested in fashion, from our spring/summer collection, today's ensemble, apart from my boots, was a crew-necked skinny-fit top teamed up with a short kilt, leaf green denim jacket, and cobalt blue tights. Practical, different but not *too* different, and way too expensive—talk about hitting the market.

It was the details I liked best in this new range, such as the skull-and-crossbones pin through the hem of the kilt. 'Get the pin in, Jake,' I told him as he checked his camera.

'Hold still,' he muttered. Cars passed and people stared as Dad flashed off a million shots. His camera always makes a soft whirring sound as it clicks. I focused on his black leather jacket and wondered what Jolene would be like. It was going to be fun having a relative come with me to After School club. I had made plenty of friends at Zetland Avenue but no one special, you know? No number one best bud. Everyone was already established in pairs by the time I got there in Year Four. I'd enjoy introducing a proper family member to everyone.

'That's it! That's excellent!' Jake effused. 'Smile— show me those beautiful teeth.'

I showed him my beautiful teeth.

'OK, now I want more punk than funk, hinnie,' Jake instructed. In Yorkshire a girl is a lass but where Dad comes from she is a hinnie. 'Here, put these on,' he said, handing me a pair of designer shades.

'Oh, cool!' I said, sliding them on.

'They fell off the back of a Porsche,' Dad joked.

'I bet,' I said. In the space of ten minutes I had to

look angry, sad, mean, angry again, and plain cheesed-off.

'Slump more,' Dad ordered, 'turn sideways, cross your feet.'

I slumped. I turned sideways. I crossed my feet.

Finally, Jake looked up and grinned. 'OK, that should do it. You're a star, Brody Miller! I have never worked with any kid more natural, even if I do say so myself. "Get India or Marlonne." I don't think so!'

I felt myself beaming with pride. Dad doesn't often give compliments but when he does, you know he means them. Between you and me, that's why I keep up with the modelling thing and don't mind missing school. Like when Sammie waited outside the mobile for her one-to-one sessions with me, times like this were my one-on-one with Dad. And they were precious.

I had to change into my uniform in the Happy Harvester Ladies Room nearby then Jake dropped me off at the school gates. 'Thanks, Brode. I'll see you tomorrow night, OK?'

'Yep.'

'You'll be all right now? Do you want me to come in and see Mrs Platini?'

'No,' I said, 'I'll be fine. I've got the absence note you wrote me.'

'OK, and remember, if Mrs Platini gives you a tough time, tell her careers come first.'

'Yeah, I'm sure she'll buy that one.'

Dad did a flashy U-turn in the road and screeched off, pipping his horn a dozen times in farewell. Such a quiet guy.

The afternoon was tough going. Mrs Platini didn't give me a hard time, exactly, but made sure I had a copy of everything she had covered that morning 'so I wouldn't fall *further* behind', which meant I missed break trying to catch up. I also knew I had After School club and another session with Mrs Morgan to survive before I could get home and start preparing for Jolene's visit.

First, of course, was Sammie.

'Hi, Brody.'

'Hi, Sammie,' I said, halting reluctantly by the mobile steps as everyone filed past.

'Your hair looks nice.'

'Thanks—yours too.' I peered closer. Actually, she had done something to it. The colour had changed, from a dull straw to a kind of Day-Glo tangerine. It was—erm—interesting.

Her face reddened as she tried to hide a bunch of dry strands behind her ears. 'I was trying to match yours but I don't think our Gemma got the right box,' she said quietly. 'Aimee Anston says I look like a carrot cake.'

'Well, tell Aimee to take a hike,' I advised, trying to peer over Sammie's shoulders and check out the indoor situation. I could just see Mrs Fryston discussing something with Mrs McCormack. 'Anyway, gotta go.'

'Brody?'

'Yep?'

'You know I gave you that headband yesterday?'

I felt instantly awful as I remembered Dad throwing it away. 'Yep.'

'You couldn't let us have it back, could you? Only it was our Gemma's and she went right into one when she found out I'd took it.'

'Oh—erm—I'll have a look for it tonight.'

That seemed to be all she wanted to hear. She grinned and let me pass.

Chapter Six

The next day, Friday, is usually my short day because I don't have any extra tuition or After School club to go to but I guess because I was so excited about Jolene arriving later on, time stretched further than melted mozzarella on a giant pizza. Finally it was three thirty and I could barely keep my arms folded straight as Mrs Platini chose which table could be dismissed first.

Then Kiersten and I had to do Sainsbury's which I usually can't stand—especially the fruit and vegetable section which takes forever—but it wasn't that bad this time because I had fun choosing packed lunch things for Jolene and me to eat next week. 'Shall I get smoked turkey or salami? Or what if she's vegetarian? Is she a vegetarian?' I asked.

'I don't know.' Kiersten frowned. 'I shouldn't think so.'

'What about potato chips—I mean crisps? What do you reckon? Salt and vinegar? Prawn cocktail?'

'I don't know—get both.'

'You don't know? Kiersten, these are basics! My grandma Tor knows my favourite brands.'

'What's that supposed to mean?' Mom snapped. She glared at me for a second before pushing the trolley further down the aisle.

I stared after her, wondering where the attitude had come from. I hurried to catch up. 'Hey, I didn't mean anything. Don't get all humpy.'

Mom threw a tub of popcorn into the trolley. 'I'm not getting "humpy", Brody, but you need to get things straight. I do not figure in Jolene's life as anything other than the woman who is married to her grandad. She certainly doesn't see me as her grandma, any more than Claire sees me as her mom—it would be stupid, anyway, given the age gap, huh?'

'I guess so. I'm sorry.'

Kiersten saw the look on my face and chucked me under the chin. 'Don't look so miserable, honey. I just don't want you playing "happy families" when we're not.'

'What are we then? Unhappy families?'

'No! Just separate families—OK?'

'OK! I get your point. I only asked what kind of potato chips I should choose.'

Mom sighed and said cheese and onion, which was a weird suggestion as those were her least favourite.

Jake got back about six by which time Mom had made dinner and I had checked Jolene's bedroom was in order. We'd put her in the guest room, next to Mom and Dad's, with its high ceilings and awesome view out on to the orchard. I added a few special touches I thought she might appreciate—magazines and books, scented candles and tiny soaps. That kind of stuff. The room looked real homely by the time I had finished.

Downstairs, Jake was checking his watch. 'Has Claire phoned at all?' he asked as it got to seven thirty and there was still no sign of them.

'Not as far as I know,' Kiersten replied, loading the dishwasher noisily.

'I could have caught a later train,' Jake complained.

Boy, he was tetchy—just like Mom had been earlier. That's the trouble with having parents who run their own businesses. They can never switch off. Anything else is an inconvenience. I sometimes wonder what would happen if I didn't actually model for Dad and was just a plain old stay-at-home daughter. Would he even remember who I was?

'How were those shots of me on Jacob's Well Road?' I asked trying to distract him.

'Better than last time—we're still working on them,' Dad sniffed as he checked his mobile for messages.

'Enough "edge"?'

'Maybe,' he said vaguely.

Then again, maybe not, said the tone of his voice but I didn't have time to go into details because a few seconds later we heard the sound of a car on the gravel driveway. Mom slammed the door of the dishwasher and stared reproachfully at Jake, who just shrugged. Claire and Jolene had arrived.

Chapter Seven

The pair stood in the doorway, squinting under the brightness of the porch's nightlight. Jolene was standing slightly in front of Claire but stepped back as Jake approached. 'Come on in,' Jake greeted them, automatically going into enthusiastic-mode and holding the door open wide so they could enter.

'Hi!' I said, pushing forward, too impatient for all those stuffy English formalities. I went

straight for Jolene and hugged her, ignoring what Mom had said in the supermarket earlier about not playing happy families. Jolene was family and I was happy to see her—simple.

My arms slid easily round Jolene's red and white striped football shirt. Wow, she was slender. She stiffened immediately, pulling back her head and shaking her long, fine blonde hair like a horse ready to bolt. 'It is so cool to have you here!' I gushed as Jake prised me off her.

'Let the poor girl breathe,' he rebuked.

The 'poor girl' stared at me through hostile greeny-blue eyes. I guess I had been a little over-the-top. 'Sorry,' I apologized, 'I've just been looking forward to your visit so much.'

Jolene didn't say a thing. She just turned towards Claire and glowered at her as if to say 'get me out of here'. I looked eagerly from my niece to my half-sister, expecting some kind of greeting, but her attention was fully focused on Jolene, whom she began to prod in the back with a sharp fingernail. 'Right, you, just remember what I've said, you behave yourself at your grandad's; I don't want any more of your nonsense. Understand?'

'Get lost,' Jolene mumbled angrily.

'You get lost!' Claire hissed back, before turning to Jake. 'Then she wonders why she's not going to Euro Disney with us!' she exclaimed.

'Ask me if I'm bothered?' Jolene retorted.

I glanced at Mom, who rolled her eyes heavenwards as if to say, 'I knew it would be like this.'

'OK, OK, let's go through into the front room and relax, huh?' Dad suggested, holding out his arm in a friendly gesture as Claire and Jolene continued to snipe at each other. Claire, who was tall and slim like Mom but with over-browned skin from what I guessed was too much time on sunbeds, broke off from her argument long enough to say she couldn't. 'No time; the flight's first thing in the morning and we've got to pack yet. Here's her stuff.' A red nylon backpack was hurriedly thrust into Jake's arms.

'Surely you'll stay for a coffee at least?' he asked nonplussed.

Claire glowered at her watch, as if to consider.

'Yeah, Mam. Stay,' Jolene said quietly and I knew that despite the argument, she didn't want her mom to leave.

'I can't,' Claire replied brusquely, again addressing Jake. 'Darryl's babysitting the lads and I promised I'd be back as soon as we could.'

'You always put them first, don't you?' Jolene muttered.

Claire retorted immediately. 'Well, whose fault's that? Maybe if you started behaving better like they do, I'd put you first.'

'Ask me if I'm bothered,' Jolene repeated but her voice wobbled as she said it.

'Hey, hey, Claire, come on, relax,' Dad said sharply.

I was glad he had interfered. The way Claire talked to Jolene made me feel uncomfortable. Claire's eyes narrowed as she turned on Jake. 'Relax? Huh! Chance would be a fine thing with this one.'

'Well, she can't be that bad. I don't see any ammo,' Dad said and winked at his granddaughter.

'That's right—undermine me like you always do,' Claire complained while Jolene fidgeted silently with the hem of her shirt. I decided I didn't like my half-sister Claire much. I mean, if I'd got this straight, the woman was dumping her daughter so she could take the rest of her family to Euro Disney. How unfair was that? Plus you could see she was itching to get away. She had barely stepped inside the hallway and even now was turning to check the car was still outside. Well, just go then, lady, I thought, and good riddance. I took Jolene by the elbow and pulled her closer to me. 'Jolene will be just fine with us, thanks, ma'am. You can leave now.'

Claire focused on me fully for the first time, running her eyes up and down me like a judge looking for faults in an exhibit. She seemed half-surprised, half-amused by me as I steadily returned her gaze. 'Ma'am? There's a new one! Get her to call me that instead of some of the stuff she comes out with and I'll give you a medal.' She shifted her gaze to the antiques in the hallway for a second before adding, 'Not that you need one.'

'Mam,' Jolene said, her voice wobbly, 'let me come back with you. I'll behave, honest.'

'No,' Claire said, shaking her head, 'it's too late for all that. You've made your bed—now you can lie in it.' Without another word, Claire turned and was gone.

Chapter Eight

None of us had expected Jolene to be left like that—so quickly and so coldly. We all stood around awkwardly in the hallway for a few seconds, then Mom and I broke out in conversation at once, both of us asking Jolene if she wanted to look at her room but our guest just stood rigidly by Dad's side, staring at the door. It was Jake who managed to coax her out of her trance. 'So, you're a Sunderland supporter?' he asked lightly.

Jolene half-nodded and I realized he was referring to the red and white shirt she was wearing. I'm not very up on soccer.

'I always followed the Toon myself, like,' Dad grinned.

I didn't have a clue what he was talking about but Jolene's jaw dropped open in horror. 'Newcastle? They're . . . ' and she used two of the foulest swear words possible to describe them.

Mom's eyes nearly shot out of her head but Dad roared with laughter. 'Well, it's an opinion!' he said, laying his hand lightly on his granddaughter's shoulder and leading her towards the warmth of the living room. 'So who's your favourite player, then?' he chatted on. I noticed Dad's Wearside accent became more and more broad as he talked, until there were 'hinnies' and 'wayayes' bouncing all over the joint. 'We could watch the pre-match reports on now, like,' he suggested, searching for the remote.

'Four-o-one,' Jolene mumbled, staring up at Dad as if she didn't quite believe him.

Dad punched in the number of this never-used channel and patted the couch beside him.

'Canny. Come and sit here then, pet,' Jake said, 'you'll get a better view.'

Cautiously, Jolene sat down, and for the next few hours her eyes never left the screen. I had the feeling she wasn't that interested in the commentary—I think it just gave her something familiar to do. She'd reply to Dad's questions warily but the several times I tried to start conversations up she ignored me completely, apart from darting me sidelong glances now and again. Dad peered over at me resignedly as if to show me he was bored too but eventually I got fed up with being blanked and I went to find Mom. Unfortunately, she was on the phone—fussing with Sarah Riley over the exhibition—so all I got from her was an apologetic smile.

That kind of set the whole pattern for the weekend. Jolene watched TV, barely spoke unless she was spoken to, and hardly acknowledged my presence at all. Dad said it was because she was shy and felt uncomfortable; Mum just sighed and said, 'What can you expect?' They had both been really kind to Jolene, despite their attitude in Piccollino's, and were bending over backwards to make her feel at home. She was even allowed Coke, because she told Dad that's all she drank.

By Sunday afternoon I was really frustrated. I'm an active kind of person and like doing things rather than watching other people do them on screen. Dad was in his study preparing for work on Monday and Mom was over at her kilns in the stable block. 'Do you want to explore outside in the orchard?' I asked Jolene. 'It's great for hide and seek and I think there are foxes living at the bottom.'

'No thanks,' she muttered, watching the credits roll by on the end of yet another cartoon.

'How about a swim in the pool?' I asked.

'Not brought me cossie.'

'I can lend you one.'

'No thanks—don't like swimming much.' She darted me one of her classic sidelong glances.

I sighed heavily and sat down on the arm of the chair near her. 'What would you like to do, then? I'll join in with anything you want.'

The girl hunched her shoulders and shrank into the couch. Anyone would think I had asked her to go sword swallowing or something. 'I want to stay here,' she said and reached out for her glass of Coke. She was about to take a drink when an advert for Euro Disney came on the screen. Her face clouded over and her mouth wobbled slightly as Mickey and Goofy waved their giant rubbery hands at us.

'I bet it's not that great,' I said, trying to make her feel better. 'I heard you have to queue for hours to get on the rides—especially Space Mountain.'

'I suppose,' she said miserably.

I tried to think of something that would cheer her. 'After School club's neat,' I said, 'we're doing film-making.' Even to me it sounded a bit lame compared to Space Mountain.

But Jolene wasn't interested. Her face hardened. 'I hope the car crashes,' she hissed, staring at the TV screen. 'I hope it crashes and Darryl and Keith and Jack get killed so I can have me mam all to myself for once.'

'Oh,' I said shocked, 'that's kind of harsh!'

'I don't care,' she declared, 'it'd be great.'

'I thought they were going by plane?' I said.

Jolene stared stonily at the screen. 'Whatever.'

She reached calmly across for more Coke and I figured a change of subject might not be a bad idea. I glanced towards the door, then took a chance. 'Jolene, do you mind if I have a taste of that?' I asked.

'If you want,' she said, and handed me her glass.

I whispered conspiratorially to her. 'I'm not

allowed it usually. Jake reckons my teeth will drop out,' and I put the glass to my lips. Just as the first drops of the delicious liquid touched my tongue I heard a door open in the outer hallway and panicked. 'Take it back, quick!' I ordered but Jolene had moved and I watched helplessly as the glass slid from my hand and into her lap, splashing Coke everywhere. She leapt up with a yell and the glass smashed onto the wooden floor.

'My shirt!' she shouted angrily, as Coke dripped down it like dark rain. 'Look at my shirt!' For once there were no sidelong glances. Her angry eyes were trained fully on me but I was too busy trying not to tread on broken glass and too worried about what Dad would say to feel the full force of her stare.

'Sorry,' I yelled, 'sorry, sorry.'

Of course, Dad rushed in, wondering what all the racket was about. He grabbed a handful of paper tissues from a nearby box and started to gather the shards in them. 'Oh, Brody, you know you need to be more careful with glass. What happened?'

'She's knacked my shirt, that's what happened,' Jolene stated bitterly before I could explain.

Jake glanced at it and told her it would wash. 'And steady with the language,' he added.

'What am I supposed to wear on top, then? A carrier bag?' Jolene demanded rudely.

I would never have dared talk to Jake like that but Jolene seemed not to care. I guessed it was what she was used to with Claire.

'Just put something else on,' Jake replied.

'Like what?' she snapped, rubbing furiously at the stain.

'Well, I suggest you change into a T-shirt or a jumper. I also suggest you change your attitude while you're at it,' Dad said, trying to sound calm but there was a tiny pulse in his neck that always shows when he's angry or irritated and it was beating rapidly.

Jolene opened her mouth to speak, glanced at me, then Jake, and thought better of it.

'Sorry,' she mumbled, 'it's just I didn't bring anything else. I only pretended to pack when Mam told me, I . . . I hadn't planned on stopping here, had I?'

'That's OK,' Jake said, more gently, 'Brody will lend you something.'

I apologized again for spilling Coke on Jolene's shirt as we headed to my bedroom. 'Yeah, well, accidents happen,' Jolene mumbled, 'though I don't know why you had to go so divvy in front of Grandad. It's only a bloomin' drink.' She gave me one of her looks but I knew there was no point explaining about how I have to take care of myself at all times. It was a model-thing and she wouldn't understand.

I tried to be cheerful. 'Anyway, this'll be fun. You can choose anything you want from my closets. I'll do your hair, too—maybe try out a few styles? It's so straight—I wish mine was straight—you can do so much more with it.'

Jolene frowned heavily. I guessed make-overs might not be her thing.

I led her into my bedroom and opened my closets. I have a whole row stretching across one wall, all arranged according to the seasons, but as I flung one outfit after another on to my bed, Jolene just pulled one sour face after another. 'Nah—too cissy, nah—too poncy,' she said. Boy, was she fussy for someone with only one shirt to wear. She wasn't even impressed by the Funky Punk outfit when I showed it to her. 'I'm just not girly,' she said flatly, 'and that's that.'

Eventually she chose a baggy old *Lakers* sweatshirt. 'This'll do,' she sniffed, leaving before I even had a chance to style her hair. I stared after her and sighed. This *so* wasn't how I had imagined the weekend would turn out.

Chapter Nine

I spent the rest of the evening in my room. I had tried again with Jolene later on but she had reverted to the eyes-glued-to-the-TV-set routine and there was no way I could face that again. Besides, I had homework to finish—a couple of projects for Mrs Platini and some vocabulary work for Mrs Morgan. Mom appeared at some stage and made supper and then took Jolene off to show her where to wash her shirt—Jolene didn't trust Mom to do it for her. I was heading back upstairs when Jake called me through into his study.

'I just wanted a quiet word,' he said, closing the door behind us.

'Hush,' I said.

'What?'

'That's a quiet word.'

He looked puzzled. 'Joke, Jake,' I explained.

His face cleared. 'Oh, right. Sorry, Brody, I'm a bit distracted.' He began packing his holdall, throwing his Filofax randomly on top of files and assorted padded envelopes.

'What gives, Jake?' I asked.

'It's about Jolene. I want you to look after her at this After School club thing this week.'

'Well, duh! What did you think I was going to do?' I asked.

He looked at me gravely. 'Hey, don't you start with the sarcasm—I need you to take this seriously. I do not have family crisis on my schedule for this week. If I don't nail this Funky Punk thing soon I'm going to be in a mess—I'm way behind as it is.'

'Oh,' I said, 'that serious.'

'Yes, that serious, so keep Jolene away from trouble, right?'

'Why would she even get into trouble?' I asked.

Dad scratched the back of his neck. 'Because she's on a short fuse, just like her mother always was—or still is. All the same signs are there.'

'You mean like with the Coke thing?'

'Yes, I mean the Coke thing and the answering back thing and the bad language thing. Claire was just the same—fine as long as she got her own way, foul if she didn't; and then, of course, it's everybody else's fault. I have no time for it—no time at all.'

'Jolene's not that bad, is she?' I said.

Dad sighed. 'I'm not saying she is, but Jolene's obviously no angel or she wouldn't be here. That gets me as well—being used like that. Claire needs to get her act together . . . and fast. Anyway, I'm just relying on you to look after Jolene. Don't let me down—I'm relying on you, Brody.'

'I won't let you down, I promise,' I told him.

'I know you won't,' he said, smiling. 'You're the daughter I got right.'

Chapter Ten

My promise to watch over Jolene was the first thing I thought of when I woke up the next morning. Not because of Dad's fear of trouble, but because she looked so edgy when she realized he had gone. 'He didn't say goodbye,' she said.

'He never does,' I explained, 'he leaves too early. Didn't he tell you last night?'

'Maybe. I can't remember.'

'He'll be back Wednesday,' Kiersten added. Jolene just shrugged, looking distrustfully from one to the other of us as if wondering who was going to pounce on her first.

'Can I make you some raisin toast?' I asked.

'If you want,' she replied dully.

'Butter?'

'Not bothered,' she mumbled.

'What would you like in your packed lunch?'

'Not bothered.'

Not bothered and a few shrugs were the best I could get out of her over breakfast but I guess some people are just not morning folk. I hoped she'd perk up once we got to After School club.

Mom dropped us off and I led Jolene into the playground. Being vacation time, the place was deserted and it was a bit spooky without everyone milling around but I knew once we were inside the mobile it would be more lively. I hoped so, anyway; I wanted Jolene to get some kind of buzz from being here.

'It'll be neat,' I reassured her, 'really.' I began filling her in with details about the film-making activity and Mrs Fryston and how cool everyone was. Just ahead, I could see Sammie waiting. 'That's Sammie—she's nice but she's got a thing about waiting there for me every day for some reason,' I whispered.

We reached the mobile steps and Sammie immediately moved aside to let us through, giving

Jolene an inquisitive stare as she did so. 'Hi, Sammie,' I said and introduced her to Jolene.

They appraised each other carefully. 'Hello,' Sammie greeted her, finally smiling broadly.

Jolene muttered something in reply that could have been a hello.

'Is Mrs Fryston here yet?' I asked Sammie.

'Yes.'

'Oh, OK, see you inside then?'

'Brody?'

'Aha?'

'Did you find our Gemma's headband yet?'

My hand shot to my mouth. 'I forgot all about it— I'm sorry, Sammie—tomorrow?'

'All right,' she said dully, glancing at Jolene who had let out an enormous yawn.

Jolene kept her head bent all the time I introduced her to the others. I guessed it was pretty hard for her,

being surrounded by new people, but she could at least have said hello. All she did was stare at the floor. Reggie, Lloyd, Sam, and even Brandon drifted away when they couldn't get a response from her.

I glanced around, wondering what I could do that might grab her attention. The guys running the film-making course, students from Bretton College, weren't due to arrive until ten thirty so Mrs Fryston had told us we could either play a game or make a photograph frame with Mrs McCormack on the craft table. I asked Jolene what she wanted to do. 'Not bothered,' she shrugged.

'How about Jenga? Or Battleships? Kerplunk?'

'I don't mind making a frame,' she whispered.

'OK.'

We sat opposite Alex and another girl. I tried again. 'Hi, everyone—this is my cousin Jolene,' I said. I knew she wasn't technically my cousin but Mom thought it would be easier to explain.

I don't think Alex was going to bother replying, what with Jolene being with me and all, until she saw Jolene's top. 'That's a Sunderland shirt, isn't it?' she asked.

'Yeah,' Jolene replied slowly and I thought to myself, not stupid soccer *again*.

'My next-door neighbour supports them. She travels everywhere to see them,' Alex informed my niece.

'Does she?' Jolene said, bucking up a little.

'Yes. She even painted the front of her house in red and white stripes once and she's called it "Stadium of Light" instead of "Prospect Place". Mum complained to the council, didn't you? So she had to paint over it.'

Mrs McCormack nodded. 'I certainly did! Smack bang in the middle of an Edwardian terrace? It stuck out like a sore thumb.'

'I think that was the whole idea, Mum,' Alex said, rolling her eyes at Jolene.

Jolene rolled hers back and something clicked between them. I felt it. Alex slid a cardboard template over to Jolene and silently passed her a saucer full of beads which had been half-hidden beneath her jumper. Jolene reached for the glue and that was that.

Over the next half-hour they seemed to do the same thing simultaneously. Alex chose blue beads for her frame; Jolene chose blue beads for her frame. Jolene opted for gold glitter round the blue beads—Alex opted for silver. Neither paid much attention to what they were actually doing—they were too engrossed in their conversation for that. Mrs McCormack raised her eyebrows at me and smiled as if to say, 'Isn't that nice?'

Forget it, lady, I thought. There was no way that relationship was going anywhere but nowhere. Dad instructed me to keep Jolene out of trouble, not leap straight into it.

When Mrs Fryston clapped her hands together for our attention and told us the students had arrived, I pulled Jolene away. 'Let's go over here,' I said and had her follow me across to Reggie.

Chapter Eleven

The three students Mrs Fryston introduced us to were called Sunreep, Will, and Denise. I liked the look of Denise immediately. She was black with the most fantastic coloured weaves in her hair that reached right down to the middle of her back. Her smile took in the whole room and I had a sudden pang of homesickness for my grade four teacher back in the States.

Will took the lead. 'OK, kids, let's see how quickly you can get into three groups.'

Jolene and I were already sitting with Reggie, Lloyd, and Brandon so I didn't have any problem telling Alex we had enough people in our group when she approached.

'One more won't hurt,' she said and plonked herself straight down on the other side of Jolene. Jolene smiled at her and shuffled up. I could see I was going to have to warn her away from Alex as soon as I got the chance.

'OK.' Will smiled, rubbing his hands together. 'Right then, let's get some action going. Who likes films like James Bond with all the car chases and special effects? Or things like *X-Men* where the characters have super-powers like morphing into another shape?'

Several hands shot up. 'OK, well, forget all that!' he said and he grinned at Mrs Fryston as everyone groaned with disappointment, just as he had expected they would. 'We're going to keep things nice and simple. This is the idea: each group will make a short film based around a traditional fairytale—you know, like "Cinderella" or "Snow White" or *Scream 2*. Each member of the group will take part by acting in it as well as dealing with the technical side, so you're all going to be very busy but the end result will be that everyone will have a video to take home. We might even have time for a film show on Friday afternoon. Bring your own popcorn.'

'This is dead smart,' Reggie whispered to me. 'I'm going to be a film producer when I grow up and I'm already getting work experience. Just think, Miller, you'll be able to tell people you knew me at school.'

I dug him in the ribs, first because I hate it when he calls me Miller, and second because Denise was heading straight towards us.

'Hello,' she said, a friendly smile on her face, 'shall we go find a space and get started?'

Our group decided we'd tackle 'Little Red Riding Hood' except it would be called 'Little Reggie Riding Hood'. There's a clue in the title as to who played the main part. I got to be the wolf, Brandon the woodcutter, Jolene surprisingly agreed to be the granny, and then a few fabricated roles were thrown in—Lloyd was Mr Hood, Reggie's dad, and Alex was Mrs Hood, Reggie's mom. The idea was to design the scenes so whoever wasn't acting would be filming.

Everyone seemed absorbed by the project from the start. Lloyd kept coming out with neat ideas about props and scenery and I was real surprised when Alex and Jolene added their suggestions, too. I began to relax. So far so good.

Reggie then suggested we begin working in pairs on the scripts. 'Shall we go over there and write a scene together?' I suggested to Jolene.

'I suppose,' she muttered, glancing at Alex.

'Can't we work in a three?' Alex wanted to know.

'Not really,' I replied instantly.

I didn't see Reggie hovering nearby. 'Er . . . person in need of a partner here,' he announced, looking straight at me.

Alex's face lit up. 'You go with him and I'll go with Jolene,' she decided and before I had a chance to say anything she linked arms with my niece and my usually don't-touch-me niece linked back as if she'd been best buddies with Alex for years. I couldn't help feeling a little sore. I mean, I'd bent over backwards all weekend to bond with Jolene and got nowhere, but two minutes with the book pincher and she's Miss Congeniality.

Reggie doled out the tasks. Boy, he was so motivated. He kept pushing his glasses up the bridge of his nose and spouting out orders. No one seemed to mind—it was Reggie, after all. He never said anything in a bossy way and it did save a lot of hassle having someone take charge. Within minutes the next Steven Spielberg had drawn up a plan of action on a sheet of sugar paper. He had Alex and Jolene work on the opening scene: 'At home with the Hoods, somewhere near the woods'; Brandon worked with Lloyd using Denise as secretary to help Brandon with the writing, on scene two: 'Wolf has lunch—Special of the Day: Raw Granny'. And finally he announced our scene was to be: 'What big eyes you've got for someone with cataracts'.

'We'll write ours in Yorkshire, Miller,' Reggie decided. 'It can get nominated for best foreign language film then. How does this sound? "Reggie Ridin' 'Ud: What great big eyes tha's got, our gran. Wolf: All the better for seeing thi' with, pet lamb".'

'Pet lamb's good,' I said. 'A hint at the character's true eating habits.'

'Course it's good—I'm a genius,' Reggie declared matter-of-factly and he began scribbling away.

Chapter Twelve

'This is the best time I've ever spent in a school,' Jolene declared as Kiersten picked us up that night. 'Except for when I set the fire alarm off during the road safety quiz.'

'Glad to hear it,' Mom grinned, smiling at me as if to say, 'Isn't that nice, apart from the fire alarm thing.'

'Do you know Alex McCormack, Mrs McCormack's daughter?' Jolene asked Kiersten chattily. It was the most animated I'd seen her round Mom since she arrived.

'Yes, I think so—by sight anyway,' Mom said.

'She's my best friend,' Jolene declared, a huge beam on her face.

'Oh, that's sweet—maybe she could come to tea before you go back home,' Mom replied.

My heart thumped painfully in my chest. 'Don't

make any definite arrangements,' I interrupted, before Jolene had time to start ordering in pizza, 'you know how unpredictable this week is for you. It would be dumb if you fixed up something then had to cancel.'

'That's true,' Kiersten agreed. 'Maybe another time, Jolene.'

Jolene scowled at me but I didn't care. There was no way Alex was coming to my house. Not for all the doughnuts in Denver.

Film-making Day Two was polishing the scripts, and adding helpful directions in the margins of the storyboard like: 'side shot of bed', 'close up of "granny's" neck being chopped— NB: use cardboard axe, not real one'. Then Denise had us all handling the video cameras. I tried hard to listen when it was my turn to learn but it was difficult to do that and keep an eye on Jolene at the same time.

She was settling in fast. The girl who had entered the mobile yesterday with her eyes drilling holes in the carpet was now laughing out loud at something Alex had said, making everyone stop and stare. I sighed, thinking how much easier my job would have been if Jolene had stuck with me. I was going to have to do something before it all got too silly. What, I didn't know.

Reggie brought me out of my stupor by rapping his knuckles on my skull. 'Hello! Anyone home?' he shouted in my ear.

'What? Oh, sorry, got other things on my mind,' I said as we made way for Brandon and Lloyd on the camera and returned to our storyboard.

'Focus, Miller—I can't do all of it, I need your help,' Reggie told me peevishly.

'Glad someone does,' I mumbled, glancing down at Jolene as we passed. She didn't even notice.

'She's not going to get lost, you know,' Reggie said.

'Who?'

'Her—that cousin of yours. You follow her round like a lemon.'

'You don't understand,' I told him.

'You're right, I don't,' he agreed. 'But I know one thing, you've turned into a right miserable mare since she came.'

'Thank you so much,' I grunted.

He pushed his glasses higher up the bridge of his nose. 'You're welcome,' he said.

Chapter Thirteen

Wednesday morning, Day Three, was the read-through for each scene so we could start thinking about stage directions and positioning of actors and cameras for when we started filming in the afternoon. The whole project was hotting up and there was a real buzz in every corner of the After School club. For my part, I had decided Reggie was right—I had turned into a 'miserable mare' this week, so I was trying to make it up to him by collaborating harder on his script. Alex and Jolene were fully occupied practising with the video camera, so I was free to work on my Yorkshire accent, which Reggie thought was 'right pathetic'.

'OK,' Reggie began, 'you're under the duvet and I come in. I put your shopping on the foot of the bed . . .'

'Are you sure Granny would have ordered lager and pork pies? It doesn't seem appropriate somehow,' I interrupted.

Reggie pursed his lips. 'It's called improvisation, Brody, and every actor worth their salt does it. Anyway, my gran lives on Baileys and Cornish pasties so I don't see why this one can't live on lager and pork pies. Now, can we get started?'

'Yes, sir.'

Reggie cleared his throat. 'My, what big eyes tha's got, our gran,' he boomed, zooming in close and staring into my eyes.

'All the better to see thi' wi', Reggie Riding Hood,' I said, stumbling across each word.

''Ud,' Reggie corrected, ''Ud.'

''Ud.'

'You've got nice eyes by the way,' he mumbled.

'Shut up,' I mumbled back.

The actor-director cleared his throat once more. 'My, what great big lug 'oles tha's got, our gran,' he boomed again, zooming in so close to my ear he filled it with his warm breath.

'All the better to hear you with, Reggie Riding 'Ud,' I said, trying not to giggle because it tickled.

''Ear you with,' Reggie corrected, ''ear.'

I threw down my script in exasperation. 'What exactly is your gripe with the eighth letter of the alphabet in this county?'

'I don't know—just get on with it, woman,' he replied and punched me lightly on the arm.

I punched him back. 'Don't start summat you can't finish!' I warned him.

He laughed and shouted across to the rest of our group. 'Summat? Eh—Lloydy—did you hear that? Miller over here said "summat". We'll turn her into a northerner yet!'

At break I walked over to the craft table to give Jolene her snack but she waved it away. 'It's all right—Alex already gave me this.' She showed me a half-eaten bar of sticky pink and white nougat. It looked gross and I felt rejected again, thinking of all that time I'd spent choosing things for her in Sainsbury's last week.

'Oh. Well, don't just fill up on junk, will you? We're having a meal in Piccollino's tonight with Jake, remember,' I said. He was coming home for his mid-week stop-over.

Jolene shrugged. 'That's ages away,' she pointed out before casually informing me that Alex reckoned Reggie fancied me. 'She says it's dead obvious.'

I got kind of defensive—I don't know why. It hadn't exactly been a secret I had liked Reggie once but I just didn't like being teased about it by Alex. 'He does not! Alex talks out of her butt,' I replied without thinking.

Jolene's face clouded over slightly but she carried on eating the gluey nougat, her eyes fixed on mine. She ate rapidly, gnawing it like a squirrel until finally tossing the remaining stump in the direction of the waste basket. It missed. 'Aren't you going to pick that up?' I asked, as Mrs Fryston looked across inquisitively.

'Nah, I'll let you,' Jolene said breezily and she walked away. My, she sure was feeling at home.

It was lunchtime when the whole thing went pear-shaped. I was eating my packed lunch with half the cast of *Reggie Riding Hood*, a quarter of the cast of *Snow Bite* (the vampire version), and all of *Pop Idols* (Sammie's group not quite getting to grips with the idea of traditional stories), when Brandon arrived, trying not to cry but not quite managing to stop the tears. 'Brody,' he sniffed, tugging at me, 'they've taken "Peas" again.'

'Who have?'

'Alex and that other girl. They've hidded it and they're laughing at me.'

My heart sank. I really didn't want to have to deal with this.

'Can't you tell Mrs Fryston? Or Denise?'

'I don't know where they is,' Brandon said, his chest heaving up and down. That book meant so much to him.

I twisted round. Sure enough, Alex had *Eat Your Peas* tucked under her arm and was heading for the cloakroom with it.

'Wait here, guy, I won't be long,' I told him.

'Thank you, Brody,' he sniffed. 'You're my hero.'

Chapter Fourteen

When I couldn't find them in the cloakroom or any of the toilet cubicles, I realized the pair had gone outside, even though it was drizzling heavily, and out of bounds. Jolene and Alex were standing outside the mobile, on the small platform leading down the steps, eating chocolate. Alex was spouting forth in a forced whisper anyone passing within fifty metres could overhear. '. . . And Mr Sharkey, who's our head teacher, right, he's going out with Mrs Fryston but they're keeping it quiet because his divorce has only just come through and it might look bad.'

Where had that juicy bit of information come from, McCormack? I wondered. Jolene nodded interestedly as Alex continued gossiping for Great Britain. 'Mrs

Fryston's told my mum she's having trouble with her two teenage daughters about it because they don't like her having a boyfriend.'

'Huh! Tell me about it!' Jolene said.

'She's never had one since her husband died, you see.'

My, she knew her stuff. Across the playing field, I could see Mr Sharkey, who had obviously forgotten he should have been on vacation, talking to the caretaker. I thought it might be a good idea to stop any further revelations in case the Head decided to 'drop in' on the Nut in the Hut sometime soon. 'Hi, you guys,' I said, stepping round the door to join them, trying to keep it light. 'How you doing?'

Their gaze told me they weren't overjoyed to see me, so I got straight to the point. 'Erm . . . is it OK if I have that book for Brandon? You know what he's like about it,' I said, addressing Alex.

She pulled it closer to her. 'No. We want it for a prop in the play. It's Mrs Hood's newspaper.'

'Couldn't you use another book instead?' I asked.

Jolene shrugged and I could tell it wouldn't have mattered either way to her but Alex pursed her lips and scowled. 'No,' she repeated, 'why should I? It's not his, like I told you last time.'

Yeah, I thought, I remember. 'Oh, chill out, Alex, it's no skin off your nose which book you use, is it?' I said. 'He's only a little boy.'

Her face paled, as if I'd said something outrageous. 'So what? Why should they get their own way all the time? It's not fair.'

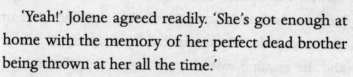

'Yeah!' Jolene agreed readily. 'She's got enough at home with the memory of her perfect dead brother being thrown at her all the time.'

'That was a secret,' Alex muttered to Jolene.

'Sorry, Alex,' Jolene replied instantly.

I tried again. 'Come on, Alex, just give me the book and I'll bring you another one, huh?'

Alex squared her shoulders and pushed the book out of reach. 'Get lost, Brody Miller. You think you rule, don't you, just because you're a model. Well, you don't!'

Where had that come from? 'I so do not think that! Get a life, Alex,' I said, becoming irritated. I turned to

Jolene. 'I wouldn't hang out with her so much if I were you—she's too immature for you.'

It was so the wrong thing to say. Jolene's eyes narrowed and her face tightened as it had when I'd spilt her Coke that time. 'I'll hang out with who I like so don't call my friends names or else,' she threatened.

Alex giggled and I felt myself blushing hard but I bit back my reply. I did not want to enter into the whole answering back deal I knew Jolene was so good at. The last thing I needed was Dad arriving at the station and getting at me for causing a commotion. Mom, too, for that matter. She was still chasing those dumb perspex units and had to travel over to Manchester to get them today. Being greeted by a report on Jolene and me arguing wouldn't go down well after a long journey in the rain. Sorry, Brandon, I thought, I can't be your hero today. 'OK, OK,' I said to Jolene, 'it's nothing to get worked up about. I'm out of here.'

I began to retreat but Jolene hadn't finished. I noticed her breathing had changed; it was now coming out in strange, rapid breaths, as if she had been exercising heavily. Distracted, I didn't see the finger which darted towards me suddenly and poked me so hard in the chest, my head bounced against the door. Alex stared too, seeming as startled as I was. 'Alex is right,' Jolene continued heatedly, 'you do think you rule and that you can boss people round all the time, don't you? You even bossed my mum around!'

'When?' I said, rubbing my head.

'When we arrived. You almost shoved her out of the house like you were the queen or something.'

'I was just trying to help you,' I said quietly, 'she was being mean to you.'

My niece focused on me once again, pushing her face closer and closer to mine so I could smell chocolate on her breath. 'My mam's not mean! She'd have taken me with her if you hadn't stuck your oar in!'

'I don't think she would—she said you'd made your bed and you had to lie in it,' I pointed out.

'Shut up, you!' Jolene roared, tears gathering in her dark eyes. 'Shut up! Shut up! You don't know anything about her. She was only trying to teach me a lesson. She would never have left me if you hadn't interfered and that's a fact, that is.'

'I didn't get that impression,' I said in a small voice.

But Jolene hadn't finished. 'Oh, you want an impression? I'll give you an impression. Who's this? "Yes, Daddy, no, Daddy, course I won't drink Coke, Daddy." You're feeble, you are. You're just a big feeble creep, like Jack and Keith. A big, stupid goody-two-shoes feeble creep who does everything you're told cos you haven't got a brain of your own!' She sprang back, stepping agitatedly from side to side, clenching and unclenching her fists, eyes trained on me, full beam and frightening.

I glanced at Alex, thinking she'd be enjoying the spectacle, but to my surprise she looked as afraid and bewildered as I felt. 'What's up? Cat got your tongue?' Jolene goaded me. 'That's a first, isn't it? Yap, yap, yap—that's all you do—talk. It does my head in! Go on, say something now!'

Say something so I've got an excuse to whack you is what she meant. I just stared at her blankly. I had never been in a fight situation before and my brain seemed to have seized up. I stood there mutely, just waiting. 'Go on!' Jolene repeated, coiled and dangerous. 'Say something!'

'She doesn't need to say nothing to you!' a familiar

voice shouted from behind me. Jolene stopped pacing for a split second as Sammie announced herself by banging the door behind her and glaring at Jolene through her orange fringe.

'Go away you!' Jolene barked at her. 'This is private.'

'Go away yourself!' Sammie barked back, standing squarely in-between Jolene and me. I had hardly seen Sammie all week—she had not even been on the steps to greet me the last two mornings—but I had been so preoccupied with Jolene and Alex, it hadn't registered. She was here now though, as solid as a stone wall. It was somehow reassuring. I cautiously edged round to give myself a little more space on the crowded platform. The drizzle had turned to rain as if to dramatize the whole sorry scene. 'Back off!' Sammie ordered. 'You can't talk to Brody like that, even if you are related! An' if anyone's feeble round here, it's you!'

'Says you and whose army?' Jolene sneered.

Alex opened her mouth to speak but closed it again. 'Why don't you go get . . . ' I began, thinking this might be a good time to find an adult. Mr Sharkey, preferably, but he seemed to have disappeared from view.

'No,' Jolene shouted shrilly, misinterpreting what I had meant, 'you get lost!'

'I wasn't going to say that!' I protested but she

wasn't listening. Whatever rage she had been suppressing finally erupted. Arms outstretched, Jolene lunged forward and pushed hard, sending Sammie careering helplessly into me. I automatically reached behind to hold on to the wooden rail as Sammie struggled to stay upright but I slipped on the wet floorboards and missed it. Sammie went one way and I went the other, toppling down the steps and onto the gravel border beside the mobile, face first.

A burning sensation seared across my mouth but it didn't really register. I heard someone scream, then I was dimly aware of Denise holding a huge towel over

my mouth and telling me to keep calm, keep calm, as she guided me to Mrs Fryston who was waiting by her open car. I think Mr Sharkey appeared at some point, ushering everyone back into the mobile, but I was already being driven away by then.

Chapter Fifteen

Mrs Fryston slid her mobile phone into her bag once more as we waited for an emergency appointment with Dr Willows, my dentist, having been directed straight there after seeing a doctor in the same medical centre complex. 'I've tried all your contact numbers but nobody's answering,' Mrs Fryston informed me worriedly. 'I'll keep trying, though. Is your mum out today?'

From somewhere in my cotton-wool brain, I registered I needed to nod.

'I expect she's at the exhibition, is she? It's very good,' Mrs Fryston told me, 'I went on Saturday with—I went on Saturday. I really liked the bowls with the seahorse design . . .' Mrs Fryston chatted nervously but I wasn't really taking any of it in and I don't think she expected me to. I felt shaky and numb and sick.

Eventually, the dental nurse called me through. 'Do you want me to come, too?' Mrs Fryston asked me. I nodded again. I needed someone familiar with me.

In the surgery, I slid reluctantly onto the black leather chair and felt even more sick and shaky as Dr Willows operated the lever to make the chair recline.

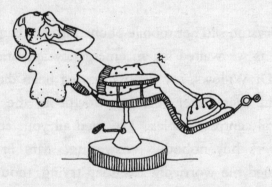

'Let's see what we've got here, shall we?' Dr Willows asked, moving her gloved hand to take the towel away. I clung to it at first, then began crying quietly as she gently coaxed it out of my grip. I already knew what she was going to find. I had run the tip of my tongue over the gap where my front tooth used to be.

The dentist grimaced when she saw. 'Oh dear, what a shame.'

'What is it?' Mrs Fryston asked huskily from her chair behind me.

She gave it to her straight. 'Her upper left incisor is broken right off, almost to the gum.' I winced and poor Mrs Fryston let out a gasp.

'Did you have the other bit of tooth with you?' Dr Willows asked.

I couldn't see but sensed Mrs Fryston shaking her head. 'I never thought to look—I just wanted to get her here as fast as possible,' she apologized.

'I doubt we could have glued it back anyway.' Dr Willows sighed. 'The tooth's broken too near to the gum, though I should be able to use the part that's left to build up a temporary new tooth to protect the damaged area until we get a veneer made. I'll have to take the nerve out, I'm afraid.' She looked at me kindly. 'It'll mean an injection, Brody, to stop you feeling any pain.'

The dentist then turned to her assistant and gave instructions. I squeezed my eyes shut and didn't look as the cold needle was slowly inserted into my gum. I tried to be brave. I tried counting to ten and thinking positive thoughts but I couldn't. I just cried noiseless,

salty tears because I knew nobody would be saying,
'Show me your beautiful smile', ever again.

Chapter Sixteen

When Dr Willows had patched me up the best she could and made me a fresh appointment for the next stage of treatment, Mrs Fryston led me back to the car. 'What do you want me to do?' she asked. 'I could drive round to the gallery and see if your mum's there, or take you back to school?'

'Mom's in Manchester,' I managed to reveal at last, my words crawling sluggishly over my thick tongue. I glanced at my reflection in the side mirror. As well as having a new fake tooth that felt like someone had stuck a house brick in there, one side of my face was scratched and grazed from where I'd ploughed into the gravel. My hands and knees, too, were gritty and sore. The girl from the States was in a state.

'Ah,' Mrs Fryston sighed, clicking in her seatbelt. 'Back to Zetland Avenue then.'

She drove slowly, even though there wasn't a lot of traffic around. 'Well, what a palaver, hm?' she mused. 'Can you remember what happened, Brody? I'll have to write out an accident form, you see. It's best to do it as soon as possible.'

I stared out of the window. The rain had stopped and everything was a washed-out dull grey. What had happened? I'd messed up, that's what had happened. Dad had asked me to keep Jolene out of trouble and I'd let him down, totally. Boy, was he going to be unhappy tonight. The thought of his reaction worried me more than any missing tooth.

I knew I was being dumb—I was the injured party here, right? But Jolene got it in one when she'd mocked me for being a—what was it?—a feeble, goody-two-shoes. When it came to my dad, I admit it, I didn't like letting him down. I would do anything to please him, from skipping school to avoiding cola. No way would I ever back-chat him the way she back-chatted her mom. Why? Because I was such a suck-up? Nope. Because I knew where I stood in the scheme of things. Jake Miller was no family guy. He put photography first, Kiersten second, and me third.

I didn't mind—it was just the way it was with a lot of creative types. But I didn't want to drop any further in the chart. Didn't want to end up like Claire, discarded like Sammie's headband because she wasn't to his liking. I mean, she was his first daughter and he hardly saw her, and Jolene was his only granddaughter and neither he nor Mom even knew what her favourite potato chips were. Call me whatever you wanted but I liked being the daughter he got right. It was a secure place to be.

But I'd messed up and he was going to be so cheesed off when he came back unless . . . my brain began spinning ideas together . . . unless I could persuade everyone it was just an accident. I mean, I fell, right? And if it hadn't been wet . . . and if Sammie hadn't fallen into me . . . 'I slipped,' I said finally to Mrs Fryston. 'We were just talking outside and I slipped.'

When we got to the main school building, Mrs Fryston nodded towards the reception area. 'Looks like Mr Sharkey's got everyone in there,' she said. 'Shall we go and get an update?'

I shrugged. Might as well face my demons one at a time, starting with Jolene. 'It all sounds very quiet,'

Mrs Fryston said to me, and she knocked on the office door.

I straightened my shoulders and walked in. I pretended I was modelling, focusing only on getting to the end of the catwalk and back. 'Hi,' I said, addressing no one in particular, 'what's new?'

Mr Sharkey, Alex, Sammie, and Jolene were all crammed together, competing with filing cabinets and computer desks and a mini pool-table for space. Everyone turned to stare as we entered. I made myself look directly at Jolene, to check out if she'd left Lake Psycho and calmed down. Her eyes met mine sullenly before she glanced away.

Mr Sharkey spoke first. 'Oh, dear, Brody, you have been in the wars, haven't you? Sit down, flower.'

Sammie was out of her seat like a shot. 'Sit here, Brody,' she said, her eyes filling with tears for some reason. I really wasn't hurt *that* much—no broken bones or anything. As I sat in her place she dragged a well-used tissue from her cardigan sleeve and blew hard.

'We're just trying to sort things out,' Mr Sharkey said, 'but we're not getting very far. Everyone seems to have taken a vow of silence—most peculiar.'

Everything did remain unbearably quiet for a few more seconds, then Alex spoke. She was sitting in the furthest corner, her head and shoulders partially obscured by a netball trophy. 'I'm really sorry, Brody,' she said timidly.

I looked at her in surprise.

'I'm really sorry—about what happened . . . outside.' She glanced from me to Jolene then back again. I remembered how distressed she had been when Jolene had lost her temper. She still seemed quite shaken.

'It's OK,' I mumbled.

'And I'm sorry for always teasing Brandon . . . you know . . . over the book. I won't do it any more.'

'OK,' I said again, not quite believing what I was hearing.

'I didn't like it when you fell. Every time I close my eyes I see it,' she explained, her voice wobbly and full of remorse.

'Forget about it, Alex,' I said, 'it wasn't your fault. It was an accident. I just skidded on the wet decking.'

'At last! A simple explanation from Miss Miller!

Hurrah!' Mr Sharkey said melodramatically. 'Alex, as you have said your piece, if you want to return to After School club, I think that would be OK,' he told her. 'If that's all right with you, Mrs Fryston?'

'Of course,' Mrs Fryston agreed.

Alex, clearly relieved, stood up to go, passing Jolene as she did so. 'See you later, Alex,' Jolene said.

Alex shook her head, not looking at her at all. 'No. I don't want to,' she said quietly. 'We're not friends any more—you're scary.'

I have seen many expressions on Jolene's face over the last few days but I had never seen the one she wore as Alex left. It was as if she had been totally crushed. Any other time, any other person, I'd have felt really bad, but not today. I wasn't that much of a sucker.

No one else seemed to have heard Alex's parting comment—the grown-ups were bringing each other up to date with what had gone on in After School club during Mrs Fryston's absence and Sammie was head-down, staring at the carpet. I turned my attention from Jolene to the girl who had tried to rescue me from her, wondering, dimly, why she was involved at all, really.

'Are you OK?' I whispered, looking up at Sammie. 'You seem upset.'

'Oh, Brody, you look so horrible,' she sniffed.

'Hey, it's like having a face-lift, only cheaper,' I quipped.

But Sammie would not let me cheer her up. She began with the waterworks again. Mrs Fryston broke off her conversation with Mr Sharkey and addressed her. 'Why don't you go back to your film-making for the last part, Sammie? You're singing a duet with Sam, aren't you?'

'No,' Sammie said firmly, 'I'm not leaving Brody. I'm on duty.'

'What do you mean?' Mr Sharkey asked.

'It's private!' she said haughtily, sniffing back tears fiercely and glaring at Jolene.

Mr Sharkey looked at me as if for an explanation but I was as clueless as he was. Mrs Fryston bent down to talk to Sammie. 'Would you like a minute alone with Brody? Would that help?'

'Yes,' Sammie agreed instantly.

'Brody? Is that OK with you?'

I nodded, feeling Jolene's eyes following us as we stepped into the corridor. 'So,' I said, 'what gives?'

Sammie feigned interest in a display of pastel drawings on the notice-board, then looked at me with huge, shiny eyes. 'I'm sorry, Brody!' she sobbed. 'I was meant to be on duty, minding you, and look what happened.'

'What do you mean "minding" me?'

'You know,' she sniffled, now resorting to wiping her nose with the back of her sleeve, 'minding

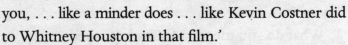

you, . . . like a minder does . . . like Kevin Costner did to Whitney Houston in that film.'

'Film? You mean *The Bodyguard*? Oh,' I said, as the penny dropped, 'oh! Is that why you're always waiting for me when I come to After School club?'

She nodded hard.

'I thought you were stalking me!'

She looked at me alarmed. 'No!' she cried. 'I was protecting you against stalkers and assassins and things. That was the whole point! Just till you got inside the mobile. I knew I wouldn't be needed inside.'

'But why?'

'Because all famous people have minders and I thought I could be yours. An' I wanted to pay you back.'

'For what?'

She glanced down at her feet. 'For what happened before.'

'Before?' I was really confused.

' . . . when you were so nice to me after I nicked your sponsor money.'

'Oh that,' I said, dragging my mind back to something that had happened so long ago I'd almost forgotten, 'that's ancient history.'

Sammie's face crumpled. 'It's not ancient history to me! You could have dobbed me in but you never. You were magic. I would never have settled into After School club if you hadn't been so nice. That's when I decided I'd pay you back one day but I didn't have nothing to give you, so I thought of the minding thing, cos it wouldn't cost nothing, then . . . then I made a fatal error that minders must never do.'

'What was that?' I said.

'I made the mistake of letting the enemy get close to you because I was fooled into thinking she was your friend. That's why I never stood outside this week and that's why the first time I was needed, I was rubbish! I fell for the oldest trick in the book.' Her shoulders heaved again and I reached out and gave her a massive hug.

'Oh, Sammie, you weren't rubbish. You were miles better than Kevin Costner, who's a real nice guy, by the way.'

But Sammie refused to be mollified. 'I hope Mrs Fryston bans that Jolene—no offence, Brody—I mean, I know she's family and all but she shouldn't be allowed to get away with shoving us around like that. She's a nutter. I haven't said nothing yet but—'

'Sammie,' I said, whispering urgently, 'I did fall. I missed the handrail, OK. If it hadn't been raining and slippery I'd have been fine.'

'No you wouldn't—'

'I would. Sammie, please, I would!'

'If you say so,' she mumbled reluctantly.

'I do.'

She gave her nose a final wipe on the back of her sleeve and shrugged. 'I suppose I'd better get back to Sam. You can't sing "It Takes Two, Baby" on your own.'

'No, you can't.'

As she turned to leave, Sammie glanced at the half-open door to Mr Sharkey's office and said loudly, 'If she starts again, though, I'll bash her in, and that's a promise, that is.'

Chapter Seventeen

No one questioned my version of the incident and it was treated as an accident. We were all given a warning about not going out of bounds, especially in wet weather, and Mrs Fryston filled in her form and Mr Sharkey got back to his paperwork and Jolene and Sammie and I returned to After School club for the last, long hour. The students had already left and packed away all the equipment. The others marvelled at my cuts and grazes and Reggie wanted details about how long the needle had been, then started telling everyone about the time he'd fallen off his bike and his shin bone had come right through the skin and even the surgeon had thrown up at the sight of it. It was easy to see the kind of films he'd be producing when he got older.

I didn't look at Jolene at all. So far she hadn't said a word to me and I decided she could take a hike. If she could do this to someone and not even say sorry, then we were through. I'd be like Kiersten was with her—polite but remote—which was still more than she deserved.

Kiersten was late. She came in all flustered from a lousy journey full of 'ridiculous' roadworks and 'crazy' lorry drivers and then she saw me and nearly dropped on the floor. After a long, long talk with Mrs Fryston she hustled Jolene and me to the car and set off for the station. 'You'd better stay in the car and wait, honey. No way are you standing on the platform tonight in this wind,' she told me.

That was not a problem.

The problem was, Jolene stayed too.

We sat side by side, separated by perspex cubes and silence. As sure as eggs was eggs I wasn't going to talk

to her, so I tried to distract myself, making up mnemonics for the car registration parked in front. MMS. Mini Macaroni Shapes. Minnie Mouse Sucks. My Mouth Stings.

'You don't have to worry. I'll tell him the truth,' Jolene suddenly announced. I jumped, having been used to the silence and not expecting her to break it.

'Who?' I said.

'Grandad Jake. I'll tell him I pushed you. I won't try and get out of it. I'm not a coward. You don't have to protect me.'

'I'm not trying to.'

'Good—cos I don't need you to. I always own up.'

'I don't want you to own up.'

'Why not? I would, if it was the other way round.'

I scowled at her. 'But it's not the other way round, is it? And it's the least you can do.'

She gave me one of her famous sidelong glances. 'I didn't mean to . . . to mess your face up like that,' she muttered.

'Gee, that's not some kind of apology, is it? Anyone get that on tape?' I snapped. I surprised myself at how much anger I was venting but I didn't care. I really didn't care.

'I didn't mean to—'

'Didn't mean to? Just what did you expect to happen when you pushed so hard?'

'Nothing. I never think that far ahead. That's the problem.'

'It sure is. Even your new best friend doesn't want to know you any more.'

She mumbled something.

'What?'

'I'm getting some help for it after the holidays. A child phsycholy-whatsit,' she said, a little more clearly.

'Psychologist?'

'Yeah—one of them. I'm top of the list in our school for anger management lessons.'

'Go figure.'

'I don't like being like this, you know—always in trouble. I can't help it. I get all worked up and then my head fills up with black and I can't even remember what happens, it's all a blur.'

Her voice trembled and I knew she was fighting hard not to cry. Jolene the tough-nut had been replaced by Jolene the . . . well . . . kind of sad. She looked small and lonely and I believed her. I believed she didn't like being like that.

All the anger I had built up since the argument drained away. What was the point of staying mad with her? She was just a mixed-up kid and she had apologized, in her own way. It left me feeling sad, too. 'I wish . . . I wish you'd just told me you were mad at me about what I did when you arrived—you know— with your mom. We could have avoided all this.'

'Yeah, well . . .'

I swallowed hard and my own voice dropped. 'All I ever wanted was to be your friend,' I told her.

There was a long pause, as Jolene considered what I'd said. 'That was never going to happen,' she said finally and I had to admire her for that. Jolene was always honest. Plus it was true. Jolene hadn't clicked with me, not like she had with Alex and you can't force people to get along if they don't click, any more than you can prevent people getting along who do. I'd just got off to a bad start with Jolene and made things worse by trying to keep her and Alex apart. Funny how a bad experience can make things so much clearer. She still shouldn't have pushed me, though!

We sat in silence again, both lost in our thoughts. The windows of the car were steamed up and I wound down the one on my side to let in the cold evening air. In the distance, I could see a train slowly pulling in on to the platform. 'Jake's here,' I said.

'Canny,' Jolene mumbled.

Chapter Eighteen

In Piccollino's, Dad gently
tipped my chin first one
way, then the other.
'You poor kid! I wish
I'd been there for
you. No permanent
damage though, hinny.
Nothing a little airbrushing can't sort out, eh?'

'I guess.'

He'd been pretty calm about my accident but what
could he do, anyhow—these things happen, right? As
long as Jolene played along, everything would be fine.

'We'll put some witch hazel on those scratches
when we get home,' Kiersten added.

Dad requested a look at my tooth. I glanced

quickly at Jolene, who had her eyes glued on the cruet set, and showed him. He grimaced immediately in the same way he had at Sammie's headband that time. 'Oh, what? I've a good mind to sue the pants off that After School club.'

'Jake, don't!' I said in alarm. He just might, knowing him.

'Relax, Brody! Just kidding!' He grinned. 'Though if it had happened a week ago I would not be feeling so magnanimous; but as it is, I have this tiny gem with me to cheer you up!' He winked at Mom and produced a flat envelope which he slid across to me. Inside was one of the pictures he'd taken of me on Jacob's Well Road. It was one where I was slumped against the wall, hands behind my back, looking away from the camera and with one DM crossed over the other. 'That's the image you'll be seeing on every bus stop and every hoarding from one end of the country to the next!' he declared. 'The designers chose it, not me—not one iota of favouritism was involved in the choosing process.'

'That was the one with the edge, then?' I smiled, feeling proud.

He nodded. 'That was the one. Miller and Miller on a roll. What a team, eh?' I smiled widely at him and he smiled widely back. When it came to work, we always clicked.

Mom leaned across and gave Jake a massive kiss on the cheek. 'That's wonderful! It means you can stop being such a grumpy old boot!'

'Hey! Less of the old!' Dad protested.

My tooth was beginning to throb. The anaesthetic had worn off and I didn't feel hungry. Part of me was a little nervous that if I bit down on my new temporary tooth by accident, it would crumble into my plate. Jolene didn't have much appetite, either. She frowned at her menu suspiciously. 'The carbonara's good,' I told her.

'I want my mam,' she mumbled.

'Your mam? I don't see her anywhere on the menu. Try the bolognese instead—it's less chewy,' Jake joked.

'Don't tease, Jake,' Kiersten said, looking concernedly at Jolene. 'Are you OK, honey? You look peaky.'

'I want my mam. I want to go home.'

Jake reached out a hand and touched Jolene lightly on the arm. 'Hey, lighten up, Jolene. We're celebrating. And listen, I'm not going back to work for a few days—I thought you, me, and bruised-up Brody here could take tomorrow off and go to the cinema or something? What do you say?'

I stared at him. I didn't want a day off tomorrow. I wanted to finish filming with Reggie. Kiersten got into a conversation with Jolene and I tugged Jake on the sleeve.

'Jake, I have to finish my project tomorrow.'

'What? And miss a day out with your old man? Never! It's not as if you're missing school. Anyway,' he said, eyeing my face, 'those scratches might be worth a couple of shots—the street urchin look, know what I mean?'

I felt my stomach clench as I prepared to turn him down. 'Thanks, but I don't want to miss After School club tomorrow. It's important.'

He looked at me and shrugged. 'OK—I'll go bug your mother at the gallery and take her to the cinema instead.'

And that was it. That was the first time I'd stood up to my dad and nothing happened. He didn't bust my chops. He didn't disown me. He didn't say I was turning out to be a disappointment just like Claire. He just shrugged. I felt so relieved, until I remembered he was on a high from finishing his project. The real tester would be if I asked for a Coke. Imogen was approaching. Would I dare? I mean, my tooth was gone, right? There was no enamel to save, was there?

But I never got that far. Kiersten was frowning at Jake, telling him something.

'What?' Jake asked.

'My mam's at home. I want to go back,' Jolene said slowly and clearly.

'What do you mean? I thought she wasn't back until Saturday?' Jake asked.

Jolene sighed hard at having to repeat what she'd already told Kiersten. 'I phoned home this afternoon from Mr Sharkey's office. I didn't expect anyone to answer but Keith did and he told me they'd come back early cos they got bored. Mam was out shopping but I'll bet she'll be in now, if you phone her to come and get me.'

She looked at her grandad eagerly and he knew she wouldn't let it drop. He ran his fingers through his hair and sighed. When Imogen arrived to take our order, he shook his head apologetically. 'Forget it,' he said, 'we'll take a raincheck.'

Chapter Nineteen

It turned out to be true. Jake phoned Claire's house as soon as we got in and she answered and admitted they had come home early from Euro Disney but they hadn't called because they didn't want to interrupt Jolene's holiday with us. Nor could they come for Jolene because their car had been broken into while they were away and it wouldn't be fixed until Saturday. Jolene became so distraught when she heard that, Jake promised he'd take her to Washington in the morning, though he told Mom who told me that Claire didn't sound too thrilled about it. 'Weird, isn't it? Anyone would think she didn't want her daughter back. I don't understand it—Jolene's such a cutie, really.'

At night-time, I knocked on Jolene's bedroom door

and asked if I could come in. She didn't reply but I went in anyway. She was sitting on the edge of her bed, ramming her few possessions into her red Sunderland bag. She looked up at me, her face content. 'I'm going home tomorrow,' she said.

'I know.'

'I can't wait.'

'I can see that.'

She glanced at me. 'Did your mam put any of that stuff on your face yet?'

'The witch hazel? No, not yet.'

'I hope it gets better soon.'

It was odd, but I think she had already forgotten who'd done it.

I looked around, not sure why I had come but I just felt I couldn't let her leave without some sort of final ending. Plus there was something a little fishy about this whole 'just got back from Euro Disney' story. 'I didn't know you'd phoned home from Mr Sharkey's office?' I began.

She shrugged. 'Oh yeah—I asked him if I could when he was marching us across the playground. I thought he was going to chuck me out anyway—I'm always being excluded from places—and I thought I'd rather go straight home than . . . '

'Than face After School club tomorrow.'

She shrugged before continuing. 'Well, everyone hates me there now—there's no point in going.'

'Yes, but if you explain about the black—'

But she wasn't interested in that. 'I phoned Nana first but she was out, then I called home, just in case she'd gone round there to clean up . . .'

'I thought your nana was in hospital?'

'Oh, she's out now and miles better.'

I looked closely at her and I just knew she was lying. 'She was never in hospital, was she?'

'She was!'

'And they never went to Euro Disney, did they?'

'Who?'

'Claire and Darryl? They never went.'

Jolene bit her lip. 'Course they did. They went on Space Mountain and everything.'

'No they didn't! You're fibbing. I can tell because you're so lame at it!'

'All right, I am,' she said in a small voice. 'They never went away anywhere but Mam said she couldn't face a week of me arguing with Jack and Keith and Grandma said she was fed up of having me in the holidays and why couldn't Grandad Jake do his turn for once? Mam thought Grandad wouldn't have me if she didn't make up something extreme. That's why she dumped me on your doorstep—she knew she couldn't keep making up details about flights and stuff when they asked. She's a rubbish liar, like me.'

I sighed hard. Poor Jolene. 'I didn't know we were such a screwed-up family,' I said.

'Yours might be, mine isn't,' she stated. I wanted to tell her that my family was her family and we were all screwed up together but I knew she'd see that as a fake thing to say so I sat on the edge of her bed and passed her a pair of socks.

Chapter Twenty

Jake dropped me off at After School club next morning before taking Jolene home. Jolene and I kept it casual, just saying 'see you' to each other when I got out of the car. I guess we didn't have much to say to each other really—everything had been cleared up last night. As I reached across for my bag, she handed me an envelope. 'Will you give that to Alex for me? It's got my address in and everything,' she said.

Our eyes met. 'I'll try,' I said, 'but I can't promise you anything.' I took the envelope then went round to Dad's side. He wound the window down and leaned out to give me a big hug.

'Take care of yourself, hinny, I'll see you tonight.'

'OK.'

'I'm sorry I'm having to do this—I'd got some quality time planned, but never mind.'

'Give it to Jolene—she needs it,' I told him, 'and find out what potato chips she likes.'

He looked at me kind of strangely but I just waved goodbye and headed for the mobile. I had a film to finish with my buddies.

Epilogue

The last two days of film-making went so fast, I barely thought about Jolene at all. Isn't that terrible? I settled right back in as if nothing had happened, unless I happened to pass a mirror. That's what I like about After School club—nobody makes a fuss but you know they all care. Weird, isn't it? I'd been thinking all this time that I didn't have any special friends at Zetland Avenue when it turned out everybody was my special friend—Sammie, Reggie, Brandon, Lloyd, Sam—even Mrs Fryston and Mr Sharkey. Sharkey and Fryston make a good team, don't they? I have a feeling Mr Sharkey knew all along about what happened out there on the steps but he was waiting to hear my angle first before he took any action. That makes good leadership, in my book.

Anyhow, we finished the films and premièred them in front of the parents on Friday afternoon. The students set up a mini Oscar ceremony. *Reggie Riding Hood* didn't win the best foreign language category but it won best costume and best screen kiss. Yep, that's what I said. Best kiss. OK, I'd better tell you about that one, though it was pretty embarrassing at the time, especially as Kiersten and Jake were in the audience.

Thursday afternoon we were on set, OK, recording the main part, where Reggie Riding Hood is giving it the 'what big eyes you've got' routine. I was sitting up in bed (two chairs pushed together with a rug over my knees), adjusting my bonnet because it was too tight for my springy hair, when Reggie delivered the 'What big eyes tha's got, our gran,' bit, then smirked and leaned in close.

'All the better for seeing you with, Reggie Riding 'Ud,' I said in my best Yorkshire accent, which still had a long way to go.

Reggie leaned in closer. 'My, what a messed-up face tha's got, our gran—it looks like roadkill,' he yelled.

That wasn't in the script but I just scowled at him in a wolf-like manner and said, 'All the better for . . . ' Then I halted because I couldn't think of how to end it. Then, before I knew what was happening, he bent down and said, 'I'd better kiss it better for thee!' and he pecked me lightly on the cheek. Lloyd, who was on camera at the time, started giggling and when you watch the film you can tell because it goes all shaky at that point. Anyway, afterwards Reggie said, 'I suppose I could go out with you; but keep the sloppy stuff to a minimum,' so I said, 'Fine, it's a deal.' Just for the record, Reggie is now my boyfriend but dating in Year Six just means we sit together on the computers at After School club and we get teased a lot in Mrs Platini's.

What else happened? Well, Sammie went back to her guard-post on the steps, watching out for stalkers and assassins attacking me from all corners of the school yard. Only now she looks the part because I gave her the shades that Jake said fell off the back of a Porsche. She was *so* delighted. Sammie has a birthday coming up soon and I'm getting her a microphone headset to go with them and before you ask, yes, I replaced Gemma's headband—three times over. I made Jake pay for them too—I told him he had no right doing that to people's property and he actually agreed. I'm getting braver at telling him when I don't want to do stuff and so far it's been OK, just like in the restaurant. I'll never get to the real heated exchanges with him, though, it's not my style. Besides, we're so busy working on the autumn/winter collection for Funky Punk we don't have time to argue.

As for Alex, she took the part of Granny and kept her promise about being nicer to Brandon. She even bought him some sweets from the tuck shop—all green, of course; Brandon only eats one kind of colour candy just as he only reads one title of book.

I don't know what she did about Jolene's letter—she never said and I never asked. I reckon she did Jolene a big favour, though, by telling her she didn't want to be her friend any more. I think it shocked Jolene into thinking about her actions much more than breaking my tooth did.

Last I heard, Jolene was doing OK but it's difficult getting news from people who don't really communicate. Still, Jolene knows my number—she's free to call any time.

Alex is up next with her story. I really don't know much about her, except she isn't as annoying as I first thought she was.

Starring Alex...

... as the girl with the voice of an angel
(who can be a little devil too)

Chapter One

My name is Alexandra Mary McCormack—Alex for short. If I had been a boy, I would have been called Daniel Timothy McCormack, after my brother who died before I was born, so I'm glad I'm a girl. It's bad enough being surrounded by him without being named after him too. Dead Daniel is everywhere in our house. I'm not trying to be disrespectful or anything but for someone who's not been around for ten years, and was only four when he died, that boy takes up way too much space. There are pictures of him on nearly every wall, with his halo of curly hair and huge blue eyes staring out at you as if to say 'Who are you?' Where there isn't a photograph, there's one of his drawings from nursery school.

What used to be his bedroom, and everyone except Mum now calls the den, is *still* full of his toys and even the garden has a bench dedicated to him. Worst of all, every night before I go to bed, I have to say goodnight to his ashes that are on the mantelpiece. I'm not kidding—talk about creepy. The only good thing about the ashes business is watching visitors' faces fall when they ask what is in the nice lacquered box and Mum says 'My son'.

Which brings me on to the other gripe I have. Visitors. Number Twelve Zetland Avenue is a magnet for them. Dad says that if he had a pound for every time the kettle boiled he'd be the richest man in Europe. Mum just tuts and tells him to stop exaggerating but it's true. There's always some sort of support group or other downstairs—Bereaved Parents, St Rose's Children's Hospice, the Meningitis Awareness Group. Tonight it's the After School Club Committee which isn't a support group, exactly, but it's the same difference.

After School club—as if I don't see enough of the place. I know I'm sounding a grade A whinger but how would you like it if on top of doing a full day at school and three hours at After School club and only having a rubbish fry-up before everyone arrived at seven, you were sent upstairs to 'entertain' yourself instead of being able to watch your favourite TV programme? It wouldn't be so bad if I had my own telly but I don't so I have spent most of the evening in my bedroom doing my Easter Garden for Sunday School. Even that's a disaster and I'm usually good at creative things. I'm very unhappy with my crosses. I've used lollipop sticks but they won't stay upright and keep toppling over as if they've been in a hurricane. I won't be able to put it on display next week at this rate.

My sister, Caitlin, is in the bedroom next to mine and I'd like to ask her for help but I'm not supposed to disturb her. Caitlin is sixteen and a sixth former at The Magna and is under a lot of pressure with exams. I can't wait to be sixteen and under a lot of pressure. You get out of doing chores because you've always got essays and you don't have to go shopping on Saturdays because you have a Saturday job and you don't have to go to church on Sundays because you stop believing in God and sleep until lunchtime instead. It's such a cushy life.

Caitlin must have finished her homework because I

could now hear Beethoven wailing through the wall. Seconds later there was a quick tap on my door and she stuck her head round and grinned at me. 'Go make us a cup of tea, Alex,' she said.

'N-o spells no.'

'Go on,' she repeated, opening the door wider and leaning her head to one side as if that was going to persuade me, especially with that hairstyle. Like me she has straight, light-brown hair, but as usual hers was scraped back in a tight, ugly ponytail that did nothing for her.

'Why do I have to do it? You're the one that's thirsty,' I pointed out.

'Because I have a psychology essay to finish then I've got to practise for band tomorrow, kind, sweet little sister of mine,' she whined.

I felt insulted. 'I am not kind and sweet,' I complained.

But she was already disappearing back to her room. 'And nab me a few biscuits—shortbread preferably,' she called over her shoulder.

I sighed and headed downstairs. I didn't really mind making her a cup of tea. I liked doing grown-up things like that. She had no chance on the biscuit front, though. I knew for a fact the shortbread wouldn't have lasted two seconds—Jan This liked them the most.

'Jan This' was my secret name for Mrs Fryston, the After School club supervisor. She's Mum's boss. Mum *loves* her. 'Jan said this' and 'Jan does that' is all we ever hear. I don't know why she's so impressed by Mrs Fryston. All Mrs Fryston does is fill in forms and suck up to the parents. It's my mum that does all the hard work at ZAPS After School club in my opinion. I bet she was volunteering this second to mend something or buy something or paint something for that shabby mobile hut, as if she's nothing else to do.

To prove it, I stopped by the half-open door of the living room as I passed on my way to the kitchen, hiding behind the bulging coats draped over the hat stand. I peered through the gap and could just make out a bunch of heads above the backs of the chairs. Mrs Fryston was talking and Tanis Fountain, Lloyd's mum, was nodding in agreement. Of all the parents there, I knew Tanis best because she's my Sunday School teacher. I don't mind her at all because she is always cheerful, which makes a change from most of our visitors.

'So, to re-cap,' Mrs Fryston banged on, 'I'll

continue setting up the e-pals project with links to other clubs. Sarah, you'll organize the sound equipment for the Pop Kids event next week and Ann, you're going to update all the registration details for us by Friday. Are you sure you don't want someone to give you a hand?'

Mum—she's Ann—looked up and shook her head. 'I'll be fine,' she said. Told you she'd get roped into something. Update all the registration details. Blinking Norah—Mrs Fryston didn't mean onto computer, did she? That would take Mum years. I peered closer. She was doing the notes again. Minutes, they're called, but they don't take her minutes to type up—she is the world's slowest typist, though she pretends she's not.

Mrs Fryston smiled at everyone, adjusted her silky neck-scarf against her fitted grey jacket as she turned from one member to the other. She does have good dress sense, I'll give her that. It's a pity it doesn't rub off a bit on Mum, who was in her horrible belted dress and bobbly cream cardy Grandma had knitted her for Christmas. It had one arm longer than the other so she had to keep the sleeves rolled up hoping no one could tell. No make-up, no jewellery. That's my mum.

'Well,' the Boss continued, 'that just leaves me to

thank Ann for letting us use her house again and to thank you all for coming. Dates to suit for the next meeting?' There was a flurry as they all dived for their diaries. No prizes for guessing where the meeting would be. I headed towards the kitchen and hoped they'd all leave quickly.

The kitchen was a right tip. All the dinner pots were still piled up because Mum hadn't had time to sort them before the meeting. Something black and disgusting floated in the grill pan that had been left to soak on the worktop. Nearby, the flip-top bin, unable to flip because it was stuffed full of rubbish, gave off a nasty fishy smell that had been getting nastier and fishier all week. I ignored it all and went to fill the water filter jug from the tap. I could hear  people leaving and shouting 'Bye' and 'See you' and finally the front door closing. I let out a huge sigh of relief as I heard footsteps approach.

'I'm glad that's over. I suppose that lazy old meanie has lumbered you with all the work again,' I called over my shoulder to Mum.

'Hello, Alex,' the lazy old meanie replied instead.

Chapter Two

Oops! I swung round with the jug in my hand, tipping water over the rim so it wet my top. 'Hello, Mrs Fryston,' I greeted her, fixing a big smile on my face and trying to pretend I had not said what I had just said.

'Where shall I put this?' she asked, indicating the tray full of beakers and plates she was carrying. The biscuit plate was empty, as I predicted.

'Erm . . . over there,' I said, pointing to the breakfast bar which just had enough space to take the tray if she budged up the wash basket full of damp clothes waiting their turn in the tumble drier.

She smiled at me again and

nodded towards the teapot I was emptying. 'Is there anything I can do to help? My lift's not here yet.'

'Not really,' I replied, now pouring water into the kettle.

She launched straight into her mind-reading act. 'I'm sorry if you've had to hide away during our meeting. It's just so much nicer sitting on comfortable chairs than squatting down on kiddies' ones for an hour and with you living just over the road from the school, it's so convenient . . .'

If she thought I was going to say, 'It doesn't matter', she had another think coming. 'I suppose so,' I said instead.

Mrs Fryston looked intently at me. '"So convenient." That sounded awful, didn't it? But your mum *does* insist.'

'I know,' I sighed.

She changed the subject. 'What do you think of the e-pals idea?'

I looked at her blankly, in case she had seen me eavesdropping and was trying to catch me out. 'That we started this afternoon? Making links with children from other After School clubs throughout the country? You filled in your "About Me" details, didn't you?' she prompted.

'Oh, yes,' I said hastily, 'I sent mine to the website's notice-board thing.'

'That's good. You might get a reply tomorrow,' she said, reaching out for an already dry cereal bowl and wiping it with a flourish.

I doubted I would get a reply. I had made my details as boring as possible so that nobody would want to write to me. It wasn't my kind of thing, e-mailing.

She must have been able to tell I wasn't that keen because she changed the subject again. 'What about the Pop Kids theme during the holidays? Are you looking forward to that?'

'Not really,' I admitted.

'No? I thought it would be right up your street. I have heard you're quite a singer,' she stated. 'Mr Sharkey was telling me how you're the star of his choir.'

'Not really,' I repeated and began to measure tea leaves into the pot. Two and a half spoonfuls. Two's not enough and three's too much. Jan This nudged me lightly in the side, trying to show how friendly she was but only annoying me instead. 'Now don't be modest, Alex.'

I shrugged. 'I'm not being! It's just that everyone

else is so rubbish so it makes me sound better than I am. Anyway, I don't know any pop songs. I only know traditional folk songs and hymns.'

'Oh,' she said shortly.

Luckily Mum came in to rescue me from any further divvy conversation and told Jan This that Andrew had arrived. 'On time, as usual,' she said, giving her this knowing look. Andrew was Mr Sharkey, my headteacher, and they're going out. I knew ages before anyone. I suppose if there is one advantage to having a mum who works at the After School club it is that you get all the inside information. They've been going out for about four months now but it's only just become common knowledge. It's not going smoothly, either, I can tell you, because of his mean ex-wife and her mardy teenage daughters, Kate and Anna.

I opened the fridge door quietly and took ages pretending to look for the milk. These were the times I found out more than I should, and pretending to be concentrating on something else helped no end, but this time Mrs Fryston just said goodbye and that was that.

I asked Mum if she wanted a cup of tea.

'Erm, no thanks,' Mum said, frowning and looking

worriedly at her notebook, 'I want to get going on these records. Jan needs them as soon as possible.'

'Do you have to? I wanted to watch telly with you.' I hated watching telly on my own. It made me feel lonely.

'What?' she said, looking at me but not looking at me, if you know what I mean. I repeated what I'd said but she shook her head. 'No, not tonight, Alex. I've got to get on,' she replied, then bit her lip. 'Must you wear that when we've got visitors?' she asked.

We both glanced down at my short, tight top with 'Bad Girl' printed across the chest. It was one of a set I had bought with my Christmas vouchers in the January sales— asking for vouchers is the only way to make sure I get decent things. Each of my tops had a different slogan like 'Bad Girl', 'Talk to the Hand', 'Whatever', and 'Up for It'—nothing rude or half as suggestive as I could have got but my old-fashioned mum disliked every one of them. 'What's wrong with it now?' I demanded.

Mum's frown deepened so that her forehead

crumpled with even more worry lines than usual. 'You'll catch such a cold,' she fussed. 'I'm sure things like that are meant to be worn under a jumper, like a vest.'

'How would you know?' I retorted, getting annoyed that the only conversation we had had all evening was where she has a go at me. 'You don't know anything about what girls wear nowadays, so don't think you can start now!'

I would never have been so cheeky to Mum if Caitlin or Dad had been around but I knew I could get away with it on a one-to-one. Mum never tells me off—she's such a pushover. 'You're right,' she agreed readily, 'I don't, but . . .'

I'd had enough. I gave her a dirty look and took Caitlin's tea and stormed out of the kitchen. I dumped Caitlin's drink next to where she was working at her desk, told her there weren't any biscuits left, and walked out. She said thanks and that I was 'a gem' but she had gone into 'essay world' and barely noticed me really.

I sat alone in my room for ages feeling sorry for myself but then I got bored so I went back to my Easter Garden. I decided to ignore the wobbly crosses and focus on the green hill instead. Mr Pisarski who ran the grocery shop six doors down had given me a piece of that imitation grass stuff he used to display his vegetables. It looked really effective yesterday when I had stuck it down over a plant pot but now I wasn't so sure. I reckoned the grass looked a bit long, so I took out my nail scissors and began clipping away. I must have been really engrossed because I didn't even know Dad was behind me until I felt a pair of cold hands tickle the back of my neck, making me nearly jump out of my skin.

I told him off for nearly scaring me to death, then gave him a hug, folding my arms round his big tummy and not letting go for ages. 'And how's my little nightingale today?' he asked, hugging me back.

I looked up at him, with his handsome, smooth face and grey-flecked hair that would be a mass of frizzy curls like Daniel's if he didn't keep it cut so short, and felt happy he was home. I liked my dad; he was always calm. 'Not bad under the circumstances,' I informed him.

He wiggled his thick, dark eyebrows. 'Well, that's good enough for me. Are you coming down for some supper? There are rumours of cheese on toast,' he said, loosening his stripy tie.

Cheese on toast? That was a good sign. Someone must have washed the grill pan. I dropped the scissors and followed him out.

Chapter Three

Downstairs, all the McCormacks were together at last. Caitlin was watching TV in one armchair and Mum was checking through her notebook in the other and I sat on the sofa and shared Dad's cheese toastie. He talked about a Georgian house he'd valued on St John's Square and how fantastic it was—Dad's an estate agent and knows all there is to know about property—and I listened. If I didn't make it as a fashion expert when I was older, I had being an estate agent down as a back-up. 'Did it have all its original features?' I asked.

'It did—right down to servants' bells in the cellars.'

'Oh—servants' bells!' I gasped, my imagination running wild. 'I'd love those.'

'Don't give her ideas,' Caitlin muttered from her chair.

'Excuse me, this is a business conversation, lassie,' I told her, and asked Dad what price he'd valued the property at. I whistled when he told me. 'Could we afford that?'

'In your dreams,' Caitlin said, flicking through the TV guide. Funny way to do a psychology essay, if you ask me.

Dad agreed with her. 'Not in a million years,' he sighed, biting deep into his toastie so the cheese oozed like Red Leicester lava.

'Well, even if we could afford it, we'd never leave here,' Mum added.

I looked at her curiously, surprised she had even been listening. 'Why not?' I asked because I'd love to live somewhere else. Somewhere detached and away from a main road so the windows didn't rattle every time a lorry went past and somewhere so remote nobody could be faffed to drive out there for a meeting. Somewhere very *in*convenient.

Mum glanced across at me and gave me a weak, far-off smile. 'Oh, I could never leave here. All my memories are here,' she said, her eyes flicking over to the fireplace.

'But if we moved, you could have new memories,' I pointed out and would have said more, but Dad

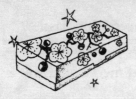nudged me and pursed his mouth in such a way I knew I had to belt up.

'So, what's on telly, Cate old mate?' he asked abruptly, changing the subject oh-so-obviously. 'Anything interesting?'

'Well, given that we have a choice of over two hundred channels . . .' Caitlin replied, pressing the remote so the menu flashed on the screen, 'not a lot.'

'No,' Mum continued, 'I'd never leave here. Never.' There was a catch in her voice, as if she was on the verge of tears.

Caitlin looked guardedly at Dad then began to flick furiously from one channel to another.

'Oh, switch the thing off!' Dad ordered jovially. 'Alex will entertain us, won't you? Give us a song, pal.'

'I don't feel like it.'

'Go on—for your old man after a hard day at work. Banish my tense, nervous headache.'

He suddenly flopped sideways across me, rubbing a mock headache with his hand and looking silly.

'The only way I'm ever leaving here is in a wooden box,' Mum informed no one in particular, 'that's the only way.'

When she started talking like that, all morose and

maudlin, we all knew it was time for distraction tactics. I shoved Dad off me and stood up, found my place bang in the middle row of the zigzags on the hearthrug, and took a deep breath. I began with Dad's favourite, 'Speed Bonny Boat', singing softly but clearly like Mr Sharkey had taught us. My voice echoed round the room and the more I sang, the more everyone relaxed. Dad leaned contentedly against the cushions and closed his eyes, Caitlin hummed along and Mum watched. She watched and listened and little by little her face lost its anxious appearance so that she looked younger and almost pretty.

After three songs, my throat began to tickle, so I gave up and collapsed onto the sofa. Everyone gave me a round of applause and I jumped up again and took a bow. 'The voice of an angel!' Dad cried. 'Despite evidence to the contrary!'

After that we watched a repeat of *Only Fools and Horses* and then it was my bedtime. ''Night,' I said, addressing everyone in turn.

'Goodnight, Alex,' Mum said, before coming out with the words I dreaded. 'Don't forget to kiss Daniel.'

I swallowed hard, knowing there was no way out of this one. We all kissed Daniel goodnight, no matter what.

I approached the mantelpiece solemnly, careful not to let my shins touch the bar of the electric fire, even though it was only on low. I breathed in deeply and stared at the bluey-turquoise lacquered box in the centre of the marble shelf where Dead Daniel rested.

Everything surrounding the box—the school photo of me on one side, the school photo of Caitlin on the other, the two wooden elephants, and even Mum's bottles of tablets—had a light coating of dust over them—but not the box. It gleamed so much from where Mum polished it every day, the glare from the light-fitting in the ceiling bounced off it, making me blink.

I so hated this. 'Goodnight, Daniel,' I whispered, my heart thudding against my ribs, my stomach heaving as I leaned forward and kissed him as quickly as I could and dashed upstairs to bed.

Chapter Four

Next day started off the usual way. Breakfast round the table with Dad in his suit and Caitlin in a book and Mum still in her dressing gown. Mornings are not Mum's best time of day. She has these tablets to help her sleep and they can take a while to wear off.

Dad leaves first, then Caitlin, then me. Since I have been in Year Four, I have been allowed to go to school on my own because it is only over the road and there is a crossing lady called Mrs Beamish to show me across.

In class—I'm in Miss Coupland's—I sat right at the back with my best friend, Jennifer Wilkinson. We are allowed to sit at the back because we don't mess about or anything. I like to just get on with my work and Jenny does too, so we make good partners. I'm as good as gold in school. It's *after* school I have trouble with.

At half-past three Mum arrived to escort me and the other After School club attendees across the playground. She was holding Brandon Petty by one hand and another kid from Reception by the other. That annoyed me straight off so I ran ahead of the group to get to the mobile first, ignoring her when she told me to wait because she hadn't called for Mr Idle's class yet.

It was Tuesday, which is a fairly quiet day at the club, so I didn't mind going as much. The mobile is not big enough sometimes, especially if it is wet out and there isn't an outside activity going on. I hate it then. The windows get all steamed up and the air feels heavy and thick, like an old man's coat. On Tuesdays, though, there are usually only about nine or ten regulars, so everyone has first choice of activities, no matter what the weather. Not that it makes much difference to me—I always choose the activity Mum's running. Partly it is because she does all the art and craft side and that's my favourite anyway but partly it is to keep an eye on her. She tends to fuss too much round the little ones and she gets carried away with them if you don't watch her.

Today I planned to get started straightaway on the necklace I had begun. I was halfway through a choker-design using tiny orange and lemon beads which were dead fiddly to thread onto cotton. I really wanted to have it finished so I could wear it to Sunday School but Jan This didn't even give me time to dump my sandwich box in the cloakroom before she called me across to the computers. Now what? I thought as I trundled my way towards her.

The usual gang were already huddled over three of the computers—Lloyd Fountain, Brody Miller, and Reggie Glazzard. Reggie Glazzard's dad had recently donated two brand new computers from his firm, to help Mrs Fryston set up this e-pal project. I reckon it was more of a guilt thing—someone must have tipped Mr Glazzard off about how his son hogged the computer area all the time and he felt bad about it.

'You've got an e-mail!' Mrs Fryston beamed at me and pointed to the vacant screen which had a picture of an unopened envelope in one corner with 'Mail for Alex' written by the side. 'You're the first one!'

'Does she get a prize?' Reggie asked, pushing his glasses up the bridge of his nose.

Then Brody, his girlfriend, said to me, 'I hate you! I spent ages and ages on my details but I haven't had one lousy response,' and smiled at me in a way that showed she wasn't at all bothered.

You do know who I mean when I talk about Brody Miller, don't you? If you don't, just go out of your house and find the nearest bus shelter and look at the poster plastered all over the side hoarding. The girl modelling on it—with the beautiful long red hair and wearing the latest swanky range of Funky Punk clothes—that's Brody Miller.

'Who's written to me?' I asked in disbelief remembering what rubbish I had put.

'Open it and find out,' Mrs Fryston instructed.

I leaned forward, scowling, and clicked on the envelope. *'Dear Alex,'* it began, *'My name is Courtney Long and I go to Burnside Primary After School club in Washington Tyne and Wear. I am not writing this because I want to be your e-pal because I already have 1 in Preston and 1 in Isleworth. Someone else here wants to write to you but she's making me write to you first. She sez she knows you but isn't sure if you want to get in touch. Her name is Jolene Nevin and her e-mail is footygirl@burnsideasc/educ/co.uk. Write to her soon pleeeeease and stop her doing my head in? CL.'*

'Huh!' I snorted and turned round to find everyone staring at me over my shoulder.

'Oh, cool!' Brody said, not even pretending she hadn't read my letter. 'Are you going to write back?'

'Not in a million years,' I said immediately and left them all staring.

Chapter Five

'You'll never guess who I've just had an e-mail from?'
I said to Mum as I sat down at the craft table and
pulled the bead tray across to me.

'Who?' she said, cutting round a picture of a
skateboard and handing it to Brandon, her only
customer, to stick on his sugar paper.

'That Jolene! Well, sort of.'

'Really?' Mum frowned.

'Jolene the bad girl?' Brandon asked.

I shot him a warning look to keep his crusty nose
out but he was too busy picking glue off his fingers to
notice.

'What did she say?' Mum asked.

'Nothing yet—she was just asking if she could
write to me.'

Brandon stuck his oar in again. 'She was nasty. She broke Brody's tooth and made her cry.'

It was true. It's a long story but basically, Jolene, who is Brody's niece, had got into an argument with Brody last half-term holiday and pushed her down the steps outside. I was there and saw it all. She pushed her so hard Brody went flying and smashed her tooth; that's a double-disaster because she's a model, remember. There was blood everywhere and for days afterwards I could see Brody fall and hear the sound she made when she hit the ground. Horrible.

The sad thing was, up until then I had really, really liked Jolene, even though she had only been coming to the club a few days. We just got on mega well right from the start and were becoming really close but when Jolene lost her temper like that, I knew it was over. I hate loud rows and scenes of any sort—they scare me. There's no way I could be friendly with someone like that. She wrote me a letter afterwards but that went straight in the bin.

'Well, it's up to you,' Mum said, 'though I never liked the girl. She was a bad influence on you.'

'Exactly,' I said, agreeing with her for once.

Brandon grabbed a handful of lentils and tried to scatter them across his picture but most of them stuck to his fingers, making him look as if he had orange fungus growing out of them. 'There—I've finished!' he announced.

'It's wonderful,' Mum smiled. I wished she wouldn't lie to him. It only encourages him to come back. The thing she just couldn't see about Brandon Petty was that he was really, really irritating. After the Brody–Jolene incident, when I'd been shaken up, I tried to be nice to everyone, including Brandon. I even bought him his favourite green sweets a couple of times but the novelty wore off after about a week. I just couldn't keep up the pretence of liking the little squirt.

Now he was creeping round Mum. 'You can have it, Mrs 'Cormick,' he announced, holding the soggy sheet out towards her.

Her face went pink for some stupid reason. 'Oh, Brandon, are you sure? Maybe your mummy would like it?' she said, her eyes shining.

He shook his head. 'Nah! Mummy says she's got enough rubbish. She throws them straight in the bin.'

'Well, I'll definitely keep it then,' Mum said gently, carrying the picture to the drying rack so carefully you would have thought it was a tray of priceless diamonds.

'Go do something else now,' I told Brandon sharply.

'Like what?' he asked, scowling back at me through his long, tangled fringe.

'Like getting lost,' I hissed.

'You're a nasty-pasty,' he said and stuck his tongue out at me.

'Back at you,' I snarled.

That got rid of him. He slid from the chair and ambled over to pester Sam and Sammie at the tuck shop instead.

Soon it was the end of the session and I had to help Mum clear away, then wait until everyone was collected. Brody's mum, Kiersten, arrived first, breezing in and smiling broadly at everyone. She used to be a model too and is still really, really beautiful. I always take note of what she is wearing so I can copy her style when in I'm in my thirties and old. Today she had on smart black trousers with a plain white shirt and pointy shoes. Simple but classic.

Sammie Wesley's mum was last to arrive, as usual. Mrs Wesley is really overweight and dyes her hair too much but even she wears trendy clothes. My mum, as usual, looked really boring and drab next to all of them. I sometimes felt as if I had been born to the wrong family.

Chapter Six

The house was empty by the time Mum and I returned from After School club but I knew Caitlin had been in earlier from the whiff of burnt toast in the air. Mum went to put the kettle on and I read a note Caitlin had left by the phone to say she was at band practice and would be back about nine and Dad would be picking her up. Beneath it was a list of missed calls for Mum. 'Caitlin's at band—Dad's picking her up,' I relayed.

'What soup do you want? Tomato or chicken noodle?' Mum asked, standing on tiptoes to reach up into the cupboard, her underskirt at half-mast.

'I don't mind,' I said.

A packet of chicken noodle came flying down. 'Here you go, love. Can you make it yourself? The sooner I finish those records the better—I only managed four last night. There's plenty of cheese and ham in the fridge for sandwiches.'

'OK,' I said dully. I would have liked a bit of attention, especially as she was supposed to have a free night tonight. Instead, she headed for the door with her hastily made mug of coffee, before pausing by the worktop. I thought she had changed her mind and was going to have something to eat with me at least, but no.

'Isn't this sweet?' she said, pointing to Brandon Petty's gunk she had brought home with us. 'Fancy his mother throwing his things in the bin. I always kept everything of Daniel's.'

'Did you keep everything of mine?' I asked immediately.

She looked at me blankly. 'What? Oh, I'm sure I did. I can't really remember.'

'Where are they?'

'What?'

'All my paintings from when I was five?'

Mum glanced back to the lentil-laden sugar paper and seemed flustered. 'I don't know—ask your father when he comes home,' she said, creasing her thick eyebrows together so that they puckered unflatteringly. 'They'll be somewhere—in the loft maybe?' She glanced from me to the wall clock, told me to be careful when I heated the soup on the hob, then went upstairs.

That left me feeling really hurt and angry. It didn't matter that I knew exactly where my drawings and paintings were from when I was five. They were where they had always been—in the bottom drawer beneath my cabin bed. What mattered was that she so obviously didn't have a clue. I stared hard at Brandon's picture for a second, then rolled it up roughly and took it out to the dustbin where I squashed it into an empty box of washing powder and then covered it with bean cans. 'Stick lentils on that, creep,' I muttered triumphantly.

I was just washing my hands and feeling a lot better when the phone rang. It was some bloke from the meningitis group. That's what Daniel died from. I don't know much about meningitis except one of the symptoms is if you've got a rash, the rash doesn't go away if you roll a glass over it. Something like that. 'I've called twice already,' the man said accusingly.

'We've only just got in one second ago,' I retorted.

Honestly—some people.

Even Mum looked perturbed when I went upstairs to give her the message. 'Oh, dear. If it's Jeff I'll be on forever. I'll never get this done by Friday.' She prodded a key with her left index finger, then prodded another with her right. 'Will you save this for me, Alex?'

'I suppose so. I have to do everything else around here,' I replied as she hurried downstairs.

I quickly pressed the disc icon on the toolbar to save the work. I could see she had hardly transferred anything on to it from the hand-written sheet nearby. On the screen, the grids under the heading 'Samantha Wesley Registration Details' were mostly empty apart from her address and date of birth.

I picked up the sheet and began to read. I knew I shouldn't really—registration forms were confidential but I had never looked at one close-up before. It was funny seeing Sammie's full name written out as Samantha Louise. At least it wasn't an embarrassing middle name. My dad's is Wally, which makes me laugh every time I think about it.

It looked as if Sammie's registration details were as bad as her mother's time-keeping. There were crossings out and added notes all over the place and there wasn't enough space for everything. From the look of it, Mrs Wesley had changed jobs about three times this year and every time the new contact numbers had been put in, the old ones had been roughly crossed out in Mrs Fryston's awful handwriting. No wonder Mum was in a flap if all the sheets were this messy.

Back on the computer, the cursor was flashing temptingly on the space left for Sammie's mum's latest emergency contact telephone number. I glanced at the original sheet and quickly filled it in, guessing one of the digits was a five, though it could have been an eight.

Mum ought to let me do these, I thought, I'd have them done in no time. I replaced Sammie's sheet and saw mine was next on the pile. Now that was novel, seeing my own name printed there. I suppose I thought because I went to After School club as Mum's daughter, not really as one of *them*, I would not have one.

I went to the open door and listened for a second. Mum was still counselling Jeff downstairs, so I knew I had tonnes of time. 'Of course you're concerned about her—it's only natural,' she was saying. Yuck. I began to read.

There was nothing I didn't know until I flipped over to the other side and saw some additional notes pencilled in by Jan This. 'Problems mixing,' it said. I frowned. Problems mixing what? I frowned again. 'V. clingy to A.M. (mother & playleader). Can be antagonistic, especially towards younger ones if they invade "her" space, making her unpopular.' Then underlined it said—'monitor'.

There was worse to come. Beneath that was another pencilled note that read: 'I agree—A.M.' A.M. for Ann McCormack—my own mother.

I lifted the dictionary down and looked up 'antagonistic' and that said 'a person opposed to or in competition with another' so that was a load of rubbish for a start because I never went in for competitions. Then I looked up 'monitor' and that had loads of definitions, including 'large, flesh-eating lizards', but the one that fitted was 'to check or supervise'.

The anger I had felt in the kitchen over Brandon's picture was nothing to how I felt now. I might have guessed Fanny Fryston had it in for me but for Mum to write 'I agree'—that was IT. They could both get bent.

I took my registration form and fed it slowly and deliberately into Dad's paper shredder, breathing short, rapid breaths through my nose. I was so angry I felt as if my brain was on fire. Then I took the next one on the pile—Lloyd's—and did the same to his. Problems mixing? Mix this, you big losers, I fumed. I reached out for the next sheet, not even bothering to see who that belonged to and shredded that. Unpopular? Thanks a lot! That was the worst. That meant *nobody* liked you. I didn't need a dictionary to tell me that.

I would have shredded every last single one of those registration forms if I hadn't turned to see Daniel staring at me. It was only a photograph on the shelf but it was one of those portraits taken by professional photographers in supermarkets. Every feature seemed magnified and gloating, especially those annoying wide, blue eyes of his. Without thinking twice, I lined that up for the shredder, too, but the card was too thick and wouldn't go down, though it did mangle the frame a bit at the bottom. I threw it back in its place and stomped out.

Chapter Seven

Nobody said anything about the damaged photo or the missing registration forms until Saturday night when Mum came into the living room looking puzzled. 'Everything all right?' Dad asked. I watched intently, my mouth suddenly as dry as sun-bleached sand.

'What?' she said distractedly, pushing her hair back from her pale, drawn face. 'Oh, yes—it's just a couple of registration forms are missing. It's a nuisance because I'd have finished the lot otherwise.'

'Whose are missing?' I asked innocently.

'Well, funnily enough, yours and Lloyd Fountain's and Sam Riley's.'

'Oh, that is funny,' I said.

Dad got up from his armchair and gave Mum a quick embrace. 'Well, that's a lucky break then—

you'll be seeing Tanis tomorrow at chapel and I think I can help you with that Alex McCormack one. Age nine going on nineteen, lives upstairs, allergic to washing up but makes an excellent pot of tea. Sings like an angel.' He winked at me.

'Yes,' Mum said and smiled at me too. 'She does make an excellent pot of tea.'

That night, when I kissed Daniel's ashes goodnight, I sent him a message telepathically. 'She never even noticed you got crumpled, Danny Boy.'

Next morning Mum and I walked across to Zetland Avenue Methodist Chapel, as we did every Sunday. Caitlin was still in bed and Dad was reading the papers. They only come if there's something special on, like me singing a solo or whatever.

Mum seemed quite happy as we were getting ready to set off and I was beginning to feel bad about the forms. If Mum said anything nice to me, I decided, I would own up, but as I was zipping up my hoodie, she scowled. 'Not that silly top, Alex, please,' she sighed. *Not that silly top Alex please* didn't count as nice in my book, especially from someone wearing black tights with white sandals, so we walked to church without speaking and I kept my secret to myself.

At least Lloyd's mum was more positive about my top. She likes to stand at the door and greet us when we arrive. 'I do like your slogans, Alex,' she said. 'I haven't seen you in that one before. "Talk to the Hand". Ha! Is that the same as talking to the wall? I seem to do that a lot in my house!'

'I don't know,' I said, beaming at her, 'I suppose so.'

'Where do you want this, Tanis?' Mum asked. Mrs Fountain smiled at Mum then peered into the carrier bag she was carrying for me. 'Oh—is this your Easter Garden, Alex? It's fantastic—I love that grass! And those crosses—so upright and regal.'

Dad had superglued the crosses for me last night so I felt quite proud of my garden now.

'Thank you very much,' I replied politely. Mum hadn't even commented on it at all, apart from saying it was an awkward shape to carry.

The garden was handed over to be put on display and Mum said she'd see me later and went round to the front door of the chapel to sit in the congregation while I lined up behind Lloyd and the rest of the Sunday School kids. Lloyd turned round and gave me a fruit pastille. I swapped it with one of my jelly babies. We always swap sweets and knock out together at chapel but don't speak much at After School club. It's just the way it is. I think I feel more comfortable talking to him here—there it seems funny.

A few minutes later we trooped across the yard from the small hall where we gather to the chapel. It was Palm Sunday, so we were given palm crosses and banana plant leaves to wave around for special effect during our hymns, 'Ride on, Ride on in Majesty' and 'Jesus Rode a Donkey into Town'.

I forgot about everything when I sang. I always do. It is as if I go into another world. Today I forgot about the nasty things Mrs Fryston had written about me and how Mum had agreed. I forgot about shredding the registration forms. I forgot I was unpopular. I faced the congregation and sang my heart out.

'I wish I could sing like you, Ally,' Lloyd said at the end of the service. He always calls me Ally for some reason. 'I sound like a parrot being choked to death.'

'Yeah, you do,' I agreed as we trudged back over to the small hall for refreshments.

There, Lloyd and I took a plastic cup of squash each and a handful of biscuits and went to look at the Easter Gardens. Lloyd's was two down from mine.

'Who's done that to it?' I
asked worriedly. 'I could
help you fix it, if you like.'

Lloyd peered closer at
the lopsided twigs and
lumpy, grey mound
that had collapsed on
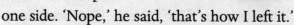
one side. 'Nope,' he said, 'that's how I left it.'

'You could have put a bit of effort in!'

'Mum thought it showed initiative,' he grinned.

'Blimey! Has she had her eyes checked recently?'

We automatically glanced across the room to
where our mums were huddled over a refectory table.
Mrs Fountain had Lloyd's little sister, Edith, balanced
on one hip and was nodding at something Mum was
saying.

'What are they doing?' Lloyd asked.

I explained about the missing registration form.
'Oh,' he said, losing interest, but once I had
mentioned it, everything came flooding back and I
found it hard to concentrate on the rest of the Easter
Gardens. Lloyd nudged my arm at one that was even
worse than his—an egg box with three matchsticks
stuck in the middle. 'That's either the worst thing I've
ever seen in my life or pure genius,' he whispered.

'It's the worst thing—trust me,' I told him.

He shrugged and moved along.

'Lloyd?'

'Yup?'

'You know at After School club?'

'Yup.'

'Who would you say was the most popular?'

He didn't hesitate. 'Easy. Brody. Everyone likes Brody and Brody likes everyone back.'

I couldn't argue with that. A fact's a fact.

'What about . . .' I paused, unsure whether I should go on, but I knew Lloyd. I trusted him. 'What about the most unpopular?'

Again, he didn't hesitate. 'Reggie. Definitely Reggie.'

That came as a surprise. 'Reggie?'

'Well, he was definitely the most unpopular where I was sitting on Friday. He'd had beans for breakfast and beans for lunch and you know what that means with Reggie. Trump, trump, trump all afternoon. Brody put a peg on her nose in the end. It left a red mark shaped like a sparrow's beak.'

'If you were being serious, though, Lloyd . . . who's really the most unpopular?'

'I don't know. I've never thought about it.'

I took a deep breath. 'Do you think it's me?'

He frowned and swallowed the rest of his biscuit. 'You? No, I wouldn't say that. You are different there, though.'

'How do you mean?'

'You're not the same as you are here. You can be a bit . . .'

'A bit what?'

He looked me straight in the eye. 'A bit snappy. Like you don't want anyone to talk to you so you snap to make them go away.'

'Oh!' I said. I felt hurt that Lloyd thought that.

'But you could work on it,' Lloyd added helpfully, seeing my face fall.

The word was still repeating in my head that night as I brushed my teeth before going to bed. What nobody seemed to get, I frothed at the cabinet mirror, was that I was only there because of Mum and sometimes I did have to tell people off round the craft table to help her out. They'd take advantage of her soft nature otherwise and mess about and pinch stuff. That wasn't being snappy, that was being responsible.

I dropped my toothbrush next to Caitlin's and wiped my mouth on the flannel. I decided Lloyd was a nice boy but had got it wrong and so had Mrs

Fryston. Very wrong. I wasn't snappy or unpopular or clingy or antagonistic. 'So back at you all!' I said out loud.

My mouth curved into a smile as an idea formed in my head. Back at you all was a genius idea!

Chapter Eight

Monday: the first day of the Easter holidays and the first of nine full days at After School club and the perfect opportunity to put Plan *Back at You* into action.

Mum and I were the first to arrive and the mobile felt cold, despite the warm April sun streaming through the windows. I rushed to turn the heating on, even though part of the plan was not to do any chores. A few minutes later Mrs Fryston arrived but she was with Mr Sharkey and spent ages chatting to him on the steps outside. When I pointed it out, Mum said it was because they were discussing plans for the new all-weather play surface. As if.

Meanwhile, Mum was trying to set up her craft table. She looked tired and yawned as she fumbled about on the paint trolley for scissors and card. Eight o'clock is early for someone not used to starting work until after three. 'Alex, have you seen the yellow tissue paper anywhere? I'm sure I put it out here on Friday,' she asked.

'It's next to the pipe cleaners,' I pointed out.

She drifted over to the flat packs of paper and placed them next to a pile of empty egg cartons. 'Tissue paper's lovely, isn't it? I like the sound it makes when you scrunch it up, don't you?'

I put my plan into action immediately. 'Oh, I agree,' I said, nodding.

Mum carried on chatting—even when she's tired she's enthusiastic about her craft ideas. 'I'm doing three-dimensional Easter daffodil cards this morning, though I suppose I'd better call them spring cards, hadn't I? Don't want to go upsetting anyone.'

'I agree,' I replied.

She began to pour herself a cup of coffee from the flask she always brought. 'Can you check if there are any bottles of orange poster paint left?'

'There aren't,' I said, quickly checking the bottom shelf of the trolley that had every colour but.

Mum glanced across to the door, where Mrs Fryston was now chatting to the first arrivals, a couple of new faces from Year Two and Three with their childminder. Mr Sharkey seemed to have disappeared.

'Oh, dear, they're coming in already,' Mum said, and poured her coffee back into her flask. Hot drink near five year olds is a disaster waiting to happen, she reckons. 'Alex, can you mix me some orange paint up using the red and yellow while I trim the card?' she sighed.

Ha! Just the wording I had been waiting for, Mrs McCormack. 'No, I'm ever so sorry but I can't,' I said, 'I'm not very good at mixing—it makes me antagonistic.'

Mum looked up at me quizzically. 'Don't be silly, Alex, there isn't time to mess about. Go easy on the red.'

I shook my head. 'I'm sorry, Mrs McCormack, I can't help you today. I'm not feeling very crafty. I think I'll go and read a book for a while.'

'Oh,' Mum said, a little surprised, 'OK, then.'

I sat in the book corner and waited and watched. It was quite interesting seeing things from the book corner for a change because I could see right into the cloakroom area. The older ones, like Brody and Reggie, arrived by themselves, dropped their stuff off and headed straight for their usual activity without any fuss. Most of the younger ones were sorted out by their parents or helpers, who came in with them and had a quick word with Mrs Fryston before they left. Brandon's mum looked cross and almost shook him out of his duffel coat. She didn't kiss him goodbye or have a quick word with Jan This before she hurried off. I bet she found the little tyke as annoying as I did; I *knew* it wasn't just me. Sammie arrived late yet stayed in the cloakroom the longest. One of her big sisters—Gemma, I think— had arrived with her and there'd been a tussle over something in Sammie's bag. In the end Gemma had gone off in a huff and Sammie stuck her middle finger up at her through the glass. Lucky for her nobody saw or she would have been in big trouble.

All in all my book corner experience was quite interesting and I might do it again in future.

Eventually, Mrs Fryston gathered everyone together and reeled off the choices for the day. 'We have,' Mrs Fryston told everyone, 'spring cards with Mrs McCormack, Quick Cricket outside with Denise, chocolate nests with me, and any of the usual After School club activities that are out. Pop Kids will start tomorrow afternoon when Mrs Riley will be bringing in the karaoke machine to set us off. Right, then,' Mrs Fryston beamed, 'let's get to it!'

Yes, let's, I thought as I approached her corner.

Chapter Nine

'Hello, Alex,' Mrs Fryston said, rolling up the sleeves of her ZAPS sweatshirt as I approached, 'does your mum need something before I start?'

'I don't know, I haven't asked her,' I shrugged, pulling out a chair and sitting down between Sammie and Tasmim.

'Oh,' Mrs Fryston said, realizing I wanted to join in, 'you've come to make a chocolate nest?'

'Yup,' I said, smiling sweetly.

'Well, you're more than welcome.'

'Thank you.'

Chocolate nests were not very challenging to make, especially when we weren't allowed to heat anything ourselves. All we were meant to do was wait until Mrs Fryston poured us each a dollop of melted cooking chocolate into a titchy bowl half filled with Shredded Wheat and stir it together, pour it into a couple of bun cases and stick a mini egg or two in the middle once it has set. It should have taken about three seconds, had I not been in a chatty mood.

'It's very *clingy*, isn't it, chocolate?' I said to Mrs Fryston.

'It can be if you're not quick with it,' she confirmed, then told Tasmim not to lick the bowl out. I glanced for a second at the dark-haired Tasmim, who was small like her mother and hardly ever spoke, before continuing, 'And hard to mix. I am *so* having problems mixing,' I said.

'Are you, Alex?' the supervisor asked, puzzled, as I pretended to find the wooden spoon very awkward and 'accidentally' flicked some Shredded Wheat onto the table. 'Oh, yes, mixing is a real problem of mine. I'm just terrible at it.'

'Just stir it fast,' Sammie said helpfully, 'you have to stir it fast when you're baking in our house or everyone nicks it before you've finished. I made a

285

recipe for lemon buns once, right, and it was supposed to make twenty-four but by the time my mam and our Gemma and our Sasha had gone past there was only enough for six!'

'Was there?' I said. 'Can I come round to your house and watch next time? I'd like to monitor that.'

'Would you?' Sammie asked uncertainly, pushing her headband away from her forehead and leaving a brown fingerprint in the middle of it.

'Definitely. Or would that make me unpopular?'

'No—'cept if you ate all the mixture and all,' Sammie replied.

'OK everyone,' Mrs Fryston instructed, 'the next step is to put a big spoonful of the mixture into your bun cases like this . . .' She broke off to demonstrate. 'And then carefully drop one or two mini eggs on top like this.' Two speckled sugar eggs, one pink, one blue, were dropped perfectly into the middle of the setting chocolate. I have to admit Jan This had made a good job of it.

'When can we eat them?' Sammie asked eagerly.

Mrs Fryston wiped her hands on a tea towel. 'I think it would be a good idea if you saved them until you got home, don't you? Show your mum what you've been up to?'

The look on Sammie's face said 'no' in capital letters but she didn't say anything.

'And make sure you all write your names on a piece of paper and put them next to your nests so nobody takes yours home by mistake,' Mrs Fryston added.

'Are you going to put "Sammie" or "Samantha Louise"?' I asked Sammie, remembering her form.

'Sammie,' she frowned. 'How did you know my middle name? I never tell nobody it.'

'Oh,' I shrugged, 'you pick up things . . .'

'I've never even told Sam,' she muttered, glancing across at Sam Riley, her best friend, who was playing Jenga with Brandon.

'Are you feeling all right, Alex?' Mrs Fryston asked.

'I'm fine, Mrs Fryston,' I said, dropping three mini eggs into my nest and squashing them down hard with my thumb. 'I'm just dandy.'

Chapter Ten

By mid-afternoon, I had run out of activities. As well as making the chocolate nests, I had played Quick Cricket, read two books, and sorted the dressing-up box into day-wear and evening-wear. Nobody could accuse me of not mixing today, I thought sourly, but I was disappointed that my 'Back at You' plan wasn't working that well. I had used every key word on my registration form and neither Mrs Fryston nor Mum had batted an eyelid.

It seemed to me that people said things or wrote things and then forgot about them, so whether I did anything good or anything bad didn't make any difference. Nobody noticed one way or the other.

Feeling miserable and a bit deflated, I headed for the only thing left to go on apart from

making spring cards—the computers.

For once, the 'it-team'—Brody, Reggie, and Lloyd —were not actually on the computers but draped over a table nearby, with Reggie and Brody on one side and Lloyd opposite. They looked quite intimidating and I had to take a few quick breaths as I approached. Reggie and Brody were the most popular kids in Year Six, after all, not just here at After School club. I was only a Year Four, remember.

'Hey,' I said as I passed and slid onto a vacant computer chair.

'Hi, Alex,' Brody replied, 'what's new?'

I switched on the computer and waited for it to load. 'Nothing much,' I mumbled, searching for the games section on the desktop icon.

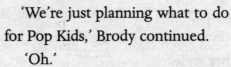

'We're just planning what to do for Pop Kids,' Brody continued.

'Oh.'

'I'm doing Elvis,' Reggie announced. 'You can't beat the

classics. Question is, how to put on twenty stone before next Friday.'

'I'm still torn between Kylie and Cindi Lauper,' Brody said, her voice troubled as if this was a real problem to her.

'Cindi who?' Lloyd asked.

'Lauper. I didn't know her either but my dad has these neat shots of her from the nineteen eighties. She was an American singer and wore these really cool dresses and had wild hair—Mom says she can easily fix me up with something similar.'

I felt a stab of envy as I loaded a CD into the disk drive. If my mum fixed me up I'd end up going as someone in the Salvation Army band.

'What about you, Lloydy?' Reggie asked.

'I don't know. Anyone who can't sing, I suppose,' he sighed, and I could feel his eyes drilling into my back as if wanting me to agree with him but I remembered what he had said about me yesterday and didn't turn round.

'I guess I'll definitely do Cindi,' Brody continued. 'I think Sammie's doing Kylie and I don't want to cramp her style.'

'What about you, Alex, who are you doing?' Reggie asked.

'Nobody,' I said, 'I'm just going to watch.'

'Why?'

'Just because,' I said, but I said it lightly so I wouldn't sound snappy.

The truth was I did not come from a pop music loving family and prancing around in silly clothes singing stuff about being broken hearted is not my idea of fun. I would rather make chocolate nests for two weeks.

I threw a quick glance towards the craft table. Mum had several customers, mainly little ones, all gluing and sticking. She seemed quite happy, sitting among them, passing them things and helping with the cutting. She wasn't missing me at all—probably hadn't even noticed I'd gone.

'I think I'll go on the computer,' Brody said, scraping back a chair noisily and coming to sit alongside me.

'Check out my e-mails,' Reggie told her, 'and if I've got one from someone called Fatmuddyboy, delete it quick. He's a freak—he eats live goldfish!'

Brody reached over and touched me lightly on my arm. 'You've got three new messages, by the way, if you're going on the e-pals website.'

'Three?'

'Aha. Two from Courtney again then one from Jolene. Didn't tell you in case you weren't interested.'

'You're right, I'm not,' I told her, 'you can delete mine, too.' But as soon as I had said it, I wished I hadn't. If there was one person in this world who understood me, it was Jolene. If she had been here, she'd have been with me all the way today. She would have *got* it.

I glanced across at Brody, to see what she was doing, but her long hair blocked my view until she suddenly glanced back at me, and smiled. That stopped me missing Jolene straight away. Brody's veneered front tooth was good, but not good enough to prevent it looking slightly different from the real thing. Again I saw Jolene's face full of rage and heard Brody's scream as she fell.

'Are you sure?' Brody asked, her finger hovering over the keyboard.

'I'm sure,' I said, shuddering.

Chapter Eleven

At least the next day I didn't have to do any of that mixing business or worry about unwanted e-mails. It was the start of the Pop Kids theme that meant all sit together and listen to instructions, boys and girls. Yuck. Yuck. Yuckity-yuck.

My heart sank as Brody handed round letters outlining the schedule for the next two weeks while we waited for Mrs Riley to plug all her cables into the right holes of the karaoke machine.

Pop Kids

Week One

Tuesday and Wednesday: Practise singing with the stars on the karaoke machine

Thursday, Friday: choose your artist, plan your outfit, learn the lyrics

Week Two

(not Monday—closed for Bank Holiday)

Tuesday: Luke and Tim with drums, guitars, etc. (and rest of week—bring ear plugs!)

Wednesday: rehearsals and hair and make-up tips with Kiersten Tor

Thursday: dress rehearsal & choreography

Friday: showtime! Performance at 4.00p.m.

'Who are Luke and Tim?' Lloyd asked from over my shoulder.

'Sam Riley's big brothers—they're in a band,' I told him dully, folding the sheet of paper and sliding it under Tasmim's shoe in front of me.

'Oh. What is it called?' Lloyd asked, taking the sheet back and rolling his eyes at me in disapproval.

'I don't know.'

'Huw's in a band. They're called the Hairy Pants,'

Lloyd whispered loudly as Mrs Riley fed the last cable into the machine and had a quick twiddle of the knobs before explaining how the karaoke worked.

Huw was Lloyd's older brother. He had an even older one called Calum but he was at university somewhere in Wales. 'I chose the name for them,' Lloyd told me proudly.

'Shh!' I said. 'Mrs Riley's ready.'

'Oh, all right. Keep your hairy pants on.'

Mrs Riley swept her eyes round the room to check out we were all listening then began. 'Now the idea of this is to get you used to timing your singing and being in front of an audience,' she told everyone, 'just follow the white ball on the television screen and let rip! It's great fun. Who'd like to be first?'

Sammie's arm shot into the air together with a loud 'ooh-ooh-ooh' sound that convinced Mrs Riley to give in to her straightaway. I'd have made her wait, myself. Anyway, Sammie leaped onto the stage blocks we had borrowed from the school hall and took the microphone then stared at it worriedly. 'Anything wrong, Sammie?' Mrs Riley asked.

'It's a bit smaller than our Gemma's hairbrush, that's all,' Sammie replied. 'I've been practising all weekend with it.'

That explained the tussle in the cloakrooms yesterday, I thought.

'I still don't know what I'm going to do, do you?' Lloyd whispered.

'I keep telling you—nothing.'

'Still? But why?' Lloyd asked, jamming his fingers in his ears as Sammie started belting out something about mountains not being high enough.

'I just don't want to.'

'I do,' he said, 'and I can't sing for toffee.'

To prove it, he put his hand up to be next when Sammie had finished. Now Sammie had been bad but Lloyd—Lloyd was chronic, as I knew from chapel. He was out of tune and at least three lines behind the words on the screen but he grinned all the way through it and everyone clapped like mad at the end, despite laughing their heads off at him.

Brody was up next, complete with so many fancy dance moves I knew Sammie wasn't the only one who had been practising over the weekend. Then Reggie had his go. He had the mike in one hand and a bag of doughnuts in the other. 'I'm going to be the King—

got to look the part,' he explained, spraying sugar everywhere.

'Does he mean Elvis or Henry the Eighth?' Lloyd asked.

After that it was the smaller ones and the performances got worse and worse but nobody seemed to mind. I shook my head when Mrs Riley asked me if I wanted a turn and I'm glad to say she didn't keep on about it when I said no. Instead, Mr Sharkey, who had dropped by for one of his 'quick words' with Mrs Fryston, put his hand up. 'Me! Me! Me!' he joked. Everyone moved out of the way as he shimmied forward. 'What shall I sing?' he asked, flicking through the songbook.

'"You're the Devil in Disguise"!' Reggie shouted out, quick as a flash.

Even I laughed at that one.

I still thought Pop Kids was a daft idea, though.

Chapter Twelve

I hadn't enjoyed my day and wanted to get home as quickly as possible but Mrs Wesley was doing one of her usuals and had not turned up. 'Did she say she might be late?' Mrs Fryston asked, keeping her voice level but glancing at her watch.

'No,' Sammie mumbled.

'I'll give her a call. Has she got her mobile with her, do you know?'

'Doubt it,' Sammie said. 'She chucked it across the room this morning cos it had run out of credit.'

'I'll try her work number then. It's just I've got to be out by seven and I won't have time to make myself look beautiful at this rate!' Mrs Fryston said, pretending it didn't matter really when everyone could tell it did.

'Sorry,' Sammie said, twirling her hairbrush round and round in her hand and looking miserable.

'Don't worry,' Mrs Fryston said sympathetically, ruffling Sammie's hair.

Meanwhile, I just sat on the wicker basket full of dressing-up clothes, listening to my tummy rumbling, feeling bored stiff. Mum was still faffing about with her glue pots, setting up for the next morning, when Mrs Fryston called out to her. 'Ann, is this contact number for Mrs Wesley the up-to-date one? I can't remember if it was Sam's or Sammie's you hadn't finished yet?'

Mum looked up and told her Sammie's was accurate. Mrs Fryston shook her head as if she couldn't understand. 'I'll try again,' she said and frowned and apologized when the person on the other end answered. 'Wrong number,' she said, 'unless your mum's in the maternity ward at Pinfields General, Sammie!'

'She'd better not be,' Sammie grunted.

'The five might be an eight,' I said, just wanting to get home. 'I wasn't sure when I typed it in.'

'Oh,' Mrs Fryston said shortly, shooting me a quizzical look and beginning to redial just as Mrs

Wesley came bursting through the door, full of apologies and excuses. 'Traffic's crackers tonight—road works everywhere,' she puffed. Road works? Huh! She hadn't used that one for a few weeks.

Mrs Fryston smiled tightly, said it didn't matter, and asked her to double-check her number before she left.

'Can we go now?' I said to Mum grumpily.

'Just a minute, Alex,' Mrs Fryston said when Sammie and her mum closed the door behind them, and asked me what I meant by 'typing it in'. I shrugged and explained what I had done, not really thinking much of it, to be honest. Mrs Fryston frowned. 'So that's how you knew about Sammie's middle name yesterday. I thought it seemed odd.'

Oh, trust her to hear that part and not one of my 'Back at You' words. She then turned to Mum and said in a bit of a snooty voice. 'Ann? You do know the records are confidential?'

Mum nodded and went slightly pink. That got me annoyed. Jan This had no right to tell my mum off. That was my job.

'It's not her fault if you give her too much to do. In case you didn't know, she's rubbish at typing, those records took her all week!' I stated angrily.

Mrs Fryston looked at me but before she could say anything, Mum butted in. 'Alex, don't be rude,' she whispered.

'I'm not being!' I fumed.

Mrs Fryston shook her head at me, then glanced at her watch. 'We'll need to talk about this later, Ann. I have to lock up.'

'I'm sorry, Jan,' Mum grovelled.

'Why are you apologizing to her? She should be apologizing to you,' I muttered loudly. 'You do all the work while she just chats to her boyfriend all day.'

'Off you go now, Alex,' Mrs Fryston said calmly but firmly, 'quickly.'

Chapter Thirteen

'How could you talk to Jan like that?' Mum asked as we waited at the pelican crossing. 'Whatever were you thinking? You were so rude.'

'She was rude to me!' I answered.

'I've never felt so ashamed,' she sniffed.

I glanced up at her to see if she was going to start crying in public, because if she did I was legging it home ahead of her. She was so embarrassing at times. 'I don't know why I'm getting all the blame. I was only sticking up for you,' I told her. 'You know you're not fast at typing. And you were the one who told me to do it anyway.'

'I asked you to save the work, that's all,' Mum mumbled, 'you know that.'

'Green man,' I said.

'What?'

'Green man! We can cross.'

She seemed so distracted I had to pull her across the road. Even outside the house she couldn't get her act together and fumbled for ages trying to unlock the door. 'Look at me,' she said, 'I'm so upset I can't even get into my own home.'

I pushed past her and into the hallway where I flung down my bag and coat and twizzled round. 'I don't see what all the fuss is about! It was only one little digit. And Sammie's mum is always late and you and Mrs Fryston are always moaning about it so don't pretend you're not because . . .'

Mum didn't let me finish. Her finger shook as she pointed it towards the stairs.

'Go to your room now and stay there until I tell you to come down,' she croaked.

Her chin wobbled as I decided whether to take any notice of her or not. 'Don't worry, I will!' I said in the end, seeing as I had to get changed anyway.

I cleared the stairs two at a time and gave my

bedroom door a mighty bang as I slammed it behind me. I waited for a few seconds, expecting Caitlin to come running out from next door wondering what was the matter. That would have been good because Caitlin would have listened and felt sorry for me and been on my side, but everything stayed eerily quiet and I remembered it was Tuesday and band practice.

I sat on my bed and stared at my trainers. I stared and stared and waited and waited but nothing happened. Mum didn't come up to apologize and tell me there was a cup of tea and a sandwich ready downstairs. She didn't even come to say I'd done wrong and don't do it again but there was a cup of tea and a sandwich ready downstairs. She didn't come at all.

After a while I got so bored I trundled downstairs and into the kitchen where I could smell something cooking.

'What's for dinner?' I asked. 'If it's chicken I'll—'

'Alex,' Mum said in a low, gruff voice, 'I thought I told you to stay upstairs.'

'I did.'

'Go back until I tell you to come down.'

'I don't want to.'

She dropped the wooden spoon she had been stirring with onto the hob where it splattered red

sauce everywhere. 'Alex, go to
your room!' she screamed.

I stared at her in
amazement and opened my
mouth to speak but she then
picked up the spoon and threw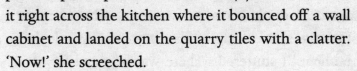
it right across the kitchen where it bounced off a wall
cabinet and landed on the quarry tiles with a clatter.
'Now!' she screeched.

I turned and fled.

It seemed a long, long time until I heard voices
downstairs and finally Dad knocked on my door and
said, 'Alex, it's me' and entered, all long-faced and
serious. 'Oh dear, Alex,' he said, 'what happened?
Your mum's really upset down there.'

'And I'm really upset up here!' I sniffed, blowing
my nose into a tissue and adding it to the pile of
others in the bin. 'Mum shouted at me and threw a
spoon.'

'Tell me what happened,' he said and sat on the
bed beside me, stroking my hair. 'And were you really
rude to Mrs Fryston?' he asked after I had told him
my version.

'Yes,' I admitted.

He sighed heavily. 'Oh, Alex,' he said and now that I had replayed the scene again out loud, even my version made me sound pretty bad. I knew I shouldn't have said that about Mr Sharkey. I liked him a lot and hoped Mrs Fryston didn't tell him what I said.

My shoulders began to judder and I began crying again. 'I don't know w . . . w . . . why everyone's making s . . . such a fuss over a silly telephone number,' I stuttered. 'There was no need for M . . . Mum to sh . . . shout at me. She knows very w . . . well I disapprove of sh . . . shouting!'

'Maybe next time you'll do as you're told the first time and there'll be no need for anyone to shout at you,' Dad pointed out.

'But M . . . Mum never shouts at me, no m . . . matter what I s . . . say,' I wailed.

'I know,' he said quietly, 'she's gone too far the other way.'

'What's that m . . . mean?'

He shook his head. 'Oh, nothing. Look, I'm going to get changed. Caitlin's coming up in a minute with something on a tray for you . . .'

'That's all right—I'll eat d . . . downstairs,' I said, jumping up, 'and I'll s . . . say s . . . sorry to Mum, I suppose.'

'No,' Dad said, shaking his head again and putting an arm out to steady me, 'eat in here then go to bed. It's best if you stay out of the way a while until Mum calms down.'

I didn't understand. 'But I n . . . never eat in my r . . . room—Mum always tells me we'll g . . . get mice,' I pointed out.

Dad cleared his throat. 'Well, we'll risk it, just this one time, eh? Anyway, the good news is, you can have a lie-in tomorrow!'

'What do you m . . . mean?' I hiccuped.

'You can skip After School club for a day and spend it with Caitlin.'

'Why?'

Dad patted me on the knees. 'It's probably best to let your mother sort things out with Mrs Fryston on her own.'

'OK,' I shrugged. I didn't fancy seeing Mrs Fryston again so soon anyway, especially the more I thought about my parting comment and her face after I had said it.

Then I realized something else. 'What, s . . . so I don't even have to c . . . come downstairs to k . . . kiss Daniel goodnight?'

Dad, thinking it worried me,

307

said no, but I could give him two kisses tomorrow night if I wanted. That really brought home how serious everyone was being and I didn't like it. My stomach, which had been rumbling with hunger, stopped immediately, as if it had been switched off, leaving me with a nasty queasy feeling instead. 'Tell Caitlin not to bring the tray—I think I'll just go straight to bed,' I said, my voice steadier now but so hushed Dad probably hardly heard it.

'OK,' Dad said and kissed me lightly on the top of my head. 'It's hard being nine, isn't it? There's so much to learn.'

'I've d . . . done all my homework,' I reassured him, hiccuping again from crying so much.

'That's not what I meant,' he said and left the room quietly.

A few minutes later Caitlin peered in and whispered my name but I pretended to be asleep and didn't answer.

Chapter Fourteen

I woke up the next morning at my usual time and was about to leap out of bed until everything came flooding back. I glanced at my alarm clock and knew Mum would still be downstairs and I didn't want to go down to face her. Even though I had said I would apologize, part of me still felt yesterday's mess hadn't been all my fault, especially when I thought about her throwing that spoon . . .

So I waited until I heard the door bang before I got up. I knew Caitlin was in bed but I still felt alone as I walked slowly past her bedroom and down the stairs into the kitchen. There was such a gloomy feeling to the house. The only signs of Mum having been here a few minutes earlier were a scattering of crumbs on the worktop from where she had prepared her sandwiches.

I don't care, I told myself at first. Ask me if I'm bothered about not going to stupid After School club? *Ask me if I'm bothered.* That's what Jolene used to say to people when they annoyed her. Jolene. Was I as naughty as her? No way. I hadn't broken anyone's tooth. I'd just been a bit cheeky, that's all.

I made myself a slice of toast and planned out my day—it was going to be good. I had the freedom to do whatever I wanted without anybody breathing down my neck. The trouble was, by half past nine I had finished doing everything I could think of—I'd had breakfast, read, watched TV, sketched, sharpened every coloured pencil I had, and tested all my felt pens to throw away ones that didn't work. Now what? I ended up watching a chat show about men cheating on their partners. It wasn't very interesting. I prefer it when they do make-overs for ugly people.

Finally Caitlin awoke and I flung my arms round her in relief as she sloped into the kitchen for her breakfast at eleven o'clock. 'Hurray—you're up!' I announced.

'I know—"put out the flags". I've heard it all before

from Dad,' she yawned as she poured herself a bowl of muesli.

'I mean it—I've been so bored. Can we do something? Go to the pictures?' I asked as she slid on to the tall stool opposite me at the breakfast bar. 'Or maybe bowling?'

She pulled a mardy face. 'You are joking, right? In case you've forgotten, you've been grounded, sister. No treats, by order of the management,' Caitlin replied, looking at me steadily and added, 'I hope you are taking this seriously, Alex.'

'I am!'

She peered at me, looking for signs. 'You'd better be! I know it's a novelty for you that they're actually following through with a punishment but I've not seen Mum as wound up as she was last night—not for a long time.'

'Well, she shouted at me!' I said in my defence. 'And she threw a spoon.'

'Huh! Is that all? Just be grateful it's not like the olden days,' Caitlin said unsympathetically.

'What do you mean?'

'She'd have gone up the wall, never mind the spoon.'

'Mum?'

'Yes, Mum. She used to scream her head off at the tiniest thing. Don't you remember? Dad too for that matter.'

'No.'

'You must do! Why do you think you hate scenes? Even now?'

'Oh,' I said, taking in this piece of incredible news.

But Caitlin didn't give me time to ponder. She carried straight on with her rant. 'Not that she's like that now, so you've no excuse for yesterday. You do know Mum could get the sack?'

That caught me by surprise. 'Could she?'

'Of course she could. All she needs is for a parent to complain about her allowing you to see private material and that's it. How would you like it if some kid in your class read all your personal details in Mr Sharkey's filing cabinet?'

I chose to ignore that uncomfortable idea. 'Well, I hope she does get the sack,' I replied heatedly, 'I hate After School club!'

Caitlin looked at me and frowned. 'Why? What's to hate? It sounds great to me—all those games and things.'

'That's only for the normal kids. I'm not a normal kid,' I told her.

'Course you are.'

'I'm not. I'm with Mum—that makes me different.'

'Well, it shouldn't do.'

'Well, it does and anyway, stop getting at me. I know I was a bit rude yesterday but—'

'A bit!'

'Let me finish!' I said, getting wound up. 'You weren't there, you don't know why.'

'Go on then,' she drawled, 'I'm all ears.'

'OK, well, I didn't even tell Dad this but Mrs Fryston wrote nasty, horrible things about me and I was only rude because I was cross about that,' I sniffed and felt tears spring to my eyes again.

'What nasty, horrible things?' Caitlin asked, seeming interested.

'She wrote on the back of my form that I was clingy and unpopular and antagonistic and Mum agreed with her. "I agree" she put, in capitals, too.'

Caitlin finished the last spoonful of muesli and looked directly at me. 'And are you?'

'What?'

'Clingy, unpopular, and antagonistic?'

'No.'

'Why would Jan write it, then? She always seems all right to me.'

'I don't know, do I?'

She gave me another long, searching look. 'Why else?' she asked.

'Why else what?'

'Why else do you hate After School club?' Caitlin repeated as if talking to a baby.

'Because . . .' I gulped.

'Go on,' Caitlin said but softer this time, pushing her empty bowl to one side.

'Because Mum always makes a fuss of the little ones, especially Brandon Potty-face and even if they make something rubbish she tells them it's good but when I make something . . .'

I went on and on, telling Caitlin one thing after another about After School club and she listened properly and didn't interrupt once, even to laugh because I was hiccuping through half of it and must have sounded funny.

'You're right,' Caitlin said when I had finished.

'What about?'

'All of it. Mum is like that. She spends all her time and energy giving to other people and forgets to give some to us. I bet I could walk into the house with nothing on but my trumpet on my head and she'd still not see me.'

'Exactly.'

Now we were talking.

Chapter Fifteen

I shuffled on my stool to get more comfortable. This was how it should be—sisters swapping complaints about their parents—supporting each other. Only Caitlin spoilt it almost immediately.

'But Mum can't help it,' she continued sadly, 'it's how she's survived since Daniel died. She wasn't like that before. Before he died she used to . . .'

But I was too excited to let her finish. 'I knew it! I knew it would be his fault! He ruins everything in this family!' I reached across so she could give me a high-five but she just stared at me in horror.

'What?' Caitlin asked, her face clouding over alarmingly.

'He's to blame—you just said so . . .' I said before stopping abruptly at the sight of her eyes which had turned as dark and dangerous as an abandoned well.

'Shut up, you little brat!' Caitlin hissed.

Her words pelted me like cold, hard hailstones. It was the final straw. My whole family hated me! I burst into tears and began to scramble down from the breakfast bar to escape but Caitlin caught me by the arm and held me fast, forcing me to look at her.

'Let's get one thing straight, Alex! You can't blame Daniel for *anything*. He was four years old! Do you think he caught meningitis on purpose? Do you think he thought, I know, I'll die and then everyone in the family will be really messed up? I'll put my mum on tablets for the rest of her life and make my dad work long hours so he doesn't have to come home, and I'll make Caitlin miss me so much she won't let me be buried properly?'

My head reeled from too many details.

'No, but . . .'

'No but nothing!' Caitlin shouted, suddenly letting go of my arm and pushing it away as if it was contaminated meat. 'I can't believe you think that, Alex!' Spit flew from her mouth as she yelled.

I flinched and leaned backwards. If I had thought Mum was bad yesterday, it was nothing compared to Caitlin now. She seemed so angry I was beginning to get that sick feeling I had just before Jolene lashed out at Brody. For the first time in my life, I was frightened of my sister.

Caitlin looked at me for a second then blinked. Taking a deep, steadying breath she lowered her voice from a shout to something calmer and less scary. 'It's all right, Alex—I'm sorry—I'm not going to hurt you,' she said, wiping her eyes roughly.

I bit my lip and nodded, but my heart was still hammering away. Caitlin put out her hand and covered mine with it and this time her eyes were as tearful as mine. 'I suppose it's harder for you to understand, because you never knew Daniel, but he was my little brother and I loved him to bits. I miss him every day and you'd better learn to respect that.'

I took a big risk and asked a question to something I had never understood. 'Even though it was ages ago?'

'It's not as bad now,' she admitted, 'but I still feel there's a bit missing, like a hole that can never be filled. We all do, especially Mum. It hit her the hardest.'

'Even with me around?' I asked in a small voice. 'Is there still a hole?'

She nodded. 'Even if there'd been ten of you around, Alex.'

There was a short pause and Caitlin, seeming to understand what I was feeling, added hastily, 'But that's not to say we don't love you, because we do. All of us.'

I knew she meant it, too, and that it was true but it hurt that I couldn't fill that hole. I should have been able to. After all, I had replaced him in the family, hadn't I? Nobody had to tell me I wouldn't have been born if he hadn't died. It was obvious. 'Would it have been better if I'd been a boy, like Daniel? Would there still be something missing then?' I persisted.

'It would have been worse, I think. For you especially.'

I pressed on. 'I suppose it's because I'm not sweet and perfect like him.'

Caitlin blinked. 'Sweet and perfect? What makes you think Daniel was that?'

'He was, wasn't he? Like an angel, Mum always says.'

'Was he heck!' Caitlin said, managing a watery smile. 'It's just that when someone dies, especially a child, people build up this ideal picture of them. Dan could be a little monster! He was always breaking my toys and you should have seen him if he didn't get his own way. He'd hold his breath until he went blue. Oh—he used to scare us silly sometimes.'

'Did he? Honest?'

'Honest. Early reports from his nursery school were that he was a bit of a handful.'

'Oh.'

'But he could also be the nicest boy in the world and when he laughed it filled the whole room.' Her eyes welled with tears again and Caitlin withdrew her hand and quickly took her bowl to the sink where she began splashing it in water from the tap. She let the water gush everywhere, not caring that she was getting wet.

'Caitlin?'

'Aha?' she said gruffly.

'What did you mean before—about not letting Daniel be buried?'

She didn't turn round but stared out of the kitchen window, into the back garden. 'I didn't want him to be buried. I didn't want him to be in the dark—he was scared of the dark—so Mum and Dad had him cremated. Then, when the ashes came, I didn't want them to be buried either, because it felt like the same thing, so they put him in my special box Grandad had bought me for Christmas and left him on the mantelpiece so I could see him every day.'

'I didn't know that,' I said. 'I didn't know it was your box. I thought it was Mum's idea.'

She turned to me and shook her head sorrowfully. 'No, it was mine. It all seems a bit babyish now but it helped me at the time. I was only six, remember. I suppose we just got used to having him there on the mantelpiece—we ought to move him really.'

'I suppose.'

Caitlin sniffed and wiped her eyes on her dressing gown sleeve. 'Blimey what a gloomy topic. How did we get on to this?' she asked.

'Tell me what else Daniel did,' I said, 'he sounds interesting.'

My sister's smile lit up her face as she returned to her seat. 'Oh, Alex, I've been dying for you to ask me! There was this one time, right, and Dad had these new spiked golfing shoes and Mum had these new cushions . . .'

Chapter Sixteen

As Caitlin told me about all the naughty things my brother had got up to, I found my feelings towards him changing. It was as if I had been given a new pair of eyes and ears to see and hear things differently. Everything associated with him I had hated before, seemed to have a story behind it, like the time Mum

 had taken him for that photograph in the supermarket and when the photographer had asked him his name he'd said 'My name is Daniel and my willy is called Tommy Sausage'. How could I look at that picture of him again and

not giggle? I didn't resent any of it now that Caitlin had helped me to see Daniel as a real person and I didn't feel jealous of him for her liking him so much because I could see why. I would have missed him, too, and stopped him from being buried in the dark if I had been around then.

I wished she had carried on with her stories but when she glanced at the clock she nearly had a heart attack. 'No! It's two o'clock! I haven't even started my English essay!'

'Or got dressed,' I pointed out.

'Teenagers, eh?' she grinned.

She reached out and gave me such a bear hug on her way out I could hardly breathe. 'You going to be OK? Do you forgive me for shouting at you?' she asked.

'I'll get over it,' I said.

'You looked so scared I felt like an axe murderer.'

'You looked like one, too,' I replied solemnly. I didn't really want to be reminded of that part of our talk but when she left I forced myself to think back to when I was little—two or three. I tried to picture Mum's angry face from yesterday then but nothing came. All I remembered was being in my bedroom a lot of the time and singing, but when I sang, I didn't feel happy, I felt anxious, and had my fingers in my ears. Sometimes I hid under my bed for some reason and Caitlin cuddled me a lot but that's about all that I could think of. Maybe I had blotted everything out. I didn't know. All I did know was I needed to show Caitlin and Dad and especially Mum how sorry I was for how I had been.

I spent late afternoon sitting hunched up on my bedroom windowsill, staring out onto Zetland Avenue, waiting for Mum to come home. I had so much I wanted to say to her I thought that I would burst. At about five o'clock her figure appeared at the pelican crossing. 'Great, she's early!' I yelped and ran downstairs.

Caitlin was in the kitchen, finishing her lunch-tea. 'Where's the fire?' she asked as I dashed past on my way to the front of the house but I didn't have time to answer.

'Mum!' I said breathlessly as I held open the door for her. 'I'm sorry about yesterday. I promise not to be rude to you or Mrs Fryston ever again. I'll . . .'

But she walked straight past, her face pale and troubled. 'Tea or coffee, Mum?' Caitlin called from the other side of the hallway.

'Coffee, please,' Mum replied in a dull monotone.

I stood nearby as she dropped her bag by the hat stand and unzipped her fleece jacket. 'I'm ready to go back to After School club tomorrow,' I gabbled, 'I'll mix and everything, I promise.'

'You can forget your empty promises,' she sighed, 'especially as neither of us is going to After School club tomorrow or the day after or the day after that.'

'Why?' I asked, then swallowed hard. 'You didn't get the sack, did you?'

I held my breath, praying she'd say no.

'Jan felt I needed a break, that's all,' Mum said, striding towards the kitchen. 'She felt working during the holidays as well as during term-time might be putting too much "strain" on me. Where she gets that idea from, I don't know, but she's the one who makes the decisions. She's the boss.'

For once I didn't leap in and take sides against Mrs Fryston. Instead I followed Mum meekly into the kitchen where Caitlin handed Mum a coffee. 'It's not a bad idea, Mum, taking a break,' Caitlin said.

'Isn't it?' Mum replied glumly.

'You can spend some quality time at home. Put your feet up.'

Mum's face registered that she hadn't got a clue what that meant. She looked so miserable and it was all my fault. I had to put it right. While Caitlin offered to make Mum a sandwich, I quietly backed out of the kitchen and headed for the front door.

Chapter Seventeen

The After School club was still busy when I burst in, all flushed from the sprint across Zetland Avenue. A few kids were in the cloakroom, packing all their things together with their parents and childminders and I had to thread my way between them to get to Mrs Fryston. Sammie and Brody, who were singing a duet in front of the full-length mirror, hairbrushes in hand, paused for a second as I barged past, then shrugged and continued their song.

I strode straight up to Mrs Fryston, who was chatting to Reggie and Lloyd by her desk. 'I'm sorry to interrupt,' I apologized as they all stared at me in surprise, 'but please don't sack my mum, Mrs Fryston —it wasn't her fault I shredded those registration

forms. I was just cross and
jealous because of Daniel and
I took it out on Brandon and
everyone else but I've got new
eyes now and I'm cured. And
I know Mum's not the most
interesting helper but the
little ones like her the best
and you know that's a fact.'
Then I left.

Back home, Mum and Caitlin were still in the kitchen.
I heard their voices murmuring as I sneaked past and
up the stairs. I sat on my bed for a while, to get my
breath back. After a minute I tried reading a book to
distract me but it didn't work. It had been a confusing
day and it was too much to take in details of made-up
lives when so much was going on in mine.

At six o'clock, I heard the doorbell ring, then
Caitlin calling for me to come down. I paused for a
second, my heart beating rapidly as I peered over the
banisters. There in the hallway stood Mrs Fryston,
and I was probably the only one who knew why she
was there. 'Wish me luck,' I telegraphed silently to
Daniel's picture on the wall.

'What's the matter, Jan?' Mum asked and I felt my stomach leap as Mrs Fryston stared up at me.

'I just wanted to check that Alex got home all right. I presumed she had come alone.'

'Where to?' Mum asked, confused.

'The club.'

'Have you just been there by yourself?' Caitlin demanded sharply.

'I crossed with the green man!' I muttered.

Caitlin shook her head at me but I knew I could explain everything to her later. It was Mum I needed to get through to right now. I turned to her, willing her to see I was a changed girl as Mrs Fryston repeated what I had just confessed to her in the mobile.

'I'm sorry, Jan, I had no idea she had shredded anything,' Mum apologized sorrowfully.

'It does confirm everything we discussed today, though, doesn't it?' Mrs Fryston replied mysteriously. No prizes for guessing who was the main topic of that discussion. I felt myself tense.

'Yes it does,' Mum said in a resigned way.

'But, Mum,' Caitlin said quietly, 'remember what I've just told you.'

Mum looked at Caitlin, then down at me. I stared back at her, trying not to cry, knowing she thought the same as Mrs Fryston, that I was naughty and spoilt. The words 'I agree' flashed before me and I waited for her to send me upstairs in disgrace again.

Instead, her face cleared and she slid her arm round my shoulder and pulled me close. 'Alex has been a bit unhappy lately, Jan. I'm going to have a talk to her tonight and get to the bottom of it.'

Mrs Fryston nodded and I was surprised to hear her say, 'That's good. That's what she needs.' I felt relief flow through me like a gust of warm air but Mrs Fryston had more to add. She bent down close and made me look into her eyes. 'Alex, you do know you must never, ever read After School club business?'

'Yes,' I whispered. Her breath smelt of peppermint.

'And that you have put your mother in a very awkward position?'

'Yes,' I whispered again.

'But it was brave of you to come and see me, so when we see you after the holidays, we can start again with a clean slate, can't we?'

'Yes,' I said but this time the whisper was so low I barely heard it myself.

'Why after the holidays?' Caitlin asked.

'Excuse me?' Mrs Fryston asked, straightening up.

Caitlin casually rubbed at a mark on her T-shirt.

'Well, if Alex has problems mixing at After School club, how's it going to help her by not mixing at all?'

'Well,' Mrs Fryston said, 'I just presumed with Ann taking a few days off, Alex would want to as well. I think a bit of time-out for her would be a good thing.'

'Time-out won't solve anything with Alex,' Caitlin continued, looking at me then back to Mrs Fryston, 'she needs time-in. She already sees herself as outside the group because Mum's there but if Mum's not around, it will give Alex a chance to show she *isn't* clingy and *can* mix.'

Mrs Fryston looked at Caitlin with a bemused expression on her face. 'I take it you're doing psychology as one of your A levels?' she stated.

'How can you tell?' Caitlin asked.

'I have one at home just like you!' she grinned.

Then she turned to me. 'What do you think, Alex? Could you cope with a whole day of Pop Kids and e-pals on your own?'

I looked into the eyes I usually avoided and saw how kind and patient they were. I realized Mrs Fryston was prepared to give me another chance, despite my bad attitude yesterday and all the other times.

'See you at half-eight, Mrs Fryston,' I said.

That night, Mum and Dad sat down with me and talked to me in a way they had never talked before. They answered all my questions, though sometimes it was difficult for them and Mum's eyes would flick towards the mantelpiece every time I mentioned Daniel.

'Is there anything else you'd like to ask?' Dad said eventually, glancing at his watch. It was way past my bedtime.

'No, just that Caitlin said you used to both shout a lot but I don't remember that.'

'Thanks,' Caitlin said, 'just drop me in it, why don't you?'

Dad opened his mouth to reply but it was Mum who answered first. 'Caitlin's right, we did. Dad and I were very hurt and angry when Daniel died and we wanted someone to blame so we blamed each other. We went through a very bad patch when you were a toddler.'

'I'm glad you're not any more,' I said.

'Well, we've got you to thank for that, pal,' Dad smiled and Mum nodded.

'Me? How?'

'Your singing. You'd sing to drown out our voices.

When we realized what you were doing and why, we knew it was time to do something about it and your mum and I went for counselling together. It helped a lot.'

'Oh!' I exclaimed as my memory of hiding under the bed and singing with my fingers in my ears suddenly made sense.

Dad began collecting the empty supper plates and cups. 'The voice of an angel you had—even then. Though we did get tired of "Row, row, row your boat" over and over again!'

'I'll bet,' I grinned and yawned loudly. 'I'm going to bed.'

I gave everyone an extra long hug and when I kissed Daniel, I meant it with all my heart.

Chapter Eighteen

If missing After School club had felt strange yesterday, the idea of going to After School club on my own felt even stranger, especially as Dad was taking me on the way to work. It was really odd, drawing up in the car with all the other parents dropping their kids off in theirs.

'Well, this is a novelty,' Dad said as he waited for Brody's mum's huge jeep-thing to move off so he could take her space. 'Have you got everything, Alex?'

I grabbed my sandwich box and nodded, feeling suddenly shy and apprehensive. It was like my first day at school all over again. 'Will you come in with me, Dad?' I asked him.

He checked his watch and nodded. 'Well, seeing as it's you, pal,' he said and got out of the car. I smiled at him gratefully.

We strolled round the side of school and then across the rear playground towards the mobile hut. 'So that's the famous After School club, is it?' Dad asked.

'Haven't you seen it before?'

'No—I've never needed to,' he replied.

'What do you reckon to it? Would it get a good asking price?'

'Not with that flat roof,' he said immediately.

We reached the bottom of the steps and Dad ruffled my hair. 'Good luck, Alex. Everything will be OK.'

'I know,' I said but I wasn't sure I meant it.

It wasn't easy, spending a whole day on my own at After School club. Sammie was definitely still angry with me. 'Done any more spying lately, *Mary*?' she asked when I went to buy my break-time sweets from her. I didn't ask how she had found out my middle name.

Brandon wouldn't let me be friends with him either. When I asked him if I could help him with some sticking, he had just looked at me and shaken his head. 'No thank you, you'll just spoil it, like always.'

I wanted to say, 'I'm not like that now,' but he wouldn't have understood. After those two knock-backs I didn't feel brave enough to join Reggie and the gang at the computers, so I read instead. Trouble was, I became worried Mrs Fryston might not think that counted as mixing, because I just *knew* she was watching me, so I played board games with Tasmim and a couple of new kids. It was a bit boring, if I'm honest, but not as boring as being at home would have been. Mum was using the time to catch up with all her support groups—not my idea of holiday fun.

In the afternoon, everyone was rehearsing for Pop Kids. Mrs Riley had taken the karaoke back and now CD players and DVDs sprouted up all over the place. I had only missed one day but it felt as if everything had changed without me. Sammie's hairbrush idea had caught on and everyone seemed to be singing into one in time to their chosen pop song. People were jigging about or concentrating on setting their CDs up properly. Once everyone got going the noise was terrible—I thought the mobile was going to vibrate so much its foundations would cave in.

I began to panic and looked for somewhere to hide. Reggie had taken over the library area, where I had been skulking, and had to be told several times to get off the table which he was using as a stage. 'I bet you wouldn't tell the real Elvis off if he was here,' he complained to Mrs Fryston.

Mrs Fryston folded her arms across her chest and looked up at him. 'You're right, Reggie. If Elvis were here, dancing on a craft table years after he'd died, I would not tell him off. I'd run out of the mobile screaming, seeing as I'm scared of ghosts. Now, get down, please, before you break your neck.'

'But I need the height,' Reggie complained.

'Use the stage blocks.'

'They're gay.'

'How can they be gay, you daft lad? What you mean is there's someone on them. Just ask people to move up.'

'Elvis does not share the stage with minions,' Reggie declared solemnly, clambering down from the table and walking off in a pretend-huff.

'Are you OK, Alex?' Mrs Fryston asked as I tried to sidle past.

'I'm fine,' I said over-enthusiastically.

'How's everything at home?' she asked carefully.

'OK. Caitlin's probably just getting up and Mum was going to visit the hospice.'

'That's Ann—always on the go.'

Mrs Fryston hesitated, as if she was going to say something else, then looked at me and changed the subject altogether. 'Have you decided which song you're going to sing?'

'Erm . . . not yet.'

Mrs Fryston touched me gently on the shoulder and twisted me round. 'Some people are doing duets, you know. Sam and Sammie over there . . .'

We turned to the dressing-up area where Sam and Sammie were dancing back to back, or trying to, but as Sammie towered over Sam it looked a bit strange and Sammie had to keep stopping and wagging her hairbrush because Sam's timing was all wrong. '. . . and so are Brandon and Tasmim . . .'

I found that hard to believe— Tasmim was so quiet I couldn't imagine her joining in but I was wrong. There she was swaying side-to-side with Brandon, singing along and laughing. 'That's nice,' I said.

I was rewarded with a warm smile from the supervisor. 'It is, isn't it? Actually, the only one I'm a wee bit concerned about is Lloyd. He keeps telling me he's OK but I get the feeling he's struggling a bit with his song. Maybe you could see what the problem is while I stop Elvis leaving the building?'

Over by the computers, Lloyd was sprawled out flat on his stomach, operating a cassette tape with one hand while chewing an apple held in the other. He didn't look as if he was struggling that much to me. He just looked like he always did. Like Lloyd.

Then I realized what Mrs Fryston was doing. I'd seen it a million times from the craft table. She was finding me an appropriate friend and edging me in like she did with all the new kids who seemed a bit lost. Before I'd always thought how bossy and interfering she was but now, with my new eyes, I knew it was clever of her. Sometimes kids did need a nudge in the right direction. 'I'll go help him,' I told Mrs Fryston.

'Good girl,' she smiled.

Chapter Nineteen

Lloyd was happy to let me do a duet with him because he said my voice would help drown out his. He had chosen a song called 'Wasted' by the Hairy Pants just so we could be different from everyone else. He played the tape to me a few times. It was very loud and very fast and Lloyd's idea of a dance routine to go with it was to shake our heads a lot as if we were being attacked by wasps then to stomp around in between as if we were killing them. 'It's a bit manic,' I said to Lloyd, puffed out after the first sing-through.

'Yeah,' he said happily, 'it's a blinder. Let's go through it again—after three—one . . . two . . .'

That kind of set the scene for the rest of the holidays at After School club. I joined in as many things as I could in the mornings, then practised my duet with Lloyd in the afternoons. At first, I really missed Mum, and had difficulty in stopping myself from telling Denise, who was running the craft table, that she was putting the equipment and materials back in the wrong places.

By Thursday, though, I had settled into a routine. I said goodbye to Dad, hung my jacket up, and just mucked in with everybody else. Sammie was still a bit distant with me and Brandon kept well away but I told myself I couldn't blame them and tried not to worry about it. I remembered Jolene telling me you couldn't force people to like you. 'If they do, they do, if they don't, hard cheese.' As long as Mrs Fryston knew I was keeping my promise, that was the main thing, I told myself.

Before I realized it, the holiday was nearly over and it was time for the Pop Kids to go live in front of all the parents and carers.

'You don't have to come,' I said to everyone at home the night before. 'Our song's not very good.'

'What is it?' Caitlin asked.

' "Wasted" by the Hairy Pants.'

'Sounds painful,' Dad joked.

'It is,' I said, 'and our dancing is even worse. In fact, the more I think about it, the more I definitely don't want you to come.'

Mum glanced up from her armchair. 'I've got to come—there's a staff meeting afterwards.'

'Oh,' I said. It was the first time she had mentioned After School club all week, apart from asking me if I had behaved myself the second I put my foot through the door.

'The meeting's not about me, is it?' I asked sheepishly.

'No,' Mum informed me, 'it's about the new all-weather surface.'

'Ooh, the excitement,' Caitlin teased.

'I think we've had enough excitement in the house, don't you?' Mum said pointedly then looked at me. 'What top are you wearing tomorrow?'

'The Bad Girl one—it goes with the song,' I replied.

'Oh,' she said shortly.

'I can wear something plain if you like,' I mumbled, though I didn't really want to.

'No, no,' she said in a clipped voice. 'You'd better get an early night, Alex,' she added.

I said goodnight but went to bed feeling as if I had let her down all over again. I knew how she hated my tops.

Chapter Twenty

The next morning was hectic. We all had to help turn the mobile hut into 'The ZAP Spot'—a pretend disco. While some helped Mrs Fryston and Mrs Riley put up flashing disco lights and glittery disco balls, others queued for Brody's mum, Kiersten, to put on their make-up. It took hours.

In the afternoon, because we didn't have to change into anything fussy like everyone else, I helped put chairs out for the parents and Lloyd watched Sam Riley's brothers set up their drum kit and keyboards off stage. Luke and Tim were supposed to have been backing everyone's songs all week but they'd been 'on the road' and only turned up today. Mrs Riley had been embarrassed and called them a pair of lazy articles.

I was halfway through the chairs when Lloyd came up to me, his face the colour of the grass in my Easter Garden. 'What's up?' I asked.

'The drum kit—Sam's brothers—they're The Mass.'

'Oh—so?'

'We can't do our song!'

'Why?'

'The Hairy Pants hate The Mass—they're deadly rivals. We can't do it—we can't do "Wasted".'

'Well, why can't we just not let Sam's brothers play it? We can use the tape we always use.'

Lloyd looked over his shoulder and whispered tearfully, 'Because I'm not supposed to have it—it's new material. I thought Huw wouldn't mind us airing it—for promotion purposes—but there's no way now. He'd kill me—lots of times and in many ways.'

'Now you tell me! Well, what are we going to sing then?'

'I don't know!' Lloyd squealed.

'Hurry up with the chairs, you two,' Denise called over, 'the parents are here.'

We were all hustled to the stage blocks where we

were supposed to sit in order of appearance. That meant I was on the back row with Sammie and Sam, then Brody, then me, Lloyd, and at the end Reggie, who was to be the final act. 'What are we going to do?' I asked Lloyd again in an urgent whisper. 'Mrs Fryston's going to call out our names—we can't just say—"We'll give it a miss, thanks".'

'Why not?' Lloyd replied miserably.

'Because,' I said, and stared out into the audience. Mum, Dad, and Caitlin were just taking their seats. Caitlin caught my eye and waved and I waved back shyly. I knew I had to sing. I knew it didn't matter what I sang but I had to sing something, for them. 'Listen, Lloyd,' I said to him, 'this is what we're going to do . . .'

'We can't,' he said, his face turning from artificial green to a genuine puce, 'everyone'll laugh.'

'It's either that or "Wasted",' I told him fiercely, 'and Huw's sitting right within thumping distance.'

I wasn't kidding, either. The Fountains had arrived late and had to sit right at the front. Huw, with cropped hair and dressed entirely in black, stared moodily ahead. Lloyd sank back in his chair and groaned.

'Right, everyone,' Mrs Fryston began, looking

347

alarming in a silver jump-suit and rainbow coloured wig, 'welcome to Pop Kids . . .'

And so the show began. It was noisy, it was loud, and it was funny but I barely saw or heard any of it until Brody sat down, all pink and flushed from her song and gave me the thumbs-up.

'And now,' Mrs Fryston announced, glancing at her running order, 'Alex and Lloyd are going to perform an original number by the Hairy Pants . . .'

There was some laughter from the audience at the name and a dirty look from Huw as Lloyd and I stepped nervously forward. 'Actually,' I stammered, 'there's been a change of plan. Due to . . . technical difficulties we are going to sing something else instead. We don't need any backing,' I added quickly to Luke who had his drumsticks poised ready. I looked at Lloyd and took his hand and nodded. 'After three,' I whispered and we began.

The words to my favourite hymn 'There Is a Green Hill Far Away' must have sounded weird that afternoon amongst all the pop songs but everyone listened intently as Lloyd and I sang our way through it, just as we had done last week on Easter Sunday. I was aware of Lloyd's voice tailing off halfway through and I realized he didn't know the words off by heart like me but I just carried on. My voice filled the room and my heart soared as it always did when I was singing words that meant something to me. As I sang I thought of Daniel up in Heaven  and I hoped he was watching and I hoped he'd be proud of his little sister.

At the end, there was a silence and I thought for a second Lloyd had been right and we should just not have gone on but then everyone broke into applause and Caitlin stood up and shouted 'Encore!' More embarrassing still was other people joined her, even Mum and Dad. Even Huw.

Mrs Fryston walked on stage, still clapping, and when she congratulated us I'm sure there was a tear in her eye. 'Well, talk about talent!' she gushed.

'I suppose that wasn't so bad,' Lloyd admitted as we returned to our seats and Elvis took centre stage. 'You were pretty rubbish, though. I had to carry you . . .'

'Thanks.'

We took our places again and Lloyd whispered: 'I thought your mum was funny, wearing that T-shirt.'

'What T-shirt?' I whispered back.

'Didn't you see? It's the same one as yours—it says Bad Girl on it!'

'No!'

Half rising, I peered into the audience and he was right—Mum was wearing an identical top to mine! So that was why she wanted to know which one I'd be wearing. Mum saw me looking and grinned, pointing proudly to the slogan. I couldn't believe it. I smiled back, knowing it was her way of telling me she loved me.

'Watch this—this is going to be epic,' Lloyd said as Reggie, wearing a white sparkly Elvis suit stuffed with cushions waddled on to centre stage.

Reggie held his arms out over his head and started clapping. 'Now before I begin I want y' all to put your hands together like this, ladies and gen'lemen, boys and girls,' he said in a dreadful American drawl. 'I wanna hear it for the best darned After School club in the country . . .'

Everyone laughed and cheered. The back row where I was sitting stamped on the floor, making the chairs rattle. And guess who was stamping and cheering the loudest?

Epilogue

Life at After School club is totally different for me now. Either Dad or Caitlin pick me up at the end of the session like all the other kids and Mum stays on to tidy up and plan things like all the other members of staff. It keeps the boundaries clearer, Mrs Fryston says. Mrs Fryston has given me a special role, though. I help any new kids settle in because I know the ropes so well. She told me nobody else could do it better, which made Mum swell with pride. It is easy to see why Mrs Fryston is a leader—she is so good with people of all ages.

Helping the new kids means I don't spend so much time on the craft table with Mum any more but I am happy about that. It lets Brandon have some one-to-one time with her because I don't think he gets much from his mum and I know how *that* feels. Brandon is still a bit wary of me but he let me help him the other day when he fell in the cloakroom and Sammie has at least stopped calling me Mary, so I know I must be doing something right.

The activities have returned to normal at After School club since Pop Kids. Or as normal as they get with kids like Reggie and Brody around. Reggie started the **E-pals Challenge of the Day** a few weeks ago. The idea was everyone had to take it in turns to find a particular kind of e-pal to write to. His challenge was to find the weirdest e-pal, because Fatmuddyboy wouldn't stop writing to him so he said there must be more of them out there and it wasn't fair he should get lumbered. Lloyd's was to find one who had the longest or shortest name, Brody's for an e-pal the same birthday as one of us. When it was my turn to think of something, I suggested writing to people who lived in places beginning with 'W'.

'Huh! I thought you'd have gone for people who live on green hills far away,' Lloyd had teased. He says he'll never get over the trauma of singing hymns during Pop Kids but you wouldn't know it to look at him.

Brody had nudged him hard in the ribs. She knew what I was up to.

So that was how I began writing to Jolene in Washington, Tyne and Wear. It was just a couple of lines at first—how are you doing? that kind of thing—then the e-mails became longer and longer until we were back to how it was and I bet you Reggie's Elvis wig that if she walked through the door this second we'd be best friends again. I know from some of the things Jolene writes that she still gets into trouble, but I'm not as scared of that now. There's more to Jolene than a bad temper. If she did get into a strop again, I would react better this time and try to calm her down before she got to boiling point. I'm a lot more tuned in to how people's brains work these days since my big talk with Caitlin.

Like Mum's, for example.

We are so much closer since I found out that Daniel was only an angel after he died and not before. Don't get me wrong, Mum and I still fall out over things like my clothes and untidiness but now if she

354

says something like, 'Daniel would never do that,' I think to myself, Yes, he would, and that stops me being too rude back.

It's funny, when I think of Daniel, I think of him as he would be now, if he were alive, and not like the curly-haired kid in the mangled photograph on my dressing table. I imagine him as really tall with a spotty face, because that would be realistic for his age. He'd be in the Hairy Pants with Huw and they'd scowl at everything together. At home, he'd wear really manky clothes that Mum despaired of and he'd stick up for me and my tops. He'd be an ace older brother, though he'd have to go some way to beat Caitlin. Caitlin's just the best, though she keeps coming out with some divvy ideas.

She reckons during the summer holidays she's going to take me to Covent Garden and make me sing outside the Royal Opera House. According to her, we'd get so much money from rich American tourists she wouldn't have to find a summer job. I told her she has no chance because I'll be at After School club. The theme is 'Get Active' and when I mentioned to Jolene in my last e-mail activities included girls' football she

355

said that was it, she was coming to ZAPS on the next bus. I wouldn't miss that for the world.

Starring Jolene...

*... as the runaway who's trying to
do a good turn (just make sure
she doesn't turn on you)*

Chapter One

Before I start, if you're one of those people who think boys are 'cool' and kittens are 'sweet' and you have hundreds of lip glosses in different flavours like raspberry ripple and pina colada, I don't think you should read my story. You won't like it—it'll be too real for you.

My anger-management counsellor would tell me off for putting that and say something like, 'Aren't you being a little judgemental, Jolene? A bit alienating?' And then I'd have to say: 'Again in English, please, miss?' and she'd remember I'm only just ten and put it into simple words like: 'Some people can like kittens and wear lip gloss and live in the real world, you know.'

And I'd say, 'Yeah, right, name me one.'

I think my counsellor might be quite new to the business. She keeps coming up with real no-brainers. Today, for instance, Friday, she told me to make a list of targets for over the summer holidays, which begin on Monday. 'Six weeks is a long time for you at home without the structure of school, Jolene, and I know you sometimes find a change of routine a challenge.'

'What do you mean?' I asked her.

'Well, if we look at some episodes from your past, changes seem to have been a trigger for some of your worst . . . erm . . . incidents. When your mum got married to Darryl, for instance?'

'What about it?'

'Didn't you run away from school several times?'

'I didn't run away. I just went visiting Spencer in Newcastle. I was worried about him,' I told her.

'Spencer?'

'Mam's old boyfriend. He works at the station in the baguette bar. She chucked him for Darryl and he was gutted.'

'But Newcastle is miles away from Washington. It was a dangerous thing to do.'

'It is when you're wearing a Sunderland shirt,' I said which I thought was funny but she didn't get it and I couldn't be bothered to explain football rivalry to her.

'Then there was the time you were sent to stay at your grandad Jake's house in Yorkshire and you attended an after-school club with your Auntie Brody,' she continued. 'Didn't you end up in some sort of trouble there? By all accounts you were pretty unmanageable when you returned.'

Flaming hot-pants, I thought, trying to peer over the top of her folder. Did she have what I'd had for breakfast written down there and all? I stared at my feet and said I didn't remember, though of course I did.

Between you and me, what happened at Brody's—she's only eleven so there's no way I'm calling her 'auntie'—wasn't one of my best childhood moments—though it certainly wasn't my worst by a long chalk—but all the same I didn't really appreciate counsellor-lady bringing it up. You'd have thought she'd have better manners.

Counsellor-lady sighed and looked at her watch. I knew the meter was ticking and she had to see loads more bad kids after me. First though, she scribbled something in her folder, then threw me an apologetic smile. 'Just try to stay out of trouble, Jolene, for six weeks. You're such a bright girl, with bags of potential. Put everything I've taught you over the past few sessions into action. Remember, if you feel yourself struggling to keep your temper . . .'

'Yeah, I know, sing a song or repeat a rhyme,' I said. 'Can I go now, please?'

Chapter Two

Straight after my session I headed for the minibus that took me to Burnside After School Club. I can't go to the after-school club at my school because I've been banned, so I am taken across town to another one where I can't put paint in the playleader's coffee or throw chairs through the window. As you have probably guessed, it's little episodes like that which have got me seeing counsellor-lady twice a term in the first place. I'm not bothered though because the club at Burnside's mint and I wouldn't have been sent there if I'd been a goody-goody.

The club's in the dining hall of the old part of Burnside Parochial Juniors. The school itself has been rebuilt in the playing fields across from it and is brand spanking new but they still keep the old bit open for community things like Slimmin' Wimmin and our after-school club.

Mick, the boss-man, is all right. He's a retired Youth Club leader and knows how to handle me. He lays on plenty of physical activities to tire me out at the beginning then lets me spend the rest of the session e-mailing my friend Alex McCormack, who goes to that other after-school club counsellor-lady mentioned. Actually, now I come to think about it, that week at Brody's wasn't all bad—I did get my one true mate out of it.

As usual, there was an e-mail from Alex waiting for me when I got to the club, with an attachment telling me what her club, ZAPS, had got lined up for their summer activities. 'Hey, sir,' I said to Mick after I had written back to her, 'what are we doing special during the holidays? At my mate's after-school club they've got football and a climbin' wall and all sorts. Can we have any of this?'

I stuck the list of activities under his nose to show him. Mick scratched his beard and looked fed up. I've never seen Mick look fed up before. 'I'm sorry, Jolene, pet,' he said, then turned to the whole group and went, 'I'm sorry, all of you. I've got some bad news . . .' Then he told us the council had found something called asbestos in the old ceilings and outbuildings and it meant they had to close down the after-school club until they'd got rid of it. 'So there won't be anything on here until September,' he said sorrowfully, 'which is ridiculously short notice, I know.'

What was it counsellor-lady said about me not reacting well to sudden changes of routine? Huh, it was Mam she should have been worried about, not me. To say she took the news badly is putting it mildly. Ballistic is more like it—I thought she was going to crash the car. 'What?' she said, trying to straighten the steering wheel, all her silver bracelets jangling at once along her arms, 'this had better not be a wind up, Jolene, or I'll kill you.'

'Looks like you're going to anyway,' I pointed out.

She glared at me through the rear-view mirror and told me to stop being so clever.

'You were going a bit fast, Claire,' Keith said in his tiny-tinny eight-year-old voice from the front. He's Darryl's eldest. There's him and his brother Jack. Jack's six. They're both wet and whingy and they hate football and never swear. We've got nothing in common.

Mam apologized for speeding immediately and slowed right down for the little slug. 'Was I, pet? I'm sorry, it's just I'd made some plans and Jolene's news came as a bit of a shock.'

'What plans?' I asked, immediately suspicious. She was always doing this—coming up with 'plans'. Mam's plans usually ended up with her going off somewhere without me. I'm not talking an afternoon shopping at the Metro Centre, neither. She left me at Nana's for four years once.

'Never you mind,' she said, going straight ahead at the roundabout instead of turning left onto our estate.

I pulled a face at the back of her head and Jack giggled until I gave him the daggers. We were heading for Nana's. That was nothing to giggle about.

Chapter Three

'What are we coming here for?' I asked as Mam pulled up outside Nana's front gate. 'Isn't Nana at work?' I was hot and tired and just wanted to go home. Nana's house always made me depressed.

'She's had today off and I've got to sort something out,' Mam said, putting on the handbrake and leaning across to check her lipstick in the mirror. Mam's very precise about her appearance. Her hair is always blonde. Her skin is always tanned and her clothes are always tight-fitting to show off her figure. She never eats bread, rice, pasta, or potatoes and never weighs above eight and a half stone. 'Now, boys,' she said as we followed her up the path, 'I want you just to watch telly for five minutes while I talk to Nana Lynne. You, too, Jolene. I've got to ask Nana a big favour and I don't want any interruptions.'

'What favour?' I demanded.

'That's for me to know and you to find out!' Mam said lightly.

Despite the heat of the afternoon, my hands felt cold and clammy. She was up to something. I could feel it.

Nana took ages to answer the door and I half hoped she had gone out. Eventually we heard the pat-pat-pat of her espadrilles and there she stood. Like Mam, Nana was always blonde, always tanned, and always wore tight clothes, though unlike Mam she had a scraggy neck and veins running down the backs of her legs like blue worms. 'Oh, it's you,' she said, tying a knot in her sarong over her bony hips, 'I was sunbathing round the back.' Her face was pink and flushed but I knew from the way she swayed in the doorway her high colour had nothing to do with the sun. 'Come on in,' she trilled, beckoning us through. 'Isn't it gorgeous weather? I bet you've been roasted in that salon,' Nana said to Mam.

'Tell me about it,' Mam replied, undoing the top buttons of the white receptionist's uniform she wears to Pluckin' Mel's Beauty Emporium.

In the kitchen, Nana refilled her wine glass with a dark red drink from a jug in the fridge. 'Help yourselves to Coke, kids—but don't touch this, will you?' she said. 'That's Lynne's special pop!' And she laughed so hard her boobs shook. Jack and Keith looked at each other, not knowing what to say. I wrinkled my nose at her in disgust.

'Where's Martin?' Mam asked, fetching three glasses down from the shelf and filling them with cola.

Martin was Nan's second husband, Mam's stepdad. He's a security guard in a builder's yard which suits him because he's a plank. 'Martin?' Nana frowned as if she couldn't remember who he was. 'Oh, he'll be back soon—he's just been out to buy some stuff for his pack-up. He's on nights this week.'

I was glad he was out and I hoped whatever Mam had to say would be quick so I didn't have to see him.

We didn't exactly get on, Grandad Martin and me. You could say we rubbed each other up the wrong way. 'You go sit in the front room now while I go talk,' Mam said, ushering us out with the back of her hand. She leaned close to me and whispered in my ear, 'Behave yourself and I'll give you a tenner.' I stared at her in amazement. Resorting to bribery so early in the proceedings? What was she up to?

Nana's front room was dark and stuffy. She never drew the curtains back in summer because she didn't want the sun to fade the furniture, so the three of us sat on her pale blue leather settee and sipped our drinks in the gloom. Outside, I could hear Mam and Nana chatting in the garden but not clearly enough over the noise from the cartoons on TV to hear the actual words.

The cartoon was boring but Jack and Keith sat and wordlessly watched every flicker, just like they'd been told. They were so obedient I reckon they'd been sheepdogs in their last life.

I couldn't stand it any longer and went into the kitchen to try and listen in on what Mam was up to, but just as I reached the back door, I heard the front door open and I quickly pretended to be getting more Coke from the fridge.

'Who's that?' Grandad Martin asked sharply, entering the kitchen and dropping a Spar carrier bag onto the table. He was a small, wiry man with sharp eyes that burned into you. I always felt I'd done something wrong when I was with him.

'It's only me. I was just getting a drink,' I said quickly in case he realized what I was up to.

He dragged out a chair and sat down. 'Pour me one while you're at it, then, Billy No-Mates. Don't take the lot,' he warned, scowling at me. See, he'd started already, teasing me. Billy No-Mates. Huh! Better than Billy No-Brains like him.

'I wasn't taking the lot,' I said, scowling right back and searching for another glass.

'Who else is here then, Billy?' he asked, his sharp eyes flashing towards the back door.

'Mam and Keith and Jack.'

'Thh! Bang goes my bit of peace and quiet before I go to work then.'

Charming. He's not like this with my cousins, by the way. He acts like a proper grandad towards them, all piggy-back rides and day trips out. It's just us he's got a downer on and me in particular. 'We're not stopping long,' I said.

He scratched the back of his shortly-cropped head and sniffed. 'Where've I heard that one before?'

I took a long sip of my drink, my hands shaking as I held the glass. We both knew what he was referring to—the time when I was two and Mam had gone off to work on the cruise ships and hadn't come back until I was six. 'Mam's just popped in to see Nana, that's all. It's what daughters do!' I said defensively.

'Huh! It might be what normal daughters do but Claire's never been normal, has she? And if she's just popped round, how come she phoned earlier to make sure we'd be in?'

He looked searchingly at me as if I had the answer but all I could do was shrug. I hadn't known about the phone call and the news of it did nothing to take away that weird feeling I had in my stomach. 'Just popped in,' Grandad Martin repeated, 'that'll be the day. Where is she?'

'In the garden.'

'Hm.' He drained his glass in one go and stood up, nodding towards the loaf of bread sticking out of the carrier bag. 'While you're here you might as well make yourself useful. I'll have two rounds—ham and mustard,' he said and headed out towards the back garden.

I was tempted to ask him what his last servant had died of but I did as I was told, though I *might* have put a bit too much mustard on the ham. Well, it came out of the jar too fast, didn't it? Mustard does that sometimes, especially the really *hot* variety. That would give the old misery-guts something to think about when he was sitting in his hut tonight, I thought with a grin.

I'd just finished wrapping the sandwiches in cling-film when Grandad Martin returned. 'Gab, gab, gab,' he said, referring to Mam and Nana and flung himself down into the chair right next to me.

'What did Mam say?' I asked, trying not to show how keen I was to know the answer.

He glared at me but didn't reply, though there was something in his eyes I couldn't quite fathom. From the breast pocket on his England T-shirt, he withdrew a rectangular pile of scratch cards which he unfolded and laid flat on the table. I watched as he took his 'lucky' coin from his shorts and began to rub the metallic-grey seals on the top card.

The first two revealed identical cash prizes of ten thousand pounds but the third didn't match up, as usual. You had to get all three to win. Exactly the same happened on the second card on the strip, and the third, and the fourth.

'Hard luck,' I said as his face clouded over.

'Hard luck? Aye, that's all I get is hard luck. Working my socks off for a minimum wage while all that fairy down south does is point a camera and he's a millionaire. Where's the justice?'

Here we go, I thought. 'That fairy down south' was my other grandad, Grandad Jake, Nana's first husband. Grandad Martin is always having a dig at him because Jake is a famous photographer and rolling in it and it annoyed him no end.

'And there's no need for you to pull that face,' Grandad Martin said sourly.

'I wasn't.'

'I know what you're thinking.'

'No you don't.'

I'd be grounded for life if he did.

'You're thinking, "I wish Grandad Martin lived in a flashy house instead of this old dump".'

'Yeah, right,' I mumbled. There was no point even trying to contradict him when he started on like this. What a pair my grandparents were. Nana sozzled one half of the time and Grandad Martin feeling sorry for himself the other half.

Absent-mindedly, he picked up one of the torn scratch cards and began to clean between his teeth with a corner of it. 'You're just the same as your mother. Nothing was ever good enough for her.'

Another familiar line, just because I'm the spitting image of Mam when she was my age. 'Mm,' I said, trying not to look at the soggy segment which, job done, he threw back onto the table. Next, Grandad reached behind him for his Tupperware box and dropped his sandwiches into it, followed by a bag of pork scratchings, muttering that he bet Jake Miller wouldn't be having pork scratchings for his supper. He then fastened the lid of his sandwich box down firmly, running his fingers and thumbs along the edge like a pastry cook finishing a pie. 'But where was *he* when your nana and me were bringing Claire up, eh? Nowhere, Billy No-Mates. Just remember that—

nowhere. Not that you'd know it from the way Claire bangs on about him.'

I began to get irritated. 'Stop calling me Billy No-Mates. It's annoying.'

'It's only the truth.'

'It's not.'

'Isn't it? Name me one friend then,' he retorted, 'cos I've never met one.'

'Easy—Alex McCormack, so there.'

'Never heard of her.'

'That's your problem,' I told him.

'No,' he said grumpily, 'my problem is I've got landed with you and your cheek for two weeks.'

My stomach clenched as his dark eyes met mine. 'What do you mean?' I asked, blinking hard.

'Caught you by surprise, has it? Why? I told you, Claire doesn't "pop in". Not without wanting something. You're staying with us for a fortnight while she goes on holiday—not that we'll get any thanks for it.'

'On holiday?'

'Yes. And bang goes mine.'

Chapter Four

It was true. Mam told me on the way home—a belated honeymoon for her and Darryl, booked on the 'spur of the moment'. Jack and Keith were already taken care of because they were at their mam's for a month so that just left me to worry about. Sure, if she'd known earlier about the after-school club closing, she might have thought twice about booking but the tickets were bought now and I'd be fine because she'd give Nana plenty of money to cover everything.

'Take me with you, Mam, I'll be good, I promise,' I asked her the next day as she packed yet another bright pink bikini into her suitcase.

'Don't start, Jolene,' Mam warned.

'Please? I don't want you to go away without me.'

Mam crossed over to her pine dresser and took out a pile of underwear, not even looking at me. 'Jolene, it's only for two weeks. Aren't I allowed two weeks off from you? What are we? Joined at the hip?' she asked, checking her watch.

'I don't want to stay at Nana's.'

'Well, who else'd have you, with your temper tantrums? I'm amazed she still said yes after I told her about the after-school club shutting.'

'But I don't want to stop with them. They're always arguing and Grandad Martin's a miserable maggot.'

Mam just glared at me. 'Look, if you're sweet to him, he'll be sweet to you.'

'I don't want to be sweet to him!' I protested. 'Being sweet's for girls!'

'Oh, just go away, Jolene—give me five minutes' peace!' Mam snapped.

 'Why should I?' I snapped back.

'Because you're getting on my nerves.'

'Ask me if I'm bothered!' I shouted, breathing the hard, shallow breaths that scared me.

Just then Darryl came into the bedroom, holding a foul orange and lime-green Hawaiian shirt over his pot belly. 'What do you think of this little number, eh?' he asked and winked at me.

He was always winking at me. Winking at me and butting in when he wasn't wanted, the daft plonker.

'Oh, Darryl,' Mam laughed, 'I'm not being seen out with you wearing that!'

'Oh, why not? What's wrong with it?' Darryl asked, pretending to be upset. 'What do you think, Jolene? Don't you think I'll knock them Benidorm lasses for six in this?'

'Who cares?' I said, glowering at him. I just wanted him to go away so I could talk to Mam in private, to sort out this whole mess.

Darryl's face fell. 'I was just trying to be friendly, pet,' he said, glancing at Mam as if to say, 'What's up with her now?'.

'Ignore her,' Mam instructed, taking the shirt and swiftly folding it against her chest. 'She's in a strop because we're having some time off together. Being with her fifty weeks of the year isn't good enough for her. She always has to spoil things.'

I stared at my mam, my ears filling with a sharp whooshing sound. Spoil things? What did she expect after a bombshell like this? Applause? A beach towel was thrown on to the bed and I swept it onto the floor. 'You never listen, do you? You're a rubbish mother, you are!' I fumed as the hailstorm passed but sparks circled round my head instead, crashing into each other and making tiny explosions.

'Oh, we're off!' Mam sighed, casually bending to pick up the towel. 'Fat lot of good those anger-management lessons are doing her. I knew they'd be a waste of time.'

I tried to think quickly about which rhyme I'd chosen for counsellor-lady but I didn't have time. All I could think about was the fact that Mam was leaving me again, dumping me without any build up, any warning. What if she was lying? Not going for two weeks at all but three? Four? A year . . .

The sparks were blinding me and I had to let go. Had to let all that anger out. 'All you care about is your stupid holiday!' I screamed, and lunged towards her suitcase, tossing all the neatly piled clothes out, throwing them across the bed, over my shoulder, at her face, every which way I could. 'You don't think about me, being left behind!' A shoe went flying into the table lamp, knocking it sideways with a satisfying clatter. The hairdryer would have been next—that was heading for the mirror—only Darryl seized it and told me to let go.

'Please, love,' he said.

'I'm not your love! I'm not anyone's love,' I shouted, dropping the hairdryer and running out.

Chapter Five

I spent the rest of the day in my room, having pushed my chest of drawers against the door so nobody could come in. Not that anybody tried, which was fine by me. I watched telly and played on my Playstation and read a bit, then went to bed. When I awoke, I felt different. A coldness had taken over my heart. If she didn't care about me, I decided, I didn't care about her. Let her go to Benidorm. Ask me if I'm bothered.

That day, Sunday, was spent seeing Jack and Keith off when their mam arrived. Her name's Tracie and she's a rubbish mother too. I once asked her how come she didn't have Jack and Keith full-time instead of Darryl and she told me to mind my own business. 'It is my business when they've taken over my bedroom,' I told her—among other things involving swear words. I'm not allowed to be around when she arrives now.

Everybody pretended to be pally and civilized as they swapped kids but then Jack got tearful when it was time to say goodbye and he clung to Darryl's neck so hard that in the end he had to prise him off and force him into the car. I could have sworn I saw Darryl brush a tear away from his eye when he came into the house. How sloppy can you get?

There were no tears from me when it was my turn the next morning. There might have been once. Last time Mam did this, dumping me on Grandad Jake miles and miles away, I was as wet as Jack had been, begging her not to leave me. Not this time, though, not even when she began making a big fuss of me before we left the house, hugging me and telling me it would soon pass. I'd had enough. Not that I let her see how I really felt. I was a hundred per cent sugar and spice when we arrived outside Nana's at seven o'clock. I had to be, if my plan was going to work.

I just hopped out of the car and told Mam not to bother getting out. 'Are you sure, darlin'?' she said, leaning out of the passenger window but looking relieved.

I fixed a big, brave smile on my face. 'Sure I'm sure.'

'We're still mates, aren't we?' she asked, stroking my Sunderland shirt sleeve. That was her way of saying she forgave me about the suitcase incident.

'Way-ay, man,' I grinned, stretching the smile as far as it would go.

Mam smiled back. 'You can be so lovely, sometimes, Jolene! And you could be so pretty if only you'd wear something else.' She shook her head and let go of my sleeve, delving into her handbag. 'Here then, take this and give it to Nana—not Grandad Martin, OK? I don't want it all to go on scratch cards.' She handed me a white envelope I knew contained my board and lodging for the fortnight. I knew Grandad Martin wouldn't have agreed to have me without it. 'And if Martin teases you, just ignore him,' she added. Her eyes darted towards Nana's house which, like all the others along the street, still had its curtains drawn. 'Be quiet when you go in—he might just have got in from work.'

'I will be,' I promised. 'Have a great time.'

Darryl then leaned across her and gave me a twenty pound note. 'And you take this for ice creams, pet,' he beamed.

'Thanks,' I shrugged and stuffed it in my pocket. Every little helped.

I opened the gate to Nana's house quietly as Darryl did a three point turn in the road. I walked slowly up the path towards the front door, put one hand towards the doorbell and turned and waved with the other. As soon as the car was out of sight, I legged it to the nearest bus stop.

By seven thirty I was in Washington bus station. By eight thirty I was at Newcastle Central Station having a nice old chinwag with Spencer and by nine o'clock I was on a train to Wakefield with a free tuna and sweetcorn baguette in one hand and an open return ticket in the other. Well, so what? I thought to myself as fields flashed by the window of the White Rose Express. Everyone else is having a holiday, why not me?

Chapter Six

It wasn't until I got off the train at Wakefield I realized I might not have thought my plan through. For example, when you're visiting a mate, it helps if you know their address. I only knew Alex lived near Zetland Avenue Primary School but I didn't know where that was. The bus station was my best bet, but I wasn't sure where that was, either. I'd only been to Wakefield once and then I'd arrived by car in the dark. Still, I hadn't travelled this far to be put off by minor details like that. Hitching my backpack higher over my shoulders, I headed out of the station and towards the town centre.

I had only gone about a hundred metres when I knew I had really screwed up. Alex would think it was mint to see me but what about her mam, Mrs McCormack? Mrs McCormack worked at the After School club and was one of those fussy women who did everything by the book. She'd have a million questions about how I'd arrived all alone and out of the blue. She wouldn't believe anything I told her.

I sighed and glanced across the road. There was a restaurant there—Piccollino's—I remembered it from my last visit. A grin broke across my face. Mrs McCormack wouldn't believe a pack of lies—but I knew a man who would.

I returned to the station and sat on an empty bench on the far side of the platform. There, I dialled Grandad Jake's mobile number from Mam's mobile which I'd pinched from her bag while she was flapping over the packing this morning. He answered instantly. 'Yep, it's Jake.'

'Hi, Grandad Jake, it's me, Jolene.'

'Jolene?' he said, sounding puzzled. Well, he would. I

haven't spoken to the guy in months. We're not what you'd call a close-knit family.

I tried to sound equally puzzled back. 'I was just wondering where you were?'

'What do you mean?'

'Well, I've arrived at the station but you're not here. I wondered if you'd got caught up in traffic or something, like?'

'Hang fire a minute . . .' There was a pause while he shouted at someone in the background. 'Not there—there—by the orange snowman. Jolene? Are you still there? What station?'

'Wakefield, of course.'

'Wakefield? Wakefield Westgate?'

'Yes. Mam did tell you . . . didn't she?' I said slowly, trying to sound calm but with a hint of panic round the edges.

'Tell me what?' he sighed. He knew, you see. He knew from last time that having his ten-year-old granddaughter turn up unexpectedly on his doorstep was not unimaginable—not with a daughter like he'd got.

'That you were looking after me for two weeks while she went on holiday.'

'What?'

'On holiday,' I repeated loudly, 'Benidorm. They should be landing in Alicante any time now. She did tell you? I know she was having trouble getting through to you but she said she'd left messages.'

'For Pete's sake! I knew nothing about it. I'm not even at home, I'm in London . . . No, not on the snowman, next to it, man! And leave those elves alone! Jolene, this isn't a joke, is it?'

'No, Grandad, course not.' As if to prove where I was, a 125 came hurtling through the station, drowning out his next sentence.

'I can't even send you up to the house. Kiersten and Brody have gone to the States already . . .' he repeated.

Result! Kiersten, Grandad's second wife, was American—they always spent summer in America. No interrogation from the missus to follow. No quizzical glances from lip gloss daughter Brody. This got better and better. 'I could always catch a train to London and meet you there,' I began. I fancied a trip to London. Madame Tussaud's was supposed to be dead good. There's this Chamber of Horrors . . .

'No!' Grandad Jake barked. 'I'm not having you travelling on your own.'

'But I've just come from Newcastle by myself . . .'

'Never mind! Claire must be crazy putting you on a train alone. Jeez! She's pulled some fast ones in her time but this takes the biscuit! And I'm up to my neck in the winter collection.'

Time to crank it up a bit, Jolene. 'I . . . I just don't know what to say, Grandad. Shall I get the next train back and wait at home until she comes back from Benidorm? I've seen this film where this boy does that and he's fine, even when burglars break in to his house . . .'

'No! No—stay where you are—no, listen, do you remember the Italian restaurant up the road we went to last time?'

'I think so. Would it be called Pinocchio's or Piccollino's or something?'

He sighed with relief 'That's it. Go there and wait for me. I'll phone Fredo the manager and tell him to watch out for you until I get there. I'll be a couple of hours at least . . .'

'OK,' I said cheerfully.

'Hell fire!'

Chapter Seven

I had a great afternoon. Fredo remembered me from before because of my Sunderland shirt and we talked football while he prepared the tables for the evening. We were just arguing about whether or not Roma or Sunderland were the best when Grandad Jake arrived. 'Haway, Grandad,' I said, trying not to laugh at his ponytail. He'd have been called all sorts for having his hair like that round us. 'Did you have a good journey?'

He wasn't in a chatty mood, though. After a few words with Fredo, he grabbed my bag and led me out to a waiting taxi, where we sat in silence for twenty minutes until we arrived at his house. Well, I say house. It's more like a mansion. I had forgotten how large it was until the taxi slowed right down to get through the narrow stone pillars of the gateway and entered the long driveway at a slow, respectful pace.

Kirkham Lodge has an orchard and a swimming pool and a stable block and that's just for starters. Grandad Jake is a very rich geezer. Nana must be kicking herself for dumping him all those years ago, though she swears he was a drippy layabout in a tatty duffel coat in those days.

'Now,' Grandad Jake said when he'd switched off all the alarm system and answered his mobile about a thousand times and finally sat down opposite me, 'tell me what's going on.'

'I told you,' I began, 'Mam's gone on holiday.'

'Yes, I know, I checked,' he said brusquely.

'You checked?'

'I phoned that place she works at.'

'Oh.'

My hands began to shake and I had to press them together to stop them from trembling. The geezer wasn't as green as I thought he'd be.

'They told me she'd gone to Benidorm, yes, but that's as much as I could get out of them. Do you have your grandma's number? She's ex-directory and

BT won't give me it and nor will that stupid salon. "It's not our policy",' he mimicked. Grandad Jake was not a happy chappie. He looked at me, puzzled and sad. 'It doesn't ring true, any of this, Jolene. How would I not know about this? How would Claire not tell me? There weren't any messages from her when I checked. In fact, I haven't heard from her in months.'

'I don't know,' I said in a quiet voice, 'all I know is she's in Benidorm and I'm here.'

Grandad sighed and rubbed his face tiredly. 'Have you got Lynne's number? Much as I hate talking to the woman I need some answers.'

I had to think fast. Believe it or not I'm not a natural born fibber—I prefer to tell it like it is but this was an emergency. I hadn't come this far to blow it now. 'No, I don't know it, honest. I'm not allowed to use the phone, see, not after I called Pluckin' Mel's pretending I was an angry customer whose lips had dropped off because they'd given me too many injections.'

'What?' he said, frowning. I knew what he was thinking. My Brody would never do anything like that; though maybe I was wrong. Was that a tiny smile I saw hovering? But then his shoulders drooped. 'The thing is, hinny, I can't look after you. I'm OK tomorrow but I'm at a shoot in Milan on Wednesday until Thursday and it's no place for kids . . . though I guess I could always ring round here . . . check out babysitters . . .'

'Yes,' I said, trying not to get too excited, 'I don't mind babysitters and it would only be evenings cos I could go to After School club here—the one Brody goes to. It's open from half eight to six. There's a girl there called Alex McCormack who'll look after me.'

'Well,' he said, and I knew he was desperate for any solution, 'I guess we can book you in for tomorrow until we sort something out . . .'

'Yes,' I agreed, 'I think that's what we should do. Sound idea, Grandad.'

'Jolene, just one thing . . .' he said solemnly.

'Yes?'

'Do you think we could drop the "Grandad" tag? Just call me Jake, OK? Grandad sounds so ancient.'

'If you want.'

Flipping heck, I'd call him Homer Simpson if it made him happy. Anything as long as he let me stay.

Chapter Eight

I slept like a log and woke up feeling fantastic—like Sunderland had just hammered Newcastle ten–nil at the Stadium of Light—that fantastic. It wasn't until Grandad—I mean Jake—pulled up outside the school railings on Zetland Avenue all the memories of my last visit came flooding back and I realized my dream of seeing Alex again might turn into a nightmare. Alex would be mint—I knew that from her cool e-mails—it was the rest of them I was bothered about.

OK, confession time. Last time I was here—February half-term—the sparks had flown and I'd lost it with Brody. It was before I'd started having my anger-management sessions, all right? I didn't have a song ready then or anything. Anyway, she'd said something and I'd pushed her down the steps outside the mobile and she'd gone flying. Long story short, she'd broken her front tooth right off and as far as I know she's still having treatment for it. That hadn't been the worst of it. Alex fell out with me for what I'd done and I never saw her again. It wasn't until we got this after-school club 'e-pals' thing going we got in touch, ages later. Then I had to reassure her a hundred times I didn't throw wobblers any more.

But what about me just turning up like this now? I knew for a fact there are at least two people in ZAPS After School club who would gladly use my face as a battering ram. Brody's boyfriend, Reggie Glazzard, for one and her so-called 'minder' Sammie Wesley

 for another. I wasn't that sure the supervisor, Mrs Fryston, would be over the moon at my appearance, either. She didn't know how to handle me like Mick did.

Jake finished yet another business call on his mobile—he might as well

have that thing welded to his ear-hole—and began to get out of the car. I was about to tell him I'd changed my mind about this whole thing when I caught sight of Alex in the wing mirror and I was just so chuffed to see her everything else just flew out of my mind.

I leapt out of the car and ran towards her. She was with an older girl I guessed was her sister Caitlin and they both looked startled as this red-and-white striped skinny thing came hurtling towards them. 'Alex, it's me!' I yelled, coming to a halt straight in front of her.

She was smaller than I remembered her, and her hair was fixed in tiny pigtails with flowery bobbles but she was still wearing her top with 'Bad Girl' written on it so I knew she hadn't gone totally girly on me.

'Jolene?' she asked and her mouth opened wide. 'Caitlin, it's Jolene!' she said, her eyes sparkling with excitement.

'Ah, the famous Jolene,' her sister grinned. I liked the look of her. A kind of 'I'll stay in the background but call if you need me' look.

Alex began firing questions and statements like a machine gun. 'What are you doing here? Are you visiting Brody? You never told me! I thought she was away? Your hair's grown really long! How long are you staying, Jolene? Jolene!'

Before I could answer, Jake put his hands on my shoulders and steered me towards the gate. 'Time to catch up later, girls, I've got to see Mrs Fryston.'

'She's not here this week—she's on holiday, with Mr Sharkey. They've gone to the Scilly Isles,' Alex said in a loud whisper, following us through the gate. Blimey, I thought, the whole world's on holiday.

'Who's in charge then?' Jake asked.

'Mum!' Alex said proudly.

'Mum being?'

You could tell Kiersten usually did all this kind of stuff.

'Mrs Ann McCormack,' Alex replied.

'A manic please-don't-let-anything-go-wrong-while-I'm-the-boss-or-I'll-freak Mrs Ann McCormack,' Caitlin added, 'so be good!' And she kissed Alex and left.

No Brody, no Mrs Fryston, no Mr Sharkey. All I needed was no Reggie and no Sammie and I'd be in heaven. No such luck. There they were when we stepped into the mobile, hitting each other with tennis rackets. It could have been my imagination but I'm sure a hush fell as I walked in. It usually does, if you must know. I have that kind of reputation. Sammie looked at me, looked at Reggie, he looked at me, looked at Sammie, wriggled one eyebrow, then shrugged.

Alex linked her arm through mine and made me go and sit with her at the craft table. 'I can't believe you're here. I can't!' she said. 'This is the best!'

'Is it?' I asked.

She beamed at me. 'Is it? Yes a million times a million! How could it not be?'

Relief poured over me like warm rain. Whatever happened when I got found out, no one could take this moment away from me.

Jake spent ages making arrangements with Mrs McCormack. He had to fill out a fresh application form and keep coming over to me to check whether I had any allergies or ailments then go back again. Eventually he was able to leave. 'I've just signed you up for the day. I don't know what we'll do tomorrow—I've got an evening flight from Heathrow booked . . .'

I stood up and gave him a hug, which surprised both of us. 'Well, I've got today, haven't I? I've got today with Alex. That's all that counts.'

Chapter Nine

It wasn't fair—the morning just flew by. There were about a million activities to choose from—outdoor and indoor. I had to admit this After School club was even better than Burnside for facilities. Alex and me spent most of our time on the climbing wall. It was tricky at first, getting used to the footholds and having to climb so high, and Alex wasn't that keen, but the instructors were good at telling us what to do and where to aim for, so we soon had the hang of it. I went up four times and Alex three.

Lunchtime was a bit embarrassing because Jake hadn't thought to pack me any food so I shared with Alex and Mrs McCormack. 'Are you sure?' I said as Mrs McCormack handed me an egg and mayonnaise roll and a banana. 'I can always phone my grandad—he's working from home today.' I fumbled in my bag for Mam's mobile which I still had with me.

Mrs McCormack shook her head. 'Oh, don't bother him. I haven't time to eat anyway,' she said, looking anxiously over my shoulder at Reggie and Lloyd and co. in the far corner who were blowing into empty bags of crisps and bursting them. I had the feeling people were taking advantage of Mrs Fryston not being around. Although there were other adult helpers, Mrs Mac was supposed to be the boss and she isn't exactly the strictest person I've ever met. Still, it was nothing to do with me. I was here for Alex and Alex only.

'Cheers,' I said, peeling the banana.

'Mum, can Jolene sleep over tomorrow?' Alex suddenly asked.

I paused mid-bite, my heart racing. I hadn't even thought of that one.

Mrs McCormack still had her eyes trained on the crisp bag corner. 'What? Sure—I don't see why not—if it's OK with Mr Miller.'

'I'll phone him now!' I cried. 'He said he had to go to Milan so he'd be dead grateful I bet!'

Before she could answer, Mrs McCormack was distracted by other events. 'Oh, Reggie, do you think that's a sensible thing to do with that bag?'

Reggie paused. 'It's just science, Mrs M,' he replied innocently, midway through blowing air into an empty bag of crisps.

'Science?' Mrs McCormack asked.

'Science—you know—an experiment to find out what sort of crisps fly best. Unless you already know the answer?'

'I don't know,' she said, falling right into Reggie's trap.

'Then allow me to demonstrate.'

 With one quick movement he clapped his hands together, bursting the bag and splattering shards of crisps all

over himself and anyone standing nearby. 'I thought so,' he laughed, picking bits out of Lloyd's hair. 'The answer is plane crisps! Get it—*plane*. Obvious really . . . unless the new Branston Pickle flavour . . .'

'Oh dear,' Mrs McCormack muttered, moving reluctantly towards the lads' corner as Lloyd handed Reggie another bag to experiment with, 'this is what I was afraid of . . .'

Alex linked arms. 'Let's go onto the field—this could turn embarrassing.'

'Yeah,' I said, linking hers back, 'let's.'

While Mrs McCormack had a 'quiet' word with Reggie, we headed for the door. Sammie Wesley was in the cloakroom as we passed, brushing her hair and chatting to another girl I didn't remember from my last visit. As we approached, Sammie swung round and glared at me. 'You'd better keep your hands to yourself while you're here,' she warned me.

Now that wasn't right. I hadn't said a thing to her. 'Or else?' I asked.

'Or you'll see what else,' she said through narrowed eyes.

A few sparks fizzed somewhere in the comer of my brain but I felt

Alex's hand squeeze my arm. 'Oh, ignore Sammie—she's in a mood because Brody's not here to hang out with.'

'Am not,' Sammie pouted.

'I don't want any trouble,' I said, 'I just want to relax.'

Sammie turned away and whispered loudly to the other girl, 'Watch her—she's as mad as a brick.'

My breathing quickened and I stared angrily at the back of Sammie's frizzy bonce for a moment. Silently, I began my rhyme for the first time. 'Five currant buns in a baker's shop,' but Alex tugged me away before I could put sugar on top. 'Come on,' she said, 'don't waste time.'

I knew she was right. I hadn't seen her for months and I might only have the rest of this afternoon with her. It was all right inviting me to a sleepover but if Jake somehow managed to get hold of Nana . . .

Quickly, I put that thought right out of my mind. We didn't want to go there, did we? 'Let me phone Grandad before I do anything,' I said, groping for Mam's phone in the bottom of my backpack and pressing his number, carefully ignoring the fact it said there were six new messages waiting to be opened.

 My stressed-out under-pressure grandad agreed straight away, just like I knew he would, especially as Thursday was taken care of, too. The sleepover meant an extra day at After School club. Re-sult. 'That's great . . . that's great,' he said. 'Headache over until Friday.'

I was sorry for giving him headaches. Not.

The afternoon was even better than the morning. We got to play football! Real football, with real players from Emleigh Ladies AFC coaching us. I was on a skills team with Alex, a little kid called Brandon, Reggie, and Tasmim somebody, led by this woman called Katie. 'Wow, you're good!' Katie said to me after we had finished doing some dribbling skills through cones.

'Thanks,' I beamed.

'Do you play at school?'

'No—at my after-school club with Mick. I'm going to play for Sunderland Women when I'm older, though.'

'Well, I'm keeping my eye on you, Speedy. We might need you at Emleigh first!'

'Are you keeping your eye on me, too?' Brandon butted in, tugging at Katie's shorts.

'Well, I'm keeping an eye on those trousers of yours,' Katie laughed. 'You must be baking in them!'

I could see what she meant. Brandon was wearing thick jogging bottoms and a heavy, long-sleeved jumper on what must have been one of the hottest days this year. 'I am a bit,' he said, pulling the round collar away from his neck, 'but Mum says I've got to keep them on because of my eczema.'

'Well, if Mum says . . .' Katie smiled and clapped her hands. 'Right then . . . let's have a match!'

Our team took on Sammie and her lot. It was only ten minutes each way and nobody took it too seriously but I loved every second of it. I loved

looking over my shoulder and seeing Alex nearby and I loved watching titchy Brandon surprise everyone by outpacing them and I loved it when Sammie tried to tackle me and I dodged her so, so easily and put the ball into their net by nutmegging Lloyd Fountain, their goalie. Not once. Not twice. Loads of times.

As I glanced across to the side of the field, I saw Katie point me out to another one of her team-mates and say something. And I felt so elated, because I knew it was all good stuff.

From about three o'clock, parents and carers began to pick up their kids. By five, there were only a few of us left. Even Caitlin arrived for Alex. 'Oh,' I said in surprise, 'I thought you went home with your mam.'

'Not now. It keeps things separate,' she replied, glancing at Caitlin.

'Oh,' I said, not sure how I felt about being left alone.

'See you tomorrow, Jolene,' Alex said. 'Bring your jammies!'

'Jammies?' Caitlin asked. 'Are you moving in?'

'Jolene's sleeping over—Mum said she could,' Alex explained.

'There goes my beauty sleep,' Caitlin laughed and tugged at Alex's pigtail. 'Come on—I've got stuff to do.'

They went, leaving me unsure what to do next. Sammie was playing 'Four-in-a-Row' on her own but I didn't fancy joining her so I decided to go and wash some grass stains off my Sunderland shirt in the cloakroom, hiding behind the partition so nobody could see me. I was making a total hash of it and spraying water everywhere when I heard Brandon ask someone if he could take his top off.

'No!' a woman's voice replied sharply. 'I told you to keep it on.'

'But I'm hot.'

'I don't care. You don't want people seeing where you fell, do you? Well, do you?'

'No,' Brandon whispered.

'Come on then—Kagan's fallen asleep at the wrong time as usual—might as well get home before he wakes and yells the place down.'

A tall woman with dark, curly hair swept past, with Brandon hurtling behind her. I watched as she clattered down the mobile steps and threw Brandon's lunch box onto a tray beneath a navy blue pushchair. Not seeming that bothered about waking the sleeping baby inside, she began pushing the buggy so fast, little Brandon almost fell trying to keep up with her. Poor kid. I didn't dwell on it, though—Jake was walking in straight towards me. I needed to concentrate.

Chapter Ten

Talk about tense. The first hour was not too bad—I chatted about what I'd done while Jake microwaved a pizza, but every time the phone rang, I jumped. Was it Nana? Was it Mam? Or even the police? I quickly dismissed the last idea. Nana wouldn't call the police, not so soon. Grandad Martin didn't exactly get on with them and she knew from all the other times I'd legged it I always turned up sooner or later. No, she wouldn't be bothering with them yet. Fingers crossed.

After the pizza and salad I went into the living room and flopped into one of the deep armchairs. I was whacked after all that running about earlier and was tempted to put my feet up on the coffee table in front of me but I daren't. This wasn't quite home.

A minute later, Jake came and sat opposite me, shoved his bare feet onto the table straight away and began tapping his thumb against the edge of his bottle of water. 'Jolene,' he said, his voice very calm but serious, 'I want you to tell me the truth.'

I looked at him and swallowed hard. I'm pathetic at proper lying to someone eyeball-to-eyeball. This was it then. Game over already.

My grandad leaned towards me, his forehead creased. 'You remember last time you came? When Claire brought you here as a punishment while everyone else was supposed to be going to EuroDisney?'

'Yes.'

'But it turned out it was a total crock—they were home all the time?'

'Yes.'

'Has she done the same again? If I were to drive you back to Washington now, would we find her at home varnishing her toenails?'

I felt so relieved I didn't have to fib. I made the sign of the cross against my Sunderland coat of arms and looked him straight in the eye. 'No, she really is in Benidorm, really. Cross my heart.'

Jake shook his head. 'I don't understand it. I don't understand how any mother . . .' He banged on about how irresponsible she was and I began to feel bad. After all, Mam had made proper arrangements for me, it was just I didn't follow them. Then the guy came out with something I had never expected. 'Still, who am I to criticize? I wasn't exactly the best father on earth to her. This is probably her way of getting back at me.'

'Yeah, I think she does wish she had seen more of you,' I said without thinking, but he just nodded in agreement.

'I'm sure she does—I hardly ever saw her when she was growing up.'

'Same as mine—he legged it as soon as he found out Mam was up the duff,' I said matter-of-factly.

'Oh, it wasn't like that,' Grandad protested. 'I tried at first, you know, after the divorce, but my work suddenly took off and then when Lynne met Martin, it became . . . awkward.' He broke off to have a sip of his water, frowning. 'Still, it's no excuse, is it? I should never have stopped visiting. I didn't see her again until she was seventeen. Maybe if I'd kept in touch . . .'

I snuggled down further in the armchair and joined him on the coffee table with my feet up. It was good this, chatting and finding out stuff about Mam. We hadn't had a chance for much one-on-one last time—Brody was always in the way.

'Still, putting you on trains on your own. In this day and age . . .'

Not again! Blimey, for someone who wore a ponytail and trendy clothes who didn't like to be called Grandad he did bang on like an old codger sometimes. 'Jake, I'm fine—I got here, didn't I?'

He glanced briefly at his watch, the same way counsellor-lady does, when the meter's ticking over. I didn't mind. He'd come through for me and that was the main thing. As rich and famous and busy as Jake Miller was, he'd dropped everything and turned up.

As I had guessed, he stood up and apologized. 'Got to make some phone calls, Jolene. Can you look after yourself for a while?'

Who me? Course I could.

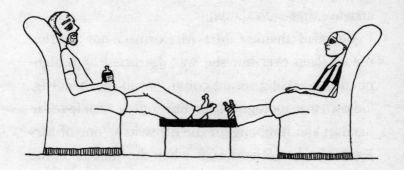

Chapter Eleven

The next morning I arrived at After School club with my backpack all ready for my sleepover at Alex's. I was early because Jake wanted to catch the London train, so only Mrs McCormack and Denise, the student-teacher helper, were there. Alex would be arriving later with Caitlin.

Grandad thanked Mrs McCormack for inviting me to sleep over but she was distracted by a high-pitched crackling sound coming from her handbag. 'Sorry,' she apologized, pulling out a walkie-talkie handset and fumbling for the off switch, 'one of Mrs Fryston's ideas for the staff when they're out on the field.'

'Good idea,' he smiled. 'Anyway, I can't tell you what kind of a hole you've got me out of,' he continued, unfolding his wallet to pay my After School club fees.

'Was Jolene's visit unexpected?' she asked.

'You could say that.'

I looked carefully at Mrs McCormack, to see if I could tell what she was really thinking. I knew she'd been caught on the hop yesterday and hadn't been really listening when Alex invited me. Maybe she wasn't that keen to have me after the Brody thing. I have had problems with friends' mums before—that's the trouble when you're on a short fuse like me: nobody wants their kids to hang out with you. They were always making excuses such as: 'It wasn't convenient', or: 'Maybe another day.' I didn't blame them, either, sometimes! I held my breath and waited.

Luckily Mrs McCormack looked back at me and smiled. 'I wish you'd come more often, Jolene—Alex actually tidied her room last night without being told to and discovered clothes under her bed she'd forgotten she had.'

I grinned. That was OK then.

'So we'll see you . . . ?' she asked Grandad.

'I'm back Thursday so I'll see you at the end of After School club—sixish? I shouldn't be any later.'

'That's fine—I'm here until then. If you're going to be any later, just call and Jolene can come back with us for tea.'

'Thanks, Mrs McCormack!' I said. What a nice lady.

I walked Jake to the door, telling him I could have paid my own fees because Mam had given me the money. I mean, it was meant to be used for stuff like this and there was plenty—there had been two hundred pounds in the envelope when I'd checked. I'd felt a bit upset when I'd seen how much there was. Other grandparents would have done it for nothing.

'It's OK, I think I can manage,' Jake grinned, and bent down to give me a hug. I automatically stiffened, in case he was going to disguise the hug as a hard squeeze that stole the air from your lungs like my other grandad would, and he looked at me strangely. 'You're a prickly one!' he said.

'I'm just not mushy like you lot!' I protested.

Straightening up, he fished in his pocket for his shades. 'See you on Thursday then, Jolene. We'll work out the next stage then.'

'Grandad—I mean Jake,' I blurted, still not really used to calling him by his first name.

'Yes, hinny?'

I took hold of his hand shyly. 'Thanks for everything. I'm dead grateful.'

He looked a bit awkward then. 'I haven't really done anything.'

'You've brought me here,' I said, 'and that's mint.'

'Mint?'

'Mint. The best. Cool.'

He ruffled my hair and looked round the mobile hut. 'Most ten year olds want Disneyland but you're happy with this . . .'

'Everywhere's Disneyland when you're with people you like,' I told him.

'Mm,' he said thoughtfully, 'that could be my new strap line for the winter range . . .' And he whizzed off down the steps, repeating what I'd said.

Chapter Twelve

Like the day before, time went too quickly and all too soon we were having another football match with Katie to finish off the skills session.

I think I was on my fourth goal when Katie blew the whistle and swapped the teams around. 'Just to get a better balance,' she said. It was Brandon, Tasmim, Alex, a couple of eight year olds, and me against Sammie, Lloyd, Reggie, and Sammie's sidekick Sam Riley—every one of them either a Year Five or Six. You should have seen the look on Sammie's face! It made no difference—we still stuffed them. Well, Brandon and I did, if I'm honest. Alex was only playing for my sake—she's not a natural—and Tasmim and the little ones were planks, but nippy little Brandon and me . . .

'Gimme some skin!' I said to him as we returned to the centre spot after yet another goal.

He returned my hi-five and grinned, sweat pouring down his hot face. He was still wearing his thick tracksuit, just like yesterday. 'We're good, aren't we!'

'We're class. You've got some pace on you for a scrap.'

He raised his head high, blinking in the sunlight. 'My daddy's in the army and I make him train me like a proper soldier so I can be strong and fit like him. We play games and combats down the park when he's home.'

'It shows,' I said. 'Is he home now?'

'No, he's in Cyprus for ages 'n' ages.'

'Aw, well, you're mint anyway.'

His eyes shone with pride and I thought for a second that if Jack or Keith had been more like Brandon and liked games, maybe we would get on better. Brandon wiped his forehead with his sleeve. 'Jolene?'

'What?'

'I didn't like you last time you were here cos of what you didded to Brody but I think you're a peach now.'

'A peach! Thanks, bud. Eh, Brandon?'

'Yeah?'

I turned round to see Reggie shrugging his shoulders as he placed the ball in the centre spot and whispered to Brandon, 'Shall we let them have a goal, so they don't cry?'

'OK.'

Unfortunately for them, Katie blew the whistle for the end of the match. 'Warm down first, everyone,' she commanded. 'One lap round the field.'

'Come on,' I said to Alex, 'race you.'

She looked at me and shook her head, blowing hard. 'I can't, my legs are like jelly. I don't know how you do it.'

'It was only ten minutes each way.'

She rolled her eyes at me, still panting. 'No way—see you inside. I need a drink.'

'Me too,' Brandon said, 'a big one.'

'Lightweights!' I shouted after them.

After two circuits of the field and a thumbs up from Katie, I went to look for Alex. I found her in the cloakroom, sitting opposite Brandon and sharing a bottle of water with him. 'Want some?' she said.

I nodded and took a deep gulp. Alex lifted her T-shirt and started wafting it to cool her stomach. 'I'm boiling—I can't wait to get home and take this off.'

'Me too,' Brandon said, rolling the sleeves of his sweatshirt as far as they would go.

'Mate, you're going to faint in that,' I told him.

'Can't you take it off?' Alex asked.

He shook his head miserably.

'Is it because you haven't got anything on under it? I bet Mum's got something in the cupboard you could borrow.'

'It's OK, I've got my army T-shirt on,' he said, and plucked out the hem of a camouflage top beneath his sweatshirt to prove it.

'Take your jumper off then, Brandon,' Alex said and she leaned across to help him.

'No, I mustn't,' he said, pulling his legs up to protect himself.

'Yes you must!' Alex teased, leaping on him

and starting to yank his top over his head; but without warning he kicked her hard with both feet and she stumbled backwards with a yell. 'Watch it, Brandon,' she scowled, 'I was only playing.'

Brandon shrank back against the wall, his face frozen hard.

'Come on, Jolene,' Alex said, 'let's leave him to his mardy.'

Normally, I would have followed her like a shot. Cut that; normally if anyone had kicked Alex like that they'd have been dead meat but instead I shook my head. 'You go,' I said to her, 'I'll be out in a minute.'

'OK,' she shrugged, 'but don't be long—Caitlin'll be here soon.'

'I won't,' I said.

We sat there for a few seconds. 'More water?' I asked, holding out the bottle.

'No thanks,' he sniffed.

'OK.'

A few more seconds passed. I glanced about, making sure no one was around. 'Brandon,' I said in a quiet voice.

'What?'

'How'd you get those bruises on your tummy?'

His eyes immediately darted towards the exit, where parents came to collect everyone. 'Haven't got none,' he said, tugging his sweatshirt top so it stretched like a woollen skirt over his knees.

'I saw them when Alex was messing about. I won't tell, I promise,' I said.

'Haven't got none. It's eczema.'

'Not where you fell?' I said, remembering his mam's reason.

He began to look distressed and I was tempted to leave it. After all, it was none of my business, was it? Only he was only five. And he was ace at football . . . 'See this?' I said, twisting my arm round to show him a scar. 'My grandad did that.'

'Did he?' Brandon asked, his eyes opening wide. 'Was it a naccident because he was tired?'

It had been an accident. Grandad Martin was a grumpy old goat but he had never actually hit me. Threatened to loads of times but never actually done it. I knew plenty of kids who had been slapped around, though. They were the ones who waited outside the office for counsellor-lady with me. I knew the way it worked. I shrugged my shoulders at Brandon and fibbed. 'Nah—no accident—it was from a cigarette to teach me a lesson, but don't tell anyone, will you?' I said. 'You're the only one who knows. Even my mam doesn't know how I got it.'

'No,' he said, 'you mustn't tell, must you, even if it is a naccident or else . . .'

'That's right. Or else . . . ?' I stared at him, as if I'd forgotten what would happen.

'Or else policemen will come and take you away and you never see your mummy and daddy and baby brother again, do you?' he completed.

'That's right,' I agreed, 'that's what they say.'

And he buried his head in his jumper while I stared at my arm.

Chapter Thirteen

'Ready?' Alex grinned an hour later, linking her arm through mine as Caitlin arrived to take us home.

'Ready!' I grinned back and laughed as we did this silly walk together down the mobile steps. Good luck, mate, I thought, as we passed Brandon's dark-eyed, gaunt-faced mam heading towards us.

What do you mean, is that it, you just left him and carried on as normal? What did you expect me to do? Just get lost—go buy a new lip gloss or put some milk out for your kitten or something. Leave me alone.

I had a great time at Alex's house, thank you very much. We played gymnastics on her climbing frame in the garden then came in for tea. Caitlin had made this chicken and orange salad thing followed by double-chocolate trifle and I was allowed two helpings because I was the guest. Her mam had to go out for a meeting somewhere but when her dad came home we played card games like 'Go Fish' and 'Uno' and I laughed because Mr McCormack was a right cheat and he didn't mind who knew it.

Before we went upstairs to bed, Alex kissed this box thing on the mantelpiece. 'What's that?' I said to Mr McCormack as I waited.

'That's our Daniel,' he said quietly, referring to Alex's brother who had died when he was little. 'We still say goodnight to him.'

'God,' I said, 'I never say goodnight to my brothers and they're only in the room next door!'

'That's a shame,' he said quietly.

'You're not kidding,' I said, 'they've ruined my wallpaper.'

'That was one of the best nights I've ever had in my life,' I told Alex later as we snuggled down to sleep. She was on a futon thing on the floor and

I was in her bed, watching the ceiling. Her house is on a main road, so every time a car passes, a beam of light travels across the room. I found it kind of hypnotizing.

'Honest?' she asked.

'Honest,' I said.

'Flipping heck—you're easily pleased,' she laughed. 'Night, Jolene.'

'Night, Alex.'

Even breakfast time felt very different at Alex's house. Although we were doing the same stuff as at home— sitting down, eating toast, getting sandwiches ready for packed lunches—the atmosphere was better. Like when Alex spilt a glass of orange juice across the table, wetting Mr McCormack's newspaper, he didn't yell at her and tell her she was a clumsy idiot, he just laughed and went, 'My horoscope said I was in for a surprise!' and that was that. And when he left for work he gave Mrs McCormack a quick peck on the cheek and said, 'See you tonight, love,' instead of kissing her on the lips for ages and whispering things in her ear that make her giggle like Darryl does to Mam. That drives me potty, that does, and I have to tell them to pack it in, then Mam frowns and tells me to mind my own business and it all starts.

'That was brilliant,' I said to Mrs McCormack afterwards.

She looked at me and blushed for some reason. 'It was just a bit of toast, love. I didn't have time to make anything else. I've got a full house at After School club today so I need to get there a bit earlier. I'd have done eggs and bacon otherwise.'

'It was still brilliant,' I said. 'Thank you very much for having me. I'll just go and pack now.'

Upstairs, Alex teased me as we brushed our teeth. 'That was brilliant,' she mocked.

'It was!'

'Jolene—that toast was as cold as an eskimo's bum and burnt to bits—I'm using my slice for a charcoal drawing.'

'I didn't mean the toast exactly,' I said.

She cocked her head to one side. 'Girl, you're a lot more weird than I remember you,' she said and spat into the sink.

'Thanks,' I said, 'I'll take that as a compliment.'

She wiped her mouth on a dark blue towel and sighed. 'It went dead fast last night.'

'I know.'

'I wish you could have stayed over longer.'

'Me too.'

'Maybe you could next time. For a whole week . . . or even a month!'

'Yeah,' I said, 'maybe.'

The idea was so fantastic, I daren't even think about it too long or I'd ache.

Chapter Fourteen

Mrs McCormack left about half an hour before us and Caitlin walked us to After School club via the newsagent's on the corner for sweets. 'Isn't this mint?' I said after we'd chosen our mix.

'Mint? I thought you'd got liquorice?' Caitlin asked and Alex and I just looked at each other and laughed.

'You two! You're like twins or something!'

I can't tell you how good that made me feel.

The inside of the crowded mobile was already warm by the time Caitlin dropped us off. Sun streamed in through the windows, and Mrs McCormack had to shield her eyes as she reeled off a list of choices for today's indoor and outdoor activities from her clipboard '. . . then for outside, as well as Emleigh Ladies continuing their coaching, Denise is taking Quick Cricket on the far end of the field. It's also the last day of the climbing wall . . .'

'That's us sorted,' I whispered to Alex, 'football.'

Alex looked at me and chewed her lip. 'Jolene? I fancy doing something else today.'

'Like what?'

'I don't know—anything as long as you don't have to move fast—or move at all, even. I might make a macaroni necklace or something.'

'All right,' I said slowly. It was the opposite to what I wanted.

'You can still do football, though,' she said.

'But I want to hang out with you.'

'But we've got tomorrow,' she pointed out.

'Maybe,' I said.

'But we have, haven't we?'

Course, I couldn't say anything to Alex but I wasn't sure how much longer we had together. Gut instinct told me my holiday time was running out. Something was going to happen soon—bound to. 'Macaroni necklace?' I said. 'Sound.'

Alex looked pleased. 'Come on, then,' she said, yanking me up from the carpet, 'before all the places go.'

'Can I come, too?' a little voice piped from behind us.

Neither of us had even noticed Brandon squatting there. Alex sighed and pulled a face. 'I suppose,' she said reluctantly, 'as long as you keep your feet to yourself.'

'Sorry,' Brandon whispered, casting his eyes towards me but I looked the other way. Don't do this, mate, I thought. Don't get attached to me.

'I'll just dump this,' I said, shoving my backpack under Mrs Fryston's desk.

The arty-crafty stuff wasn't too bad, I suppose. I managed to make something that could have passed for a necklace, if you kept it in a dark box and didn't look at it. Alex, though, was in a different league. No stringing orange and green macaroni on a bit of cotton for her—oh no. She was weaving all these delicate red and white threads together on this metal frame thing. It was slow going—by lunchtime she still only had about six centimetres of her pattern completed but I was well impressed.

'What is it?' I kept asking.

'Not telling,' she kept saying.

'They're my favourite colours.'

'No? Really?'

'Yes, really.'

'What a coincidence.'

At lunchtime we all sat outside to eat our sandwiches. We tried to find somewhere apart from everyone else, though Brandon stuck to us like paste to wallpaper. I think Alex was a bit narked but it didn't matter, really. He didn't butt in or anything—he was happy just to sit and listen to Alex and me telling jokes and laughing over nothing. A couple of times I noticed Sammie and a few others glancing across at us but I ignored her, just like I had all week. Not that I'd forgotten what she'd said about me, like. I never forget. I just didn't want any hassle.

'Alex,' I said towards the end of the break.

'Yep.'

'I just want you to know, whatever happens, you're my best friend,' I whispered.

'You're mine, too,' she whispered back, 'forever and ever.'

'Amen,' Brandon added.

Chapter Fifteen

The mobile was stuffier than ever when we returned for the afternoon session despite every door and window being wide open. Mrs McCormack tried to take the register but it was noisy and I could tell she was getting stressed out when nobody would settle. 'Listen carefully, children, please,' she began, 'I have to get this right. There are some new people with us this afternoon and some from the morning session have gone home and I mustn't get them mixed up in case there's a fire.'

She continued droning on about rules and respect and litter on the field, sounding too much like a teacher, which isn't what after-school clubs were about. Nobody was listening. A button on her blouse had come undone and her underskirt dipped below the hem of her dress. Even her clothes disobeyed her, I thought. Normally I'd have got bored and ignored her or shouted out to tell her to wind her neck in but it was Alex's mum, after all. 'OK,' she said finally, 'on to this afternoon . . .'

I had resigned myself to more macaroni stringing when Sammie came up to me just as I was taking my seat. 'Jolene?' she said, a grumpy look on her face.

'Yeah?'

'Katie asked me to fetch you.'

'Why?'

Sammie stuck out her chin. 'She thinks you're a good role model for other girls.'

Me? A role model? That was a first. I glanced across at Alex and she just shrugged and said, 'Go on, role model, what you waiting for? I'll join you when I've finished this.'

'Can I come too?' Brandon asked, scrambling out of his chair and coming to stand next to me.

'Course you can,' Sammie said and she held her hand out for him but he just shook his head because he wanted to go with me and she flounced off in a huff.

'Jolene?' Alex said in a hushed voice as I was about to leave.

'Yes?'

'You'll be OK, won't you? With Sammie?'

'Course I will. It's not like last time.'

Her face flushed pink, as if she was embarrassed to even mention it. 'I knew that,' she said.

I did feel a bit uneasy without Alex at first but my stomach soon filled with bubbles of excitement once the match started. As well as Reggie and Sammie and the other regulars, there were some older kids playing this time, Year Sixes who'd come from another school somewhere. It gave me more of a challenge and I had to work harder for the goals, avoiding some rough sliding tackles from the new kids that had Katie shouting words of warning to them.

One kid in particular, a lanky lad with floppy hair, called Nat, seemed to take it personal when I nutmegged him a few times. 'Someone thinks they're special,' I heard him mutter.

I just laughed and crossed to Brandon. Brandon took it forward but just as he was about to pass back the floppy haired cheat cropped him from behind, taking his legs from right under him. Brandon fell to the parched ground with a thud and started crying.

'Sorry, mate,' the kid said, holding his hands out in surrender as Katie advanced towards him and started giving him an earful.

Brandon was still curled up on the floor, holding his left leg and rocking backwards and forwards.

Sammie got to him first. 'You all right, Brandon?' she said, leaning towards him.

'It hurts,' he sobbed.

'Let's have a look,' she said, reaching for the zip near the ankle of his jogging bottoms to see his legs.

'No,' he screeched, batting her hand away.

'Just to check if it's bleeding or owt,' she said.

'No!' he repeated and his eyes sought mine, like I knew they would.

I had the ball and began bouncing it up and down. 'Leave him alone,' I said to her, 'he's all right.'

She spun round angrily. 'Who asked you? For your information I'm helping him.'

'He doesn't want your help,' I said, coming to stand in front of Brandon but continuing to bounce the ball. Sammie pulled herself up to her full height and glared at me. If looks could kill, I'd have been smoke. A few sparks fizzed in my head and I stared right back. The atmosphere around us grew still and tense.

'Since when have you been the boss of him?' Sammie demanded.

I stopped mid-bounce, and looked at her. Oh, she was up for a fight, this one. I didn't blame her. I knew she still hated me for what I'd done to Brody and maybe if she knew how sorry I was about that she might have cut the attitude, but this wasn't about Brody. This was a different deal altogether. 'I'm not the boss. I'm just telling you to back off,' I said. And I said it quite calmly, for me.

Sammie's mouth almost disappeared into her face and she stepped just that bit too near to me. 'And who are you? The Queen of Sheba?'

I'm sorry, counsellor-lady. I know the rhyme thing's supposed to help but, to tell you the truth, rhymes are rubbish in an emergency. When you've got someone in your face like Sammie was at that moment, those five currant buns just stay in the baker's shop.

I threw the ball to the side and went to smack her one but, amazingly, she got there first and punched me right in the mouth. Though it wasn't a full swing and didn't hurt that much, I was too surprised to punch her back. Nobody had ever swung at me before—they're usually too scared. Besides, Katie was already on the case and pushed us angrily apart. 'Stop it,' she said, 'stop it now!'

'You're dead!' I yelled, darting towards Sammie. 'You are *so* dead!'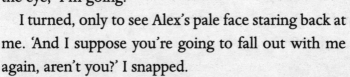

'Time out, time out!' Katie barked.

'Don't worry,' I said, glaring at Sammie who didn't have the decency to look me in the eye, 'I'm going.'

I turned, only to see Alex's pale face staring back at me. 'And I suppose you're going to fall out with me again, aren't you?' I snapped.

She didn't answer but for someone who didn't like sport much she was off like a hare, racing across the field and disappearing into the mobile without a backward glance.

I followed but didn't attempt to catch her because I didn't know what I'd say if I did.

All I knew, when I reached the bottom step outside the mobile and flopped down onto it, was that my stomach had the familiar churned up feeling I always got when I'd messed up again. Brandon came hobbling up a few seconds later and sat right next to me. I slid my arm round his shoulders and we just sat there, like the two outcasts that we were.

Chapter Sixteen

A few seconds later Mrs McCormack poked her head round the door, the walkie-talkie crackling away in her ear. 'No, no, they're here now, sitting on the steps,' she said, looking down at us with a pained expression on her face. 'Thank you, Katie. Yes, I'll wait for her.' Mrs McCormack gave me a disappointed shake of the head.

Here we go, I thought. Same old same old.

I stood up, shrugging as she told me Sammie was on her way over and was very, very upset. 'What a shame, Jolene,' Mrs McCormack began, 'after you'd behaved so beautifully this week.' She glanced over her shoulder into the room where I guessed Alex's sudden arrival had probably tipped her off that she could say goodbye to a relaxing end to the day.

'Sammie biffed Jolene first,' Brandon told her.

'Why don't you go and sit down, Brandon. Katie says you had a nasty knock,' Mrs McCormack replied.

'Not going anywhere,' he said sullenly, folding his arms across his chest.

'Brandon?' Mrs McCormack said, her voice wobbling because he was ignoring her.

'Go on, mate,' I told him and he disappeared inside without another word.

When Sammie arrived I couldn't believe the state she was in. She was blubbering and out of control. What was her problem? I hadn't touched her. 'Calm 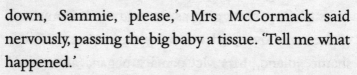 down, Sammie, please,' Mrs McCormack said nervously, passing the big baby a tissue. 'Tell me what happened.'

Fine, I thought, ask her first. She's a regular, right, and I'm just the bad guy. To be fair, the story Sammie managed to get out in between sobbing everywhere was pretty accurate. She even admitted having a pop

Chapter Seventeen

When I entered the mobile it was like one of those scenes in a school drama lesson where everyone takes up posed positions you just know are fake. Alex was reading a book upside down, Brandon was drinking from an empty beaker and a group of kids were playing Jenga without touching any of the pieces. They were all waiting to see what the nasty girl would do next. Well, the nasty girl was too tired to do anything—sorry to disappoint you all.

'I'm going to just sit and wait for Grandad,' I mumbled to Mrs McCormack.

'I think that's a good idea,' she said, sounding relieved.

'Don't worry, Mrs McCormack,' I told her, 'you'll soon be rid of me.'

'It's not that, Jolene,' she began but I was already in the furthest corner of the book area I could find.

The rest of the afternoon passed slower than the last match of the season, when you've already been relegated and there's nothing to play for, but I stuck it out without budging. I just sat with my arms round my backpack and waited for Grandad Jake to arrive. I kind of guessed Alex would come across but when she did I felt all tongue-tied and couldn't look at her. 'Jolene,' she said quietly, 'I'm going now.'

'OK,' I said, not turning round. I was in what counsellor-lady called 'defensive mode' where I put up a barrier to protect myself. Even I couldn't figure out why I wanted to protect myself from Alex but I did. Next time I glanced up, she was gone.

So that was that, then. I was Billy No-Mates again.

At last the time came we had all been waiting for. Grandad Jake arrived, earlier than expected and not looking exactly delighted with the world either, to take me away from ZAPS After School club forever. I knew there was no way I was coming back here again. Sammie was spot-on: I'd ruined it. For her, for me, for everyone. 'Ready, Jolene?' he said.

I looked up. Mrs McCormack was hovering behind him—she'd have given him the good news about my behaviour, bet you.

I headed straight for the exit, not looking right nor left, up or down. I strode straight through the playground and into the parking area where Grandad's flashy car was waiting to take me away. 'Home, Jake,' I said, giving it a false smile when he finally caught up with me.

Like Queen what's-her-face, he was not amused. He pointed his key to the car and unlocked the doors. 'Not quite, Jolene. You've got a bit of explaining to do first,' he said, chucking my backpack into the boot.

Great, I thought, just what I needed.

Chapter Eighteen

'So what did she say?' I asked as soon as he started the car engine.

'Who?'

'Mrs McCormack—I suppose she told you about the fight?'

'Fight? Hell's bells, Jolene, you haven't been in a fight as well?'

'As well as what?'

'Here—listen to this,' he said and laid his mobile on my lap. 'Press star.'

I listened, my heart sinking fast as Nana's high-pitched voice screeched on and on and on. 'So then when she hadn't turned up by night-time, I phoned our

Claire at the hotel—I'd been trying her mobile all day but she said she'd lost it—had it pinched at the airport, she reckoned. Anyway, you can imagine the state she was in when I told her Jolene hadn't turned up. "Try that no-mark Spencer at the station," she said, "that's where she always goes first," but of course he'd finished work by then and we couldn't get hold of him till Tuesday morning . . . blah-blah-blah.'

'Press again,' Grandad said when Nana finally finished.

This time it was Mam, more or less continuing the story. 'So he said she'd mentioned Wakefield and so I presume she's headed straight to you so I'd appreciate a call if you're not *too* busy . . .'

'Nice messages to receive in the middle of Milan,' Grandad said.

'Yep.'

'Why did you do it?' Grandad asked.

'What?'

'What? What do you mean, "what"? Run away like that!'

I shrugged. 'I just wanted a holiday.'

'A holiday?'

'Yes—a holiday—you know, one of those things with buckets and ice creams.'

'So you came to Wakefield?'

'Why not? It's as good a place as any, though that walk to the beach is a killer.'

He looked at me sternly. 'Jolene, this isn't a joke. You can't just take yourself off on a whim! You are ten years old! And think how I feel—here's me yelling at Claire when all the time I should have been yelling at you!'

'Well, you'll have to join the queue then, won't you?' I shouted and burst into tears.

I don't know who was more shocked, me or my grandad. Once I started, I couldn't stop. I was miles worse than Sammie. Never mind a main bursting—I could have filled a valley twice the size of Lake Windermere with my waterworks.

On and on I sobbed, blindly ripping tissue after tissue out of the  box that Jake had handed to me. 'Jolene, hinny,' he kept saying, 'I'm sorry. I won't yell at you, I promise. It was just a figure of speech. It's not my style.'

'It's not that!' I managed to sob eventually. 'I'm just tired.'

'Tired? Didn't you sleep well?'

'Not that kind of tired! I mean tired of always being in trouble and tired of everybody hating me and tired of losing friends like I just did over there. Every time something's going all right, right, something rubbish happens and I'm fed up of it. It wasn't even my fault this time. I knew I wouldn't have long before Nana caught me and I wanted every minute to be magic with Alex because she's my best friend and I never get to see her. And I behaved, I did, honest. Katie said I was a role model.'

'So what happened?'

'Nothing!'

'Well, clearly something must have. You said there was a fight?'

'Sort of. It wasn't what I'd call a proper fight but it was bad enough. That Sammie sticking her nose in . . .'

'Listen, Jolene, if something happened at After School club, perhaps we need to go back inside and clear it up now.'

'I'm not going back in there!' I sniffed.

'Well, the thing is, you are. I've booked you in for tomorrow again.'

'I'm not going. You can't make me.'

Jake rubbed the back of his neck. You could tell he was new at all this. 'Whatever happened can't have been that bad,' he began in this corny 'let's-all-calm-down-guys' tone. 'Don't you think it's best to face up to things instead of running away all the time?'

I wiped my eyes clear with the back of my hand, annoyed now. What was the point of telling him anything? He only understood about dumb things like airhead models and orange snowmen. Besides, he had no room to talk, did he? 'Well, everybody else runs away, why can't I?' I told him.

'What do you mean?'

'You ran away and left my mam when she was little and Mam ran away and left me when I was little. I'm only keeping up the family tradition, aren't I?'

'It wasn't like that,' Jake began but I wasn't going to listen to him.

'. . . and you like Brody better than Mam, even though they're both your daughters, just like Mam likes Keith and Jack best instead of me. And don't pretend you don't because you know you do!'

The sparks were coming now, fast and furious. I twisted away from him, pressing myself up against the door as he started the car engine. And then I saw her. Mrs Petty, Brandon's mam, coming to fetch him from the club. This was all her fault. I'd still have that happy feeling and be mates with Alex if it wasn't for her. I wouldn't be leaving here like this, all messed up. 'Wind down the window, Jake,' I grunted.

'There's air conditioning . . .'

'Please!'

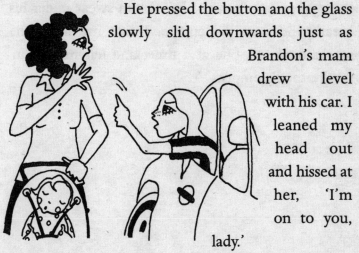

He pressed the button and the glass slowly slid downwards just as Brandon's mam drew level with his car. I leaned my head out and hissed at her, 'I'm on to you, lady.'

She turned, startled, just as Jake began pulling away from the kerb. 'Yes,' I said, jabbing my finger, 'I know what you do to him.' Her hand flew to her mouth and I withdrew, my heart hammering in my chest.

'Now what was that about?' Grandad barked, stalling the engine.

'Nothing!' I barked back.

He stared in disbelief as Mrs Petty quickly disappeared into the school playground. 'I don't believe you sometimes, Jolene.'

'Ask me if I'm bothered,' I said, without much conviction, as he glanced in his rear mirror, as if trying to decide whether to get out and follow Mrs Petty or just go home. I heard him swear under his breath and start the engine. Inside my head, the sparks died out, one at a time, and left me feeling totally, totally empty.

Chapter Nineteen

Brody's dad—I had decided that's who he was from now on—drove home in silence, which was fine by me. As soon as we entered the hallway I tried to go up to my room. I just wanted to be by myself. I didn't have sparks in my head but it was full of something just as confusing. I couldn't describe it, but if I drew it, it would be a mass of black squiggles like a cartoon raincloud. All I could figure out was I wanted to be alone, but when I made for the stairs, Brody's dad put a hand on my shoulder to hold me back.

'Jolene,' he said quietly.

'What?' I muttered.

'You're right.'

'About what.'

'About the running away and the favouritism. You're absolutely right and I'm sorry.'

I looked at him and was about to shrug when I got the shock of my life. He had tears in his eyes now. He was as big a wuss as Darryl!

'Don't worry about it,' I said. I felt really confused. My feelings towards him changed all the time.

He cleared his throat and gave me a feeble smile. 'Listen, hinny, I've got something I want to do. How about giving me half an hour and I'll call you down, hey?'

'Fine.'

'Why don't you have a long, cool bath?' he suggested.

Baths are not my thing but I couldn't think of anything else to do so I did as I was told. I felt a lot better after, especially when I dried myself in one of their gigantic white fluffy towels. Trouble was after I only had my Sunderland kit to put back on and that was well grubby so I put on the only other clothes I'd brought with me—my pyjamas—and went downstairs.

'What happens next then?' I said to Grandad Jake, which is what I had decided to start calling him again. It was the name with which I felt most comfortable.

He was sitting on the sofa and had, thank goodness, packed in with the tears-lark.

'First things first,' Grandad Jake said and passed me the phone. 'Claire's waiting to talk to you—just press star.'

'Do I have to? She knows I'm safe.'

'Yes, you do. Don't worry, she won't have a go at you—I've already had a long talk to her. I'll be in the kitchen if you need me.'

I stared at the handset for ages. The last thing I felt like was an ear-bashing live from Benidorm. Mam *not* have a go at me? Who was he kidding? Reluctantly, I pressed 'star' and waited.

The phone had hardly rung once when Mam answered. 'Jolene, is that you?' Her voice came across all muffled and strange.

'Yes. What's wrong with you? You sound funny. Have you got a cold?'

'No, I'm a bit . . . a bit upset that's all . . . after talking to Dad.'

Not her, too! What was this? National Blubbing Day? 'Go on then,' I sighed, 'get it over with.'

'Oh, Jolene! I do not like those two boys more than you.'

It was not the opening line I'd expected but I was definitely not going to let that whopper pass. 'Give me a break,' I said.

'I don't!' she hissed. 'Hang on a minute . . .' In the background, I heard a door bang shut. 'Darryl's on the verandah. I don't want him to hear. Listen, I don't, they get right on my nerves if you want to know the truth. It's just, I have to make a fuss of them because Darryl does.' She took a deep breath. 'He's such a good dad and I want him . . . I want him to think I'm a better mother to them than Tracie or he won't stay with me.'

That was original, I'll give her that. 'Is that supposed to make *me* feel better?' I asked.

She tutted irritably down the line. 'No! But you don't help much with your attitude, do you? Causing atmospheres all the time and running off. Here's me trying to make a happy family and all you do is spoil everything.'

Now I might have bought that a week ago. I know I'm not the easiest kid to have round the house but I'd seen how Alex's family worked. I had something to compare ours to and I knew which one I preferred. The one where if you made a mistake, like spilling orange juice, it was turned into a joke not a fight.

'Maybe you should talk to me differently and I wouldn't spoil things,' I suggested.

'Oh, really?' she said, all prickly.

'Yes—really. And I think you should know that good mums don't have favourites—especially fake favourites,' I told her quietly. 'Alex's mam treats her kids equally, even the dead ones.'

'Oh, does she? Good for her. Maybe she's a more natural mother than I am, then.'

'What do you mean?'

'I mean, some mothers take to it better than others. I'm not a natural mother. I admit it. Do you know what else I know? I hate even *being* a mother! I've hated it right from when you were born, having to be there twenty-four-seven while this little alien clung to me and cried and cried. How's that for a confession?'

It's a start, I thought. Now, I know a lip gloss type would be in shreds if their mam had just admitted she hated being a mam, but the thing is, I wasn't a bit surprised. Let's face it, Mam was only stating the obvious. It wasn't even personal, in a way.

'So what did you have me for then?' I asked out of curiosity.

Mam blew her nose loudly near the receiver. 'Honestly?'

'Yes.'

'Because I wanted some attention from Dad after Kiersten had her baby.'

'That's daft.'

'Well, I know that now, wise girl! I was jealous, all right? You try competing with a supermodel stepmother who's only five years older than you are.'

I should have known it would come back to Brody's mam. It always does, just like when Grandad Martin starts it always comes back to Grandad Jake. Ever since I can remember, Mam had compared herself to Kiersten Tor, and no matter how many times I told her she was pretty and looked young, she never believed me and would get out a photo of Kiersten taken years ago and say, 'Not that pretty,

though.' She even called me Jolene after some stupid song about a woman that takes another woman's bloke away. It does my head in. Still, at least now it was all fitting together.

'Jolene? You still there?' she sniffed.

'Yes, course I am. I'm just listening and taking it all in.'

'Well, that makes a change.'

Now, see, normally with that sort of put-down, I'd have been hurt and said something nasty back and it'd be the start of a row, but I still had the spilt orange juice memory in my head so I just said calmly, 'Yes, I know, I'm learning fast.' Learning to be long-tempered instead of short-tempered.

'Oh,' Mam replied and you could tell she was surprised because she'd been expecting me to kick off, too.

'Tell me more about when I was little,' I said, 'like why you left me.'

'Not that again.'

'It's important.'

She took a deep breath. 'Oh, I just couldn't cope, especially when you got to two and still wouldn't sleep through the night, so I looked for a way out. I took that job on the cruise ships as a chambermaid.

The pay was lousy but anything was better than being at home.'

'Was I such a bad baby?'

'No! This is about me, not you. You were just normal—then anyway.'

'Thanks.'

'I know I should have stuck it out and I know Mam and Martin aren't the best people in the world to leave a toddler with.'

'Huh.'

'But maybe when I get back we can start fresh, eh? You, me, Darryl, and the lads?' The lads. Poor Jack and Keith. Lumbered with two half-baked mams.

'I'll make a deal,' I said.

'What sort of a deal?'

'You stop dumping me at Nana's and I'll try harder to make your job easier.'

'My job? At Pluckin' Mel's?'

'No, your job at home—being a mam.'

There was a long pause before she spoke again. 'Darryl wanted us to get the next flight back, you know,' she announced.

'Did he?'

'Oh yes—he was well worried about you, even when I told him you were like me, a tough little survivor.'

'Oh.'

'Jolene, are you still there?' Mam prompted. 'I've never known you this quiet.'

'I'm thinking about things,' I replied. 'I'm a role model now—that's what we do.'

'Oh, get you!' she said cheerfully. She'd perked up no end. 'Listen, pet, if you want us to come back early and cut our special holiday short, we will do. Though Jake did say he'd look after you until we got back . . .'

Her voice had that wheedling tone she uses when she says one thing but means another. She might be all bright and breezy now but I thought of the mood she'd be in if I said, 'Yeah, catch the next flight out.' Besides, if Grandad Jake was taking the week off, that was a bonus. Ponytail or not, the guy was beginning to grow on me. 'No, I'm fine—you stay in Benidorm,' I told her.

'If you're sure.'

'I'm sure.'

'Will you phone me tomorrow?'

'If you like.'

'Anytime.'

'OK.'

'Love ya, Jolene.'

And I think she meant it, in her own way.

I hung up. I reckoned that was the longest conversation I'd ever had with my mam without it ending up in an argument. And you know what? I felt really proud of both of us.

'Everything all right?' Jake asked, peeping round the doorway.

'Yes,' I said, holding the phone out for him to take. He shook his head.

'What?' I asked.

'One more call.'

'Who?'

'You know who.'

I pulled a face. 'Why? They don't care.'

'Dial,' he said, and went out again.

Like Mam, Nana answered immediately but her conversation was way more predictable. She ranted on and on about me not turning up and what a worry I was and how I'd put them all in an early grave.

'Go have a drink of your special pop, Nana,' I told her in the end just so she'd put a sock in it.

'Your grandad wants a word first,' she said gruffly and handed me across.

I took a deep breath and waited for him to start. 'I suppose you've spent all that money,' he began and I couldn't help it—I just laughed out loud.

'I knew that's all you'd be worried about.'

'Is it?' he snapped. 'How come I spent two nights searching Barlow's Wood for you, then?'

'Did you?' I said in surprise. Barlow's Wood was well spooky—you wouldn't catch me there in broad daylight, never mind night-time. Even muggers avoid Barlow's Wood. 'Oh,' I said shortly, 'thanks.'

He mumbled something about me wanting a good hiding then hung up. I smiled into the receiver. There was another turn-up for the books—Martin Nevin actually doing something that showed he cared about me. Blimey.

Chapter Twenty

This time when Jake entered the room he was carrying a huge glass sundae dish full of different flavoured ice creams topped with fudge sauce and chocolate flakes.

'Waoh!' I gasped. 'Is that all for me?'

'Well, you are on holiday—what's a holiday without ice cream, eh?' he said, sliding the dish towards me. Yep, this guy was definitely growing on me.

'Wow,' I said, aiming straight for the vanilla, feeling very hungry all of a sudden. 'Jake?'

'Aha?'

'Can I start calling you Grandad again? It feels better.'

He smiled. 'Course you can, hinny. It's what I am, after all.'

'Exactly. You've got to do what feels proper, haven't you?'

'You do.'

'Grandad Jake?'

'Aha?'

'What did you say to my mam on the phone to make her cry?'

'I told her what I should have told her when she was your age.'

'What's that?'

'That her daddy loves her.'

'Urgh! That is so cheesy.'

He blushed. 'Cheesy? Maybe but . . . it just felt . . . proper.'

'I think you did the right thing. I think it will stop a lot of problems.'

'Really?' he said and waited for me to explain but I didn't elaborate.

The thing is, when I thought about it, Grandad Jake had caused a lot of problems. If he hadn't become so famous, Grandad Martin would never have been so bitter towards him, and if Jake had kept in touch with Mam, she wouldn't have been so insecure and jealous of Kiersten. You never know, she might even have liked being a mam more. But then it wasn't all Jake's fault, because Nana told me she booted him out, not the other way round, so really it was her fault . . .

I broke off from my thoughts and started in on the pink ice cream. It was delicious. I remembered what counsellor-lady says when I tell her the latest scrape I'd been in hadn't been my fault. 'I'm not blaming you, Jolene, I'm trying to understand.' She was right. In the end no single person was to blame for the mess-up in our family. The thing was just to not make it worse. 'Mam said you'd taken next week off?' I said to Grandad Jake to change the subject.

'That's right.'

'Cool.'

'I need you out of my hair for one more day, though, hinny. Calls to make, models to book—you know.'

'Yeah—whatever. I'll just go for a swim or something.'

'Er . . . not possible, Jolene. I need to do lunch with some clients.'

'So I have to buzz off?' I asked, finishing off the strawberry and starting in on the green ice cream that was turning slushy.

'Yep.'

'You mean After School club, don't you?'

'I do mean After School club.'

'Have I got a choice?'

'No.'

'OK,' I sighed, thinking how thrilled everyone would be to see me turning up again. I couldn't quite see Sammie putting the flags out.

'Hey,' Grandad said, tapping me on the knee, 'just remember it hurts less if you take the plaster off in one quick go.'

'Oh yeah?' I replied, wrinkling my nose at the unexpected taste of the melted dollop of pale green ice cream.

'What's the matter? Is it too tart?'

'No,' I laughed, 'it's mint!'

Chapter Twenty-One

'Ready?' Grandad said the next morning as he parked on the yellow zigzag lines outside Zetland Avenue Primary.

'Yep,' I said, breathing deeply as Reggie and Lloyd went past, eyeing me suspiciously.

'Want me to come in with you?'

'No.'

Grandad handed me a brown bag and grinned. 'Packed lunch. Mrs McCormack mentioned it.'

I managed a smile, even though I had butterflies, moths, and bluebottles flying round my stomach. I think there might have been a couple of bats in there as well. And a parrot. I felt as sick as one anyway but I didn't want to worry Grandad Jake. 'You're getting good at this,' I told him.

'I am, aren't I? Good luck, hinny,' he said, ignoring the ringing tone on his mobile, 'you'll be fine. Remember—one quick go.'

'Thanks,' I said, sliding out of the car and closing the door behind me.

One quick go sounded like a good plan to me. I walked fast, across the playground, straight up the steps of the mobile hut and straight up to Mrs McCormack, who was wheeling the tuck shop into place. 'Mrs McCormack,' I said, 'I just wanted to say I'm sorry about yesterday. I promise nothing like that will happen again. When I think of you, I'll always think of orange juice.'

She blinked a few times, clearly not having a clue what I was talking about, brushed her grey fringe out of her eyes and smiled. 'Well, that's very mature of you to tell me, Jolene. Thank you.'

'That's OK,' I replied, glancing round. I knew Alex wouldn't be arriving until about nine with Caitlin so I scanned the room for Brandon. I couldn't see him anywhere. 'Is Brandon around, Mrs McCormack?' I asked.

She began loading tubs of sweets onto the tuck shop counter. 'No, he's not coming in today. He's not well.'

'Oh,' I said, my mind racing, 'what's wrong with him?'

'I'm not sure, love. His mum didn't say.'

'Is he often away?' I asked.

'No, no he's not. It's unusual.'

'Oh,' I said, trudging slowly to the book corner to have a think. This didn't feel good—this didn't feel good at all.

I waited anxiously for Alex to arrive, pouncing on her nearly as soon as Caitlin had waved goodbye and she entered the cloakroom. 'Alex!' I whispered, pulling her into one of the girls' cubicles.

'Oh, so you're talking to me, are you?' she said as I bolted the door behind us.

It was a bit of a squash but I didn't have time to worry about that. 'Course I'm talking to you— you're my most favourite person in the world—but I haven't time to go into all the making-friends-again stuff. Look, I want to explain about yesterday.'

She flicked a pigtail out of the way. 'No need—I saw what happened. I wasn't cross with you, you know—you just jumped to conclusions.'

'All right, all right, I'm an idiot, I know.'

'Well, now that that's sorted, can we go find somewhere more comfortable to talk than in here?'

'In a minute, I want to explain why I went into a radgy first.'

'Go on then, surprise me,' she said and folded her arms across her chest.

Oh, I surprised her all right. Her eyes opened wider and wider as I told her about Brandon and his bruises and why I'd argued with Sammie and what I had said to his mam outside the gates. 'And he's not here today and I think I've dropped him in it,' I finished lamely.

'Poor Brandon. That's horrible.'

'Do you know where he lives?'

'Why?'

'I thought, if it's not far, I could go round and peer in the windows or something.'

She chewed her lip and looked doubtful. 'That's a bit dodgy, isn't it? I think we should just tell Mum . . .'

'I do, too,' Sammie said from the other side of the partition. This was followed immediately by the sound of a toilet flushing and then a banging on the door. I had no choice but to open it and face her.

'This is a secret, right?' I hissed at her.

'Chill out, Jolene—I'm on your side.'

'What, even after yesterday?'

'Yes,' she nodded.

'Why?'

Sammie began tucking her T-shirt into her jeans. 'Because I believe you. I knew there was something funny going on this week. That daft tracksuit . . . it makes sense now, when you think about it. He usually wears shorts and those army T-shirts, even when it's freezing.'

'I believe you, too,' Alex added. 'Brandon wouldn't have followed you round like that if he didn't trust you.'

'Thanks,' I said, 'thanks for believing me—especially you, Sammie. I know you can't stand my guts.'

'Your guts are all right—it's your face I have problems with!' she grinned.

And I grinned, too, for a split second, before remembering what this was all about. 'Anyway,' I said, 'about Brandon. We've got to keep this between us three, right?'

'No way,' Sammie said urgently, 'you've got to tell. I saw this thing on *Trisha* once—you know, the chat show—and she said the worst thing you can do is keep things like this secret.'

'I'll get Mum,' Alex said and slipped past us.

Mrs McCormack appeared in the cramped cloakroom, a puzzled look on her face as Alex closed the door and said, 'Go on, Jolene.'

I hesitated for a second. This went totally against the way I'd always done things. You put up and shut up. You kept adults out of it because they never believed you and anyway it only led to bigger trouble. And besides, this was Mrs McCormack—Mrs McCormack, who couldn't keep Reggie from blowing up bags of crisps never mind deal with something as major as this. What if she made things worse? 'Tell her, Jolene,' Alex urged, 'tell Mum.'

That's what persuaded me. I wasn't telling Mrs McCormack, the soft teacher type, I was telling Mrs McCormack the mum, who shared her sandwiches and gave people second chances and knew what it was like to lose a little boy. So I repeated everything I knew and watched as Mrs McCormack's already pale face turned paler and paler. I waited for her to tell me she didn't believe me but she didn't do that. I waited for her to go into a panic and say she couldn't possibly do anything until Mrs Fryston returned but she didn't do that, either. 'Are you very, very sure, Jolene?' she asked me and I told her I was and she nodded.

'OK,' she said, 'all back in the mobile now. I'll take it from here.'

A few minutes later she called everyone together, as usual, and went over the morning's choices. 'Now, listen, everybody, I've got to pop out for a while—Denise is in charge until I get back and Mrs Riley and Mrs Fountain are also on hand if you need anything.'

Nobody fussed or asked her where she was going. Only the three of us knew and I'm telling you, it was a long, long morning. There was no sign of her by lunchtime or when Katie turned up to take football.

'No fighting today, you two, all right?' she joked.

Sammie and me both looked at her miserably. 'We won't—we're friends now,' Sammie said dully.

'Yeah,' I said, equally as dully, 'we are.'

'Blimey, what a pair of miseries. Where's that little ray of sunshine Brandon to cheer us up?'

We didn't find the answer to that until we had finished the match. Mrs McCormack arrived back at After School club about three o'clock but of course nobody could ask her anything until nearer home time, when it was a bit quieter. She called the three of us over to the book corner where she could talk in private but all she said she could tell us was that they were all OK. 'Everything else has to remain confidential, I'm afraid,' she explained but added, 'You did the right thing, Jolene.'

'Told you,' Sammie nodded, wandering off to help pack the tuck shop away.

Alex sat with me in the book corner. 'You're not happy, are you?' she said.

'No,' I whispered.

She sighed. 'You know how Caitlin brings me to ZAPS now?'

'Yes,' I said, wondering what that had to do with anything.

'That's because I was reading stuff I shouldn't have been—files and things about it. After that, Mum and Mrs Fryston thought it would be better if I was treated more like everyone else—you know, started at the same time, finished at the same time, kept my nose out of private papers.'

'Oh.'

'So I don't go into Mum's things any more.'

'Course not.'

'I promised.'

'OK.' I still didn't know what she was getting at until she leaned over and cupped her hand to my ear.

'I never promised not to listen to phone calls, though. I'll call you as soon as I know what's happened.'

That girl! She was such a bad influence on me.

Chapter Twenty-Two

The call came just after breakfast the next morning. 'It's for you,' Grandad said, looking surprised.

'Thank you!' I said, almost snatching the phone from him. 'I'll take this in my study, if you don't mind,' I said, marching into the hallway. There, I sat on the bottom step and listened.

'Jolene?' Alex whispered.

'Yeah. What have you got?'

'Everything! Mum's been calling every blooming support group and helpline and agency she knows. Our phone bill's going to be on *Record Breakers*.'

'And? Tell me about Brandon!'

'Oh, right, OK . . .'

This is what Alex Superspy found out. When Mrs McCormack went round to Brandon's house, she found his mam huddled on the sofa with him, staring into space. The baby was crying in the pram and the whole house was a tip. It was obvious she wasn't coping and hadn't been for a long time. Apparently Mrs Petty's mum used to help but she went back to live in Ireland, and Mrs Petty was a quiet woman who kept herself to herself, so there hadn't been anyone else to turn to.

When Alex's mum asked her if what I'd said about Brandon was true, she nodded and burst into tears. She said she never meant to, she just was so tired and stressed she took it out on him, but she swore she never hurt the baby. She told Mrs Mac that what I'd shouted at her had terrified her, in case social services took the kids away, so she didn't dare go out. 'I love them so much,' she kept saying. I began to feel a *bit* sorry for her when Alex told me that.

Anyway, Mrs McCormack has been in touch with all these different people who are going to go round and work things out. The best news Alex overheard her mam telling Mrs Fryston, who only got back first thing and must have been well miffed to be greeted with all this, was the army was going to let Brandon's dad come home on compassionate leave as soon as possible.

'Brandon'll like that,' I said.

'I know,' Alex whispered, 'and Brandon's coming back to After School club next week. Caitlin's picking him up and babysitting for Kagan during the day so Mrs Petty can get some counselling. Oh, Jolene—can't talk. Mum's coming up—gotta go. See you Monday.'

'Yeah, see you Monday.'

'See who Monday?' Grandad Jake asked, looking down at me.

'Oh!' I said, jumping because I hadn't seen him. 'Alex—at After School club.'

Grandad came and sat beside me on the step and handed me some leaflets. 'But, hinny, I've taken the week off. Look, I've just printed these off the Internet. I thought we could go somewhere nice. Devon or Cornwall—France maybe. We could even go to Kiersten and Brody in the States.'

I glanced at the colourful pictures of sunny skies and golden sandy beaches, then shook my head. 'Nah, you're all right—save your money. I'd rather stay here.'

'But wouldn't you rather go somewhere more exciting—somewhere with a bit more of a holiday atmosphere?'

'Nah,' I said, 'but thanks, like.'

He stared sadly at the leaflets. 'Well, what am I supposed to do while you're at After School club? Twiddle my thumbs?'

I grinned. 'Grandad Jake, I know exactly what you can do!'

Chapter Twenty-Three

The second week of my holiday was miles better than the first. It was bound to be, wasn't it? I'd got my head cleared out of all that emotional stuff that stopped me enjoying myself. I was just like everybody else now—one of the crowd.

I spent every morning doing arty-crafty stuff with Alex and nearly every afternoon playing football with Sammie and Brandon. Sammie admitted one of the reasons she'd been in a mardy with me, apart from the Brody thing, was that I was better at football than her. She had been the best girl until I had turned up and 'taken over'. I didn't know what to do about that—a fact's a fact; but Katie settled it by presenting

Sammie with a trophy for best girl player on the course and me with best overall player.

The weather changed towards the end of the week and it rained a couple of times. That was when things got embarrassing because I let Brandon and Alex dress me up in daft clothes from the dressing-up box. I had a long pink bridesmaid dress on with this dumb flowery hat and—wait for it—lip gloss. It wouldn't have been half so bad if Grandad hadn't been there to catch me on camera. Still, I only had myself to blame for that as I was the one who roped him in to take some holiday 'snaps'. Well, I'd reckoned if I had to stare at ones of Mam and Darryl on the beach and Jack and Keith on wherever they'd been with Tracie it was only right they should see me in my element, too.

Of course, my grandad being Jake Miller meant when he had the films developed they weren't the usual pictures with red eyes and half your head missing and a thumb instead of the thing you had meant to take a picture of in the first place. No way, man. These were smart. He had some football scenes blown into poster size and one group shot outside the mobile made into proper postcards with 'Greetings from Zetland Avenue After School Club' printed across the bottom. Mrs McCormack and Mrs Fryston were really impressed with them, especially as Grandad Jake donated a stack of them to the club to use for promotional purposes.

I liked all the photos he took that week but two were my favourites. One was where Alex and me were giving Brandon a fireman's lift. He was wearing a yellow plastic fireman's helmet and a purple tutu and wellies and he just looked so happy.

The second, which is my favourite favourite, is one of me just with Alex. Grandad took it on the last day during lunchtime. We're just sitting on the grass, back to back, chatting. I've got the friendship bracelet on Alex managed to finish at last. I knew that thing she was doing was for me because it was in red and white, I just couldn't tell from the pattern exactly what it was

Greetings from Zetland Avenue After School Club!

going to be. It's really clever, with the letters J and A woven all the way through it. I'll never take it off, ever.

Anyway, I was twirling that round and round and she was wearing my Sunderland top I'd given her and Jake Miller the famous photographer yelled 'smile' and we both turned round at the same time and did just that. It's a brilliant picture. I have it in a frame on my desk, next to my football trophy. What? No, I'm not in the nuddy on the picture or wearing my pyjamas because I'd given Alex my shirt. Very funny. If you must know, Grandad Jake had forced me into clothes shops on that weekend and bought me all sorts of stuff. I'd told him I could just borrow something of Brody's but he said as the one who had carried her suitcases to the airport he could vouch for the fact she had nothing left in her cupboards.

That was the other thing I did that week—I talked to Brody on the phone a lot. I didn't want her getting jealous of me spending time with her dad like my mam had with Kiersten. Brody's not like that, though—she's a laid-back type who takes everything in her stride. When I apologized to her about the tooth thing, she said, 'Oh, forget it.' The only thing that did seem to be bothering her was missing time with Reggie. I had to report back to her every detail of what he was up to during the day. Even what he had in his sandwiches. Urgh! I'm glad I'm not into boys—as far as I'm concerned, they're only good for one thing: tackling.

Epilogue

'So, Jolene,' counsellor-lady said to me next time I saw her, 'how did you get on during the summer holidays?'

'All right,' I said.

'Did you manage to make that list of targets like I suggested?'

'Nah.'

'Oh, well never mind. Did you manage to keep out of trouble?'

I scratched the back of my head and whistled a little tune, making her smile.

'I see. And what about your temper? Did you need to use your rhyme?'

I rolled my eyes at her. 'Yeah, a couple of times, miss, but I have to tell you, as ideas go, it's a no-brainer. No offence, like, I just thought you should know for in future.'

'Well,' she said, glancing at my folder in front of her, 'something must be working. Your teacher says that you have settled into the new year very well indeed, that you are being co-operative, attentive, and sociable and your after-school club leader says simply that you're a star.'

'I'll agree with all that,' I said.

'Well, I think it's fantastic. You won't be needing me soon at this rate.'

'Thanks.'

'Well, come on, Jolene, tell me what your secret is so I can pass it on to the others waiting outside.'

'Oh, it's simple. You just need a good friend to talk to and people who'll listen and believe you and if the sparks start just think of spilt orange juice and when your daft grandad calls you Billy No-Mates just shove a photo of Alex McCormack in his mush.

'Oh, and if you've got a mam that's not very good at being a mam, don't worry—you're not the only one and it's probably not their fault because they probably weren't shown much love when they were kids so the thing to do is find another role model. You can get them in schools or after-school clubs or they might even be in the same family right under your nose. They might even start off as an enemy called Sammie that turn out to be all right in the end.

'Then, if you have good role models, you can become one. Like I'm a role model to Jack and Keith, right. They can both do keepy-uppies now without crying about it and I've got them supporting Sunderland. You can't give anyone a better gift than that. Oh, and Jack e-mails Brandon at after-school club, so he's got a new friend, and having friends is just the best thing ever.'

Counsellor-lady looked a bit stunned as I stopped to catch my breath. 'Goodness! That must have been some holiday,' she said.

I grinned back and twisted my friendship bracelet. 'It was. Can I go now, please, miss?'

Helena Pielichaty (pronounced Pierre-li-hatty) was born in Stockholm, Sweden but most of her childhood was spent in Yorkshire. Her English teacher wrote of her in Year Nine that she produced 'lively and quite sound work but she must be careful not to let the liveliness go too far.' Following this advice, Helena never took her liveliness further south than East Grinstead, where she began her career as a teacher. She didn't begin writing until she was 32. Since then, Helena has written many books for Oxford University Press. She lives in Nottinghamshire with her husband and two children.

The girls are back...

It wasn't my fault!

*All I did was try to bring everyone together again.
I just wanted it to be how it used to be—before Dad left.
That's not so wrong, is it?*

*But as usual, it all went pear-shaped. Why does
everything I do turn into a complete nightmare?
I feel like such an idiot.*

*I bet everyone else's families are perfect. Well, they
would be, wouldn't they—their lives are all brilliant
compared to mine . . .*

ISBN 978 0 19 275377 9

Brody's
Back

—the girl who's got it all
(well, that's what everyone
else thinks)

Helena Pielichaty

Life sucks!

*Everyone's always depending on me—Brody the Reliable.
Expecting me to sort out their problems, but when I need
help even my best buddy lets me down. Well, fine, if that's
how he wants to play it, he can take a hike.*

*And that goes for all the others too. I'm through doing
things just to please other people, and that includes
being captain for the Big Book Quiz. Let Mrs Fryston find
some other loser . . .*

ISBN 978 0 19 275378 6

What a nightmare!

All I want is a quiet life – but do you think that's possible? No chance.

It started off fine. With one best friend and out-of-school stuff kept to almost zero, I had no worries. But then it all went wrong. First there was the secret, then the secret about the secret . . . and now everything's out of control!

The only time I feel calm is when I'm talking to my brother Daniel – at least he never answers back. OK, so he's been dead for years, but I don't have a problem with that – unfortunately my family obviously does . . .

ISBN 978 0 19 275379 3

Jolene's Back

—the girl who knows what
she wants (and won't stop
till she gets it)

Helena Pielichaty

It's crunch-time!

*I'd been really looking forward to visiting Brody, Alex, and
the rest of the gang—but now I'm not so sure I should have
come at such a major time. My mum and stepdad, Darryl,
aren't getting on. She's such an old nag—I don't know how
Darryl puts up with her.*

*Well, if push comes to shove I know exactly where I want to
be. And it's not with Mum, that's for sure. If she can divorce
Darryl, then I'll divorce her—end of story! And until they sort
it out I'm staying down here with my mates, even if it means
doing another runner . . .*

ISBN 978 0 19 275380 9